## Praise for *To Catch a Killer*

"A twisty, cold-case mystery custom-made for fans of Sara Shepard, *Pretty Little Liars,* and *Veronica Mars*! The edge-of-your-seat plot, sinister backstory, and smart, brave, and irreverent main character make this whodunit unputdownable."

—*Justine*

"A compulsive read. Scarborough has created a thrilling book brimming with life, murder, and adventure."

—Carrie Jones, *New York Times* bestselling author of *Flying*

"An intense, engrossing debut." —*Booklist*

"*To Catch a Killer* is a tense, storming heartbeat of a thriller. Scarborough's tightly woven story merges forensic intrigue with friendship, romance, and family, nailing the dynamic stylings of *Veronica Mars* and the playful spirit of *Bones*. I could not put it down."

—Cori McCarthy, author of *Breaking Sky*

"The fast-paced plot and *Veronica Mars*–esque protagonist make this book a good fit for avid mystery readers."

—*School Library Journal*

"A relatable cast and well-thought-out plot make this mystery a Sherlockian puzzle sure to impress the most hardened crime-procedural fanatic." —Mary Elizabeth Summer, author of *Trust Me, I'm Lying*

BOOKS BY **SHERYL SCARBOROUGH**

*To Catch a Killer*

*To Right the Wrongs*

# To Catch a Killer

## Sheryl Scarborough

A Tom Doherty Associates Book
New York

TO CATCH A KILLER



A Tor Teen Book
Published by Tom Doherty Associates
175 Fifth Avenue
New York, NY 10010

www.tor-forge.com

Tor® is a registered trademark of Macmillan Publishing Group, LLC.

The Library of Congress has cataloged the hardcover edition as follows:

Scarborough, Sheryl, author.
To catch a killer / Sheryl Scarborough.—First edition.
p. cm.
"A Tom Doherty Associates book."
ISBN 978-0-7653-8191-0 (hardcover)
ISBN 978-1-4668-8548-6 (ebook)
1. High school students—Fiction. 2. Murder—Investigation—Fiction.
3. Mothers—Death—Fiction. 4. Mystery and detective stories. I. Title.
PZ7.1.S33 To 2017
813'.6—dc23

2016286184

ISBN 978-0-7653-8192-7 (trade paperback)

Our books may be purchased in bulk for promotional, educational, or business use. Please contact your local bookseller or the Macmillan Corporate and Premium Sales Department at 1-800-221-7945, extension 5442, or by email at MacmillanSpecialMarkets@macmillan.com.

First Edition: February 2017
First Trade Paperback Edition: February 2018

Printed in the United States of America

0 9 8 7 6 5 4

To Gordon Kent, who believed long before I did.

# Acknowledgments

It takes a village to produce a writer capable of turning out a book. Here are my thanks, in no particular order.

To my editor, Melissa Frain, thanks for your keen insight and passion for this book. *Your* fingerprints are all over it. Amy Stapp, thanks for staying on top of everything and for keeping the bones of this process lined up. To Diana Griffin and the Tor publicity team, the evidence is in, you guys delivered in every way possible.

Jessica Regel, my rock-star agent and partner in crime. Thanks for everything you do and the classy way you do it! I'm actually lucky enough to have a second rock-star agent and partner in crime, Yfat Reiss Gendell—your amazing friendship changed my life.

Thanks to my writer's group, Ingrid Sundberg-Gearheart and Melle Amade-Melkumian; you were like a forensic team, willing to get down in the muck of lousy drafts. You were harsh, but always with love. This wouldn't be a book without you.

Beta readers are Luminol to a writer. They shine a light on mistakes and things that don't work. I'm blessed with the best and grateful for every one of you: Beverley Bevenflorez, Celia Bonaduce, Jennifer Bosworth, Stephen Bramucci, Edith Cohn, Janie Emaus, Marge Engessor, Stuart Fox, Bryan Simon, and Ariel Woodruff.

To "My Girls" Billie Jo Mason, Denise Cruz-Castino, and Yvette Bou—you gave your support, you showed up, and you were the best brunch-bunch eve-ah. Muchos besos!

There's a saying that when the student is ready, the teacher will appear. Thank you to my teachers/advisors: Rita Williams-Garcia, Tom Birdseye, Susan Fletcher, Sharon Darrow, Tim Wynne-Jones, and A. M. Jenkins. Parts of each of you exist in the DNA of my writing and ultimately in this book.

Pit Crew (every writer needs one): Alan and Diane Williams, Cheryl and Michael O'Leary, and Crystal and Jesselyn Yaeger. Thanks for all you continue to do.

Thanks to my family. It is largely because of them that this book exists. Jerry Piatt, Mason Faulk, Jazmine Piatt, Caden Piatt, Stuart Fox, Lois Freeman-Fox, Royce Bauder, and Ron Weyers.

Special thanks to Christina Neff, for key genetics research information.

# To CATCH A KILLER

# ▸ 1 ◂

High school's supposed to be fun.

—MISS P

I soothe my forehead against the icy car window and breathe out a path of fog. If I squint one eye, the neon splashed across the rain-slicked street forms a wide, cruel mouth.

It's after 2:00 a.m. and we're just now pulling up to the police station. They took me to the hospital first, even though I swore that not a single drop of the blood all over me was mine.

A hospital would be lost trying to treat my wounds.

The trip wasn't a complete waste, though. They let me clean up and swap my bloody sweats for scrubs. Now come the questions, hard and fast. They'll expect me to have answers. But all I have are more questions.

Beginning with, who killed Miss P?

As soon as the car stops, I grab for the handle but swipe an oddly smooth panel instead. It's like trying to locate a missing limb. You know it should be there, but . . .

The young officer bends low, checking me out through the window. He opens the door and offers his hand. "Let me help you." His voice is low and horror-movie shaky.

I wish he could help me. I really wish he could.

Lurching out of the backseat, I bend over the gutter and gulp the cool morning mist until my stomach calms.

The older cop takes his time groaning his way out of the driver's seat. "Looks like rain again." He scowls at the sky as if his grumpy attitude could make it stop.

Dude, Iron *Rain,* Oregon is like ninety miles from Portland. It rains here constantly. Deal with it.

At least by now I'm completely cried out. All that's left are some sniffs and huffs and they seem to control me more than I control them. My escorts are so relaxed we could be dropping in for a late-night donut and cup of coffee. From the way the old one hikes his belt up over his belly, I'm sure he'd prefer that to dealing with me and my dead teacher.

*Same here, buddy.* And she's not just some corpse to me, either. But I doubt he cares. With a sweep of his arm he waves me through the door. A desk sergeant leans heavily on the high counter and quietly tracks us with his eyes as we pass him and enter through a plain, unmarked door.

These guys probably don't realize that I practically grew up in this building. Once Rachel gets here, they'll connect the dots. Still, it's a shock to see the squad room so alive.

Two or three officers are clustered around every desk with telephones and cell phones pressed to their ears. Tears spring to my eyes when I spot my principal, Mr. Roberts, helping out by delivering steaming cups of coffee.

I hope he knows I tried to help her. I really did. But there was nothing I could do.

Once Mr. Roberts sees me, everyone turns to stare. Their gaze is awkward, like a face full of acupuncture needles. Not painful exactly, but not entirely comfortable, either. He threads his way over to me through the maze of desks.

"Oh, Erin. Are you okay?"

My voice sticks in my throat. "Miss P," I croak and press my hands over my mouth, fighting to keep back another round of tears.

"I heard . . . over the police scanner," he says. "Is she—?"

Unable to speak, I nod.

He steps forward as though maybe he wants to hug me, but he doesn't.

"Excuse us." The older officer guides me around Mr. Roberts, pointing toward a hallway at the end of the room. I hesitate for a second because I really wish Mr. Roberts could come with us. He's been in my life for so many years I hardly remember a time without him. I'm sure he would come, too. He's always been helpful like that. But neither of us knows what to say, so I wave good-bye to my only friend in this whole mess and move off toward the hallway. The officer leads me to the door of an interrogation room. "For privacy," he says.

The room is small—one table and four chairs. I turn away from the mirror. Everyone knows there's a secret room on the other side of that glass. Why do they even try to hide it?

The young officer pulls out my chair and offers water or soda. I shake my head. He slips out quietly.

Old Guy transfers his hat to the table and runs his hand over his threadlike hair before dropping into the seat across from me. He flips open a notebook. "Just so you know, they put in a call to your mother and she's on her way." He keeps his eyes down on his notes instead of up on me.

"You mean guardian." This is not meant to disrespect Rachel; it's just a habit. "She's not my mother," I add.

"Yeah. Whatever number you gave us, that's who we called." He pats and digs around in his various pockets for a pen. "If it's okay, I'm going to get started here. Understand that you're not in any trouble. I just want to take your statement while it's fresh in your mind. Can I get your full name for the report?"

I stiffen. This is the moment when things always change. My eyes drop to his badge: Baldwin. His name isn't familiar, but he's definitely old enough.

"Um. I'm Erin Blake." I let it hang there. The silence is for emphasis.

Shock dawns as Baldwin's eyes rise slowly and he looks at my face for the first time. "*The* Erin Blake?"

I stare at the table. This reaction is not something you get used to. Or, at least, I never have.

"So that means—" He snaps his fingers. "What was her name? Oh—Sarah. Sarah Blake was your mother?" I think I detect a tinge of awe in his voice, even though that would be highly inappropriate.

I nod.

"Wow." His chair whines as he leans forward, resting his cheek on a meaty hand. "We all remember that one." His tone is reverent but his eyes darken, as if the pain of recalling the details of my mother's murder is almost too great. I know this look, too. The next question is never asked out loud but I do him the favor of answering it anyway.

"I don't know why he didn't kill me, too."

"And they never caught him, right?"

I shake my head. But I will . . . someday.

"What about your father, where's he?"

I offer a shrug.

Baldwin's head twitches. More shock. "He just took off?"

I shrug again. It's all I've got. "Mom never told anyone who he is. I guess she was independent like that."

"Wow. That's got to be tough."

"It is, kinda. My life's like this huge blank." I lay my palms flat on the table, framing a dark expanse of space between them.

His eyes—light chocolate, flecked with moss—study me quietly and without pity. "Tabula rasa, sweetheart."

"What?"

"You were an innocent baby when all that went down. A blank slate. You don't have to let any of it affect you."

I push my lower lip up into my upper one. It's the closest I can get to a smile. Adults always say this, as if it's true.

He shakes his head. "And now this. So, this Laura Peters was your science teacher?"

"Biology."

He frowns. "You don't have any reason to believe your mother's . . . uh, death could have anything to do with this, do you?" I notice the way he sits, shoulders hunched over the table and legs tucked back under his chair. He forms the perfect human question mark.

A dizzy thrum rises in my ears. He just labeled the giant ball of worry I've been avoiding since the moment I knew there was another murder. I grip the edge of the table. "I don't know how they could be connected, but I guess there's always a chance."

He looks up toward the ceiling while thinking this through. "Yeah, I don't think they're connected, not after all this time."

I desperately need him to be right about that.

His gaze drops to the dark rings of blood so caked into my cuticles that even a thorough scrub at the hospital couldn't remove them. "What can you tell me about Miss Peters? Was she a good teacher? Did you like her?"

I slide my hands off the table and tuck them under my legs. Miss Peters always said I reminded her of herself when she was younger, and it felt so important to finally be *like* someone. Especially her. I picture her darting from lab table to lab table like one of those birds on the beach, pecking at our projects. "She was the best," I say, my voice a ragged whisper.

"And your relationship was . . . ?"

"Normal."

"When was the last time you saw her?"

"You mean . . . ?"

"Alive. When did you last see her alive?"

"Today, last period. Well, maybe I should say yesterday."

"So, Thursday at . . . ?"

"Two-ten to three-oh-five."

"Do you remember the last conversation you had?" he asks.

I actually can't stop thinking about it. Just before the final bell, she had moved close to my lab table. Her glasses were on top of her head, tangled in a mass of blond curls held in place by chewed pencils. She'd tipped her head close to my ear. "Listen, Cookie, this isn't the only way, you know."

But it was. She's the one who showed me how it worked. "It's my best shot. You said so yourself," I argued. "Besides, what have we got to lose?"

A savage cramp twists my stomach. It was such an easy thing to say at the time.

She'd handed me an orange from her pocket, clicked her fingernails on the Formica, and pointed at me. "Be careful."

I looked back once before heading out the door. Her smile had urged me on. There was no way I could fail.

I realize Baldwin's waiting for my answer but a lump the size of a walnut has swelled in my throat and it's a few seconds before I can talk again. "Um." My voice cracks. "She basically just said to be careful." I don't care if telling him that makes him suspicious. It's what she said. I wasn't. And now she's dead.

"Careful of what?" Baldwin's eyes narrow as he scribbles notes. "Was she worried about something?"

I shake my head. "It was just her way of saying good-bye. Like, bye, be careful."

We'd made a deal. She would run the test if I promised two things. One: I wouldn't do anything illegal. And two: I'd go to the prom. The legal thing was easy. If someone throws something in the trash, it's not illegal to pick it up. And as for the second, she knew I wasn't the prom type, but she pushed it because I couldn't say no. "High school's supposed to be fun," she said.

"You said you were passing her house and saw the door open. Why so late at night?"

"I left some things in her mailbox . . . for a science project."

His head snaps up. "What kinds of things?"

"Some trash with DNA on it. It was like an extra credit thing." I make sure to add the part about extra credit because if he checks, he won't find any other students with the same assignment. And he is going to check.

He squints. "DNA, like, from a person?"

I bob my head slowly. I want to be honest but I worry where this will take me.

"Are you in one of those forensic classes?"

"Sort of."

He frowns. "Did this DNA belong to anyone in particular?"

I shrug. "No. It was just kind of random."

My first lie.

There was nothing random about the cigarette butts, coffee cup, and bloody towel I left in Miss P's mailbox. But I can't tell him that, and there's no way he'll find out now. It was only supposed to be three quick stops for bits of trash from three specific men.

"Are you saying your biology teacher *told* you to leave an assignment in her mailbox in the middle of the night?"

"She said where to leave it but she didn't say an exact time."

"Hang on. I want to call over there and make sure they get those things from the mailbox." Baldwin rises from his chair and disappears out the door.

*Dead*. The word hammers in my head. Along with *Who did this?* And *Why?*

I can't think of anyone who didn't love Miss P. I rest my elbows on the table and stare quietly at my reflection in the secret mirror.

# 2

Basic eyewitness testimony is only accurate about half the time.
Science has a much better track record than that.

—VICTOR FLEMMING

Up until nine months ago, I could count the things I knew about my mother on one hand. I knew she had curly brown hair and brown eyes. She traveled all over the world as a fashion photographer and Italy was her favorite assignment. She was twenty-five when I was born and twenty-seven when she was murdered. Her killer has never been caught.

Growing up, I was given two Polaroid photos of her: one from when she was in high school, posing with her best friend, Rachel, and the other from the hospital the day I was born. The rest of the details of her life are as hazy as those photos. And somehow Rachel expected me to be okay with that.

I'm tall, like my mother was, but my hair's the color of rust, and if I don't clip it back, it hangs straight over my right eye like a veil of death. My eyes are a weak blue, not brown like hers.

I want someone to tell me I have Aunt Ginny's cheekbones and Uncle Ralph's crooked toe. Hell, I want to know if I even have an Aunt Ginny or an Uncle Ralph. My mom was an only child and her parents are both dead. But unless I am a clone, there's a whole other mystery family on my father's side.

Who really believes that a couple of blurry snapshots are enough to know where you belong? That somehow I should just carry on like nothing bad happened? Grow up, be a teenager . . . go to school . . . have friends.

My mother's life was about documenting things. But all I have are a couple of Polaroids? It doesn't make any sense. I once asked Rachel what happened to all my mother's stuff. She got a blank, faraway look on her face and said we would save that conversation until I'm older. In Rachel-speak that means never.

She pretends to be open and honest and willing to talk about anything in the world . . . except my mother. She won't even tell stories about when they were kids growing up. She claims it's because there's an active police investigation. As if the police ordered her not to say anything. Why would they say that? And if they did, I'm sure they didn't mean she couldn't talk to me. I was there. As far as the investigation goes, it's turned up nothing in fourteen years. Not even the identity of my father. So I wouldn't exactly call it active.

Miss Peters became my total hero when she showed me how DNA could answer my questions about my father. And maybe someday even tell us who killed my mother. Tonight was supposed to be the beginning. We were going to take it to the next level. But something went wrong.

The door slams open against the wall with a loud bang. I drop to my hands and knees and skitter under the table, then realize it's only Baldwin. He catches the door with his elbow because he's holding a steaming cup of coffee in each hand. His notebook is wedged under his arm. "Do you use cream or . . . oh, shoot, are you okay?" His eyebrows ride high on his forehead, giving him an owlish look.

Shaking, I slide back into my seat and hold up two fingers. "Two sugars, please."

He sets the coffee on the table and backs toward the door. "Sorry if I scared you. When I get back, I'd like to talk about the classmate of yours you saw at the scene." He slips out, this time keeping his hand on the door until it closes gently.

Once he's gone, I reach for one of the coffees and pull it toward me. I wrap my trembling fingers around it.

*The classmate of yours.*

▾ ▾ ▾

Today started out as a perfectly normal Thursday.

I was in my usual spot on the wide cement banister at the top of the cafeteria stairs. Mostly I try to look like I'm just hanging out, but really that's the best spot to catch Journey Michaels as he arrives from the parking lot and walks across the quad to the basketball courts.

Watching Journey arrive is bearing witness to a tidal wave of popularity as it engulfs the campus. Every guy he passes high-fives him or punches him in the shoulder. And every girl offers a hug or a coffee or a bite of muffin. This morning he snagged a whole bag of cookies—the little frosted-animal kind you can eat by the handful.

I'm pretty sure my interest in Journey is not the same as everyone else's. I'm oblivious to the way the sunlight plays off the caramel streaks in his hair. And I hardly even notice how his thin, white T-shirt clings to his athletic abs.

Okay, that's a lie. I appreciate both of those things. It's just that that's not all there is for me. What intrigues me most is how he moves through all those people. He almost makes it look smooth, as though he's completely comfortable in his skin. Almost. But I'm convinced his cool-kid moves are a lie.

"Man, you are obsessed with him."

I was so immersed in silent Journey worship I hadn't noticed my best friend, Spam, had joined me.

"Who?" I wasn't ready to discuss the depth of my Journey obsession with her.

Her smirk called BS. Then she ripped off a wolf whistle loud enough to set dogs barking a block away. Once she had everyone's attention, she hollered, "Oooh, Journey. *Work it.*"

Her final insult was to drop down behind me when he looked up.

That was the first time he had ever looked directly at me, so I'm not sure if I only imagined the little sizzle as his eyes met mine. He smiled, though. Shook his head and kept walking.

"Screw you, Spam," I said through clenched teeth.

"Hey, I got him to look at you," she bragged.

It was true. Despite the fact that she was wearing rainbow suspenders and matching over-the-knee socks, she still managed to make *me* the attraction. Spam's idea of fashion is an extension of her personality—sort of shock-and-awe chic.

"You don't have to pretend with me," she said. "I know you want to marry him and bear his freakishly tall basketball-star children."

▾ ▾ ▾

Baldwin returns with the sugar. He's careful with the door this time, allowing it to close all the way before crossing the room and dropping into his chair. He pauses to take a sip of his coffee, then opens his notebook. "Are you okay? Can we continue?"

I give him a weak smile and set about adding the sugars to my coffee.

"So, it was dark. You had just stumbled across this horrific scene with your teacher. You had to be extremely upset," he says.

The pleasant images from this morning dissipate.

Baldwin's chair groans as he settles in further. "Then you see someone running away. And you recognized him as a classmate."

"Journey Michaels."

"What?" Baldwin asks.

"That's his name. Journey Michaels." I press my fingers into my eye sockets. Of all the people in this world, why did it have to be *him*?

"And you're sure it was him?" Baldwin says.

I nod, keeping my fingertips against my eyelids as if that could block some of the horror.

"What makes you so positive?"

I reach for my coffee. "Well." My voice trembles. I dig my thumbnail into the Styrofoam and carve a curved line resembling a stretched-out letter *C*. "Um. He goes to my school." Baldwin waits, pen poised above paper. "And I see him every day." Baldwin's still not writing. How do I explain it? I carve another squiggle on the other side. Will it be enough to simply say that Journey is the boy every girl wants to notice her? Will it mean anything to Baldwin that I make a point not just to see him every day but also to actually study him?

Baldwin waits as I stare at the shape I've carved into the cup. It's not a heart, exactly. The lines are too far apart and not even close to symmetrical. Maybe it's my heart, weak and dysfunctional.

"Um, okay. It's hard to explain. It's like he has this way of moving forward with one shoulder sort of tilted in." I demonstrate, twisting in my seat and leaning my right shoulder forward.

At first Baldwin looks as though he understands but then the folds between his eyebrows deepen. "You're saying you knew it was him because he tilts his shoulder?"

"Most people just walk. But not Journey. He always looks like he's pushing a giant, invisible boulder uphill with his shoulder."

Baldwin shakes his head but proceeds to write down my description. "Tilted shoulder, pushing boulder."

For the first time in a long time I need someone to get it . . . to get *me.*

I lean across the table, hands cupping the air in front of me. "It's just, every day I watch this guy move through the world, and even though he's all cool and everybody loves him, he looks exactly like how I feel. Life's a huge strain, but everyone everywhere tries to hide it. Not him, though. He plows forward, jamming that invisible boulder out of his way. It's like he's saying: Force it. Make it happen."

Baldwin's face lights up. "Ah. You're saying he has a chip on his shoulder?"

It's actually the exact opposite of that, but as I open my mouth to refute him, a squawk comes from his radio.

"Sorry, I have to take this. I'll be right back." He pulls the brick-shaped device off of his belt and heads for the door. "On my way."

The door stutters shut behind him and I'm once again wrapped in the disapproving silence of the room, only now I'm steeped in thoughts of Journey Michaels and the things I saw versus the things I didn't see.

# 3

The hardest thing to teach new crime-scene techs is not to cover the body. But dignity can destroy evidence.

—VICTOR FLEMMING

I go back through it again.

It was just about midnight. The moon hung low and large in the sky, like a giant Olympic gold medal. Its glow felt like praise. As predicted, I had acquired all three of my targeted DNA samples.

Miss Peters's mailbox sat out by the curb on top of a short post. I opened it and shoved the bag of evidence inside. She didn't want to know which sample came from whom. Only I would have that information. She called it a blind study.

As I was leaving, her front door blew open.

"Miss Peters?"

I edged up the walk. Even though she lived in an average neighborhood only a few miles from mine, the late hour gave the area a graveyard hush. As I approached her porch, a faint shadow in the shape of a cross bobbed low against the baseboard, sending terror through me like a drop of ink in water. Even once I realized it was just the moon shining through the slats of Miss P's trellis the panic was overwhelming.

Then the smell hit me.

That smell triggered a memory so vivid and deep that it dropped me to my knees. It was a strong, raw scent, like shoving your face into a vat of pennies mixed with freshly ground hamburger.

It was the smell of blood.

*Lots of blood.*

And there she was, lying on her back inside the doorway. She floated on a huge sea of red.

I might have screamed. I don't know. White noise filled my ears and my vision slid to gray. I crawled to her side, ignoring the wash of blood. I was there, but nowhere. I was breathing, but holding my breath.

"Oh, Miss Peters . . ."

A motion light in the front yard blinked on, shattering the dark. Someone was watching me from the shadows. Once he triggered the light, he ran. But I saw him clearly, and when I realized who it was, my insides filled with lead and sank all the way to my knees.

▾ ▾ ▾

The interrogation room door bursts open, introducing a whoosh of fresh air.

"Oh my god, Erin."

Rachel drops her purse and coat and rushes to me. Her arms circle my neck. She was my mother's best friend and the one who found her lifeless body. She scooped me up that day and ever since, she has stood between me and any harm that might come, large or small. I know she would literally throw herself in front of a train for me. Without her, who knows where I would have ended up?

"I'm sorry you had to get out of bed for this." Even though

I feel bad, I'm grateful to have Rachel's warmth enveloping me. Now that she's here I don't have to pretend to be so strong.

"Shhhh. I'm fine. Just worried about you." Rachel brushes the hair off my face and runs her hands over my back and my arms as though she has to feel for herself that I'm really in one piece.

Hovering near the door is Detective Sydney Rankle, Rachel's best friend. At the station she acts more formal, but when she's at our house she calls herself *Aunt Sydney.*

"I'll take it from here," Sydney says to Baldwin. "But come get me when they bring him in."

Rachel takes my face between her hands. "Sydney says you know the boy who did this?"

I open my mouth to speak but Sydney beats me to it.

"Alleged. We can't say he did it. Not yet."

"But you know him, right? He goes to your school?"

I nod.

"That settles it. We're changing schools," she says.

"No." It comes out frantic. "I can't change."

"You don't know what's at work here," Rachel says.

What I want to say is: *I was there,* and *You don't know what's at work here, either.* But now's not the time for that.

"We shouldn't knee-jerk, remember?" That was my therapist's go-to phrase. Good for any occasion. I stopped seeing him a year ago. We weren't getting anywhere anyway. But I still use his words when they suit me. Changing schools is not an option. Rachel needs to hear that.

She keeps her hands on my shoulders and holds me out away from her while she scans my face. Then she squeezes me in close, rocking us both from side to side. "I'm so sorry this happened; you must've been terrified."

I was. What if I caused it, and Miss P's death is my fault? What then?

There's a light knock. Sydney opens the door. It's Baldwin. He nods his head toward the squad room. "He's coming in now."

"I'll be right there." Sydney glances at us. Rachel's arms are wrapped tightly around me. "Take her home," she says. "Keep her home tomorrow. I'll be in touch."

Baldwin leads a group past the door. One in the middle is taller than the others and his hands are cuffed behind his back. Caramel tufts of hair curl against a chiseled profile that's pale beneath the tan.

There's a quick jolt of recognition. I wasn't expecting to see him here like this, and I definitely hope he doesn't see me.

Journey Michaels's jaw tightens. His gaze sweeps the room, looking for who or what brought this down on his head. For the second time today, he looks directly at me, only this time instead of sizzle, his expression reveals an anger so hot it could melt tungsten.

I expected him to look different to me now. I mean, if he's a killer he should look different. Right? I can't help it, though—I still feel a tug. There's something about Journey Michaels that draws me to him.

I bury my face in Rachel's shoulder and she strokes my hair. "Hey, it's okay to cry, you know. This is one of those times." Rachel means well but she never totally gets it.

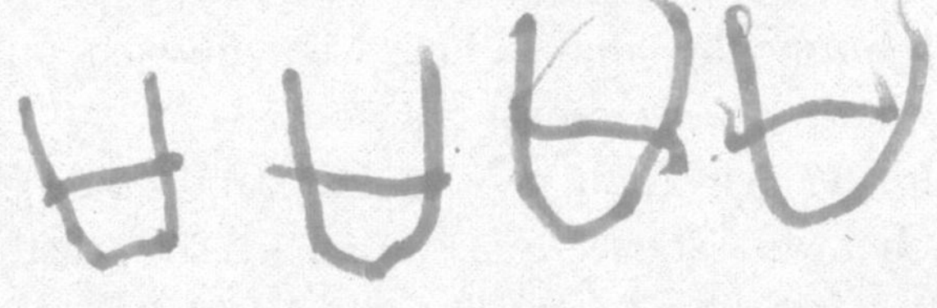

# ▸ 4 ◂

The crime scene tape will separate you from everything
but the emotional impact. You still have to be
able to deal with that.

—VICTOR FLEMMING

I wake to the potent scent of orange.

There's a pile of orange peels on my nightstand—Miss P's orange. I'd savored it in the dark. It was sweet and salty, mixed with my tears.

I pick up one of the peels and pinch it under my nose, memorizing the scent and packing it away. I vow that for the rest of my life, every time I smell the scent of orange I will think of her and it will remind me of the bright orange safety goggles she wore when using ultraviolet light. It also brings to mind her sunshiny outlook on life.

By pairing the image of an orange with Miss P maybe one day I can forget my final image of her, lying still just inside her door, several officers standing guard.

What I won't forget though are all her cute mannerisms, like the large pair of glasses she was always pushing up onto her nose, and how she kept her scrunched-up bun in place with strategically placed pencils. In the same way that Mr. Roberts isn't just a principal, Miss Peters wasn't just a teacher. Not to me, anyway.

I hear Rachel rattling around in the kitchen, but before I go join her I swipe the orange peels off my nightstand and drop them into a small potpourri basket. Then I wander down to the kitchen in search of some quiet comfort. I'm greeted by the smell of coffee and Rachel's worried look. "Did you get any sleep last night?" she asks.

"A little. How about you?" I sit down at the table and take a fresh orange from the bowl. I press it to my nose, inhaling deeply even though the smell makes my heart hurt. I wonder if Rachel will ever mention Miss Peters to me again or if my favorite teacher will now join my mother on that list of things Rachel deems too dangerous for us to discuss.

She brings her coffee to the table. When she doesn't say anything right away, I look up and find her staring at me.

She rubs the spot between her eyebrows with two fingers, as if trying to erase difficult thoughts. "Last night was—" She pauses, and then begins again. "Sydney doesn't want us to talk too much about what happened because she might need to interview you again and she wants what you say to be fresh and not rehearsed. But she asked me something and I didn't have an answer. Erin, what were you doing at your teacher's house after midnight?"

I sit up slowly. I should have a Rachel-ready lie to roll off my tongue. She was asleep when I snuck out and I wasn't planning on getting caught. I know I owe her the truth, but it's been so long since we've been honest with each other, I don't know what she can handle. I do know she can't handle me wanting to delve into my past. She closed the door on that a long time ago. I'm supposed to just forget it and go on. As if.

I roll the orange back into the bowl and shutter my eyes to look extra exhausted.

"I couldn't sleep, so I left here around midnight." I've had insomnia for years and she knows this. "I just went for a little drive . . . to clear my head and get sleepy."

"Alone?" she asks.

"Yes."

"You weren't with anyone? Not even Spam . . . or maybe a boy?"

I shake my head. Here we go—Rachel's denial in action. How can she even think I could sneak out to be with some boy like a normal teenager? She's seen the way people act when they hear my name. How the recognition lands in their eyes like cherries in a slot machine. The looks of pity that wash over me as they think, but never say, *Oh, she's the one.* Rachel sees all of that but thinks I should just ignore it.

Miss Peters got it. She understood how the stigma of a notorious unsolved crime kept me from getting close to people—especially boys.

I bite into the skin of the orange, releasing even more of its rich scent.

When I finally do have a relationship, I want it to be honest. How can I tell someone everything about myself when I don't even know the most basic facts? Miss P agreed that I deserved to know everything that was possible to know.

Rachel blows on her coffee before trying again. "Just be honest with me, Erin. This is no time for secrets."

I widen my eyes and aim a searing look directly at her.

"I need words, not pop-eyes," she says.

"I said I was alone." Clearly, seeing Journey Michaels doesn't count.

"Okay. Just checking." The hand bringing coffee to her lips trembles. I sense she's holding something back. Guess what, that makes two of us. Her gaze drifts around the kitchen as if she's seeing it for the very first time. Then she stops and pins me with her own hard look. "Did you really leave a bloody towel in Miss Peters's mailbox?"

Crap. I forgot they'd tell her about that, too.

"It's not Miss Peters's," I say quickly. "The blood, I mean."

"Whose is it? Sydney said there was a lot of it." Rachel's knuckles turn white against the coffee cup.

"It was just some random DNA that I picked up." It's partially true. "For extra credit."

"Erin." Her eyes stay locked onto mine in a gaze so direct I have no choice but to look away. "You honestly expect me to believe that you went through a stranger's trash and *touched* a bloody towel?" Rachel frowns. "I know you. You wouldn't touch it if it was your own blood."

Usually I pretend I'm telling the truth and Rachel pretends to believe me, even though I'm sure she really doesn't. In the end, we agree I won't do the things that worry her, like sneaking out of the house, and she won't nail me to the wall with punishments. We keep it very civilized. But today is different. Neither of us is pretending in quite the same way.

"I was wearing gloves," I say, adding an indignant tone, as though I only did what anyone else would've done.

"You understand the problem, right? If you know more than you're saying, they're going to find out. Sydney is probably testing that bloody towel right now."

"She doesn't have the equipment to test blood. The best she can do is to send it to the FBI. They won't get the results for at least a week. Probably more."

"How do you know that?" Rachel adjusts her sweater, wrapping the fabric tighter around her neck. Her expression is a combination of scared and proud.

"How do you think? Uncle Victor's books."

"I can't believe you've actually read those gory things."

At least now Rachel's "the world's gone mad" look isn't all about me.

"And I can't believe you haven't. He sends us autographed copies."

Miss P might have introduced me to forensics, but the blow-by-blow instructions came directly from my uncle's books.

"Those books exploit the tragedy of real people," Rachel says, slapping the table. "You shouldn't put my brother on a pedestal like that."

"Solving crime is his job."

"No. Your grandfather was a police detective. *He* solved crimes."

"My grandfather?" I force one eyebrow into a higher arch than the other. It might be mean, but sometimes Rachel needs to be reminded that we're not actually related by blood.

She makes a pruney face. "Don't get smart. He was the only grandfather you ever knew." She tightens her jaw, which makes her voice sound strained. "What my brother does is process evidence to be used in court, and that's different. Trust me. Dad was never thrilled about Victor going with the FBI instead of the police academy."

I know I won't win this argument, but I still have to try. "If you had read even one of his books you would understand why Uncle Victor does what he does. He does it for the survivors and the families of the victims. He believes they deserve to know the truth about what happened to the ones they loved." I let that statement hang there for a minute, leaving the obvious unsaid. Uncle Victor believes the survivors deserve to know all of the things Rachel thinks I should ignore.

She starts to interrupt but I hold up a finger, keeping her silent for one more second. "He does it because he believes that in all cases, good should triumph over evil." I sit back in my chair. There, let her deal with that.

Rachel's face turns to stone. "After what you've been through, Victor's books are not appropriate reading material for you. Case closed!" Then she turns her attention to cleaning out her purse, a signal that our discussion is over.

I fume silently. Maybe someday she'll understand that I am not a case. I can't be closed.

"I have to go in to work for a couple of hours. You—"

"I know. Stay here."

She opens the back door and pauses with her hand on the knob. "Should I put in a call to Dr. Engle?"

"No more therapists." I add wide, laser eyes. "Unless you're willing to open up and gut it out with me."

Rachel leaves the door standing open and comes back to give me an awkward hug. Awkward because she's five foot four and I'm five foot eight. I bend my knees to make it easier for her. "I'm sorry. I simply can't relive all of that again," she says. "I wish I could wave a magic wand and make you understand that none of the past has anything to do with who you are."

And I wish I could make her understand that she's wrong. It has everything to do with who I am.

"No worries, Rach. We're good," I say.

"We're better than good." She gives me a pat on the cheek. "Lock the door, okay?"

# ▸ 5 ◂

**Most people believe that forensic evidence is the ironclad truth but they're ignoring the fact that it's handled by humans.**

**—VICTOR FLEMMING**

Back in my room, I sink into bed and wrap a pile of blankets around me like flotation devices. When I was little we tried a bunch of things to jump-start my memory, including therapy and hypnosis, even acupuncture. Doctors said there was a chance I could remember the murder one day. But that never happened.

For my part, I just wanted to remember something—anything—about my mother.

I've read the report describing her cold, stiff body, lying on her back in an area of blood the size of a child's swimming pool. They believed she had been dead for three days. Apparently the trail of my footprints, stamped in blood, told them how I survived three days alone by raiding the low shelves of the refrigerator and drinking toilet water. Two-year-old me, terrified, hungry, and dehydrated, but left alive, by whom and for what reason? The report is hard enough for me to stomach all these years later. Rachel was hit with the real deal. Who wouldn't want to forget that?

Now I have a grasp on what she's been dealing with all these years.

It's hard, but I can read about my mother's death scene because I don't remember it. But I'm afraid the vision of Miss Peters, arms outstretched and golden curls floating on top of a seeping red sea, has become a permanent scar.

I even understand Rachel's constant fear for me.

When I was ten, she sat me down and explained how the man who killed my mother had never been caught. Her tone was comforting, but her words were very blunt. He's still out there walking around. He could be watching you every day and we would never know. He could come after you at any time. It was the most difficult and terrifying conversation of my life.

To keep me safe when she wasn't around, Rachel actually gave me my first training in forensics. She taught me to pay attention to details by constantly reminding me to think about where I was and whom I was with. Over time my eyes became like a camera and my brain a recorder. I learned to speak less and listen more. I didn't just think about my mother's killer, I obsessed over him. Is he tall? Short? Mean? Nice? Old? Young? He could be any man walking down the street.

Someone pounding on the back door startles me out of my thoughts. I throw off the covers and slip down the stairs, cautiously scanning gaps in the front curtains for a familiar car in the driveway. I relax when I see a sliver of red.

I unlock the back door and Spam shoots through the opening with the speed of an alien popping out of a corpse. She's wearing a short, puffy vest that's gray and clear. Looking closer, I realize she made it out of duct tape and Bubble Wrap. She flings her arms around my neck and hugs me so hard that one whole side of her vest explodes. She doesn't let go, even as I stumble backward into the kitchen. Our other friend, Lysa, steps in quietly behind her and closes the door.

Of the three of us, Lysa is the one who looks like she just stepped off the page of a magazine. She always wears a pair of crisply pressed designer jeans paired with hoodies, tanks, Vans sneakers, and socks that all color-coordinate. Today she's decked out in five different shades of teal, which nicely complements her flawless, golden-brown skin.

I pry one of my arms out of Spam's iron grasp and hold it out toward Lysa. She joins us in a quick group hug.

"You heard?" I ask.

Spam pulls back and squints, inspecting me all over.

"I'm okay." I break from the hug and move toward a chair at the table. Lysa joins me, nervously gnawing on a cuticle.

Spam heads for the refrigerator. "We would've been here sooner but they had us in an assembly all morning."

"Grief squad?" I ask.

Lysa slides her hands down the side of her face, dragging her skin into an exaggerated, sad look.

"They brought us all to the auditorium and just dropped the news on us." Spam moves things around in the fridge.

"I still don't believe it," Lysa says.

Spam settles on a tub of spicy hummus and a bag of baby carrots, bringing them to the table. "Oh." She stops and digs around in each of her pockets. "Before I forget, I know the timing sucks but we got a Cheater Check this morning." She pulls two small Ziploc bags out of her back pocket and slides them across the table. "Hair analysis."

Cheater Checks is a little side business we run. My obsession with forensics started by reading my Uncle Victor's books. Following his detailed descriptions I taught myself the basics, how to lift fingerprints and analyze hair. Then freshman year

I entered a chromatography test in the science fair comparing different shades and brands of lipstick. About that same time, we had a friend who thought her boyfriend was cheating on her. We tried the lipstick chromatography test on his shirt and proved it! Word got around about what we could do and people were willing to pay us to do it for them. So, we combined my forensic skills with Spam's computer savvy and Lysa's profiling ability and our little underground business was born.

We take on all kinds of jobs for our friends at school, like outwitting spying parents and neutralizing brothers and sisters who like to snoop. But we get the most requests for Cheater Checks—girlfriends and boyfriends who want proof they're dating cheaters.

I hold up the bags. Inside each one is a single blond hair about five inches long. One bag is labeled with the letter B, the other reads TRAMP. I shake my head. "Brianna found a random hair in Mark's car again?"

Spam chuckles. "I think this one came from inside his jacket."

"How will you do this without Miss P to let you into the lab on Monday?" Lysa says.

I roll my head from side to side, contemplating the changes I know are coming. "It's okay. I can do it here."

"How?" Lysa asks. "Don't you need a—"

"Microscope? Yeah. I have one up . . ." I catch myself. "Anyway, I can do it." I set the bags aside and grab another orange out of the bowl.

Spam curls one leg under her on the chair. "What were you doing at Miss Peters's?"

"Yeah, why didn't you call us?" Lysa asks.

"Or text us . . . or IM us . . . or FaceTime us?" Spam adds.

I freeze. I'm not ready to talk about last night. I need more time to get everything straight in my own head. "How'd you even know I was there?"

"You're kidding, right?" Spam crunches a carrot. "You being there is all over school." She pops the last bite into her mouth.

For the second time in less than twenty-four hours, my internal organs slide into a dark abyss located somewhere around my knees. I press my nose to the orange and inhale deeply. I get it. Discovering a murder has to be the pinnacle of gossip-worthy news. Seriously, what could trump that? I've been so crushed over Miss P I haven't considered what being the one to find her body will do to me. All that attention and pity . . . again.

I smooth the place mat in front of me with my finger. "What are they saying?"

Lysa pats my hand. "Don't worry, it's really not about you."

Spam gives Lysa a wide-eyed look. "Dude. It's totally about her."

"It is?" I squeeze Lysa's hand. I don't think I can deal with this.

Lysa frowns. "Go easy, Spam. She's been through a traumatic experience."

"You guys, I can't talk about this right now." My eyes fill with water but I hold perfectly still to keep it from spilling down my cheeks.

"It's okay. You don't have to. We can talk about something else." Lysa lays her other hand on top of mine, but I notice she passes a pointed look to Spam.

"Right." Spam glances away from Lysa and settles into a soothing tone. "It's just you *did* sort of become an instant legend, but that's not really important right now."

"L-l-legend?" I can barely speak.

"God, Spam, stop it! You're making it sound like she won prom queen or something. Just get to the point," Lysa says.

"She kinda did," Spam says with a grin. "Everybody knows who you are now." Lysa's glare causes Spam to drop the humor. "But we want you to know we're really, really worried about you. And we know you must have been investigating something important at Miss P's. We just don't understand why you didn't tell us about it."

This is so hard. I hate lying to them. "It's not what you think. And it didn't have anything to do with you guys."

"Are you sure?" Lysa asks carefully. "Because you know we *think* it has something to do with the box . . . and if that's the case then we are involved. Big-time."

I need to say something but I can't seem to dredge up a new lie.

"Come on. We helped you steal it, and if that box caused what happened with Miss Peters, you can bet we're going to get grilled about it." Lysa's voice gets higher and louder, a clear sign that she's starting to panic.

"Miss Peters was murdered by a person, not a box. No one even knows I have it. I promise."

"Erin, my father's a criminal attorney. I know *all* the ways that this can go wrong for us," Lysa says.

"Where's the box now?" Spam asks.

"It's in a safe place," I say, my voice barely above a whisper.

"Maybe you should give it to one of us," Spam says. "For safekeeping."

"No!" My tone is sharp and nonnegotiable. The box is mine. I'm keeping it. "It's fine where it is."

"Where exactly is it?" Lysa asks. "Since we're involved, I think we should know."

I push away from the table so fast I bang the chair against

the wall. "I should be resting." I manage a shaky half smile. "Rachel agrees that I probably have PTSD. Don't worry about the box; it's hidden in a place where no one would think to look."

I stand like I'm going to walk them to the door. Spam and Lysa rise and ease in that direction, but then Lysa turns back for one more question.

"When did you first suspect there was something weird about Journey Michaels?"

"Huh?" I freeze, and the image of him walking past the interrogation room door leaps to my mind. Pale and sullen, his hands cuffed behind him. "I never suspected anything about him. Why?"

"Because isn't it weird that just yesterday you were watching him?" Spam says.

"The same day he killed Miss Peters and you found her body," Lysa adds.

"Allegedly," I say, stuffing my hands in my pockets to keep them from shaking. "You can't say he did it. Not yet."

Lysa and Spam exchange a tight-lipped frown that suggests there's something seriously deranged about what I just said, but I'm done talking for the day.

"I need to lie down." I wait quietly while they slip back out the door. Then I flip the lock behind them and race up the stairs to my bedroom, bringing the Cheater Check bags with me.

# ▸ 6 ◂

If you want to spot a liar, just remember that concealing the truth is like swallowing a slow-acting poison. It might take a while, but it will get them in the end.

—VICTOR FLEMMING

I check the time and wonder how long I have before Rachel will be home. I can't risk her catching me with the box, so I usually restrict my time with it to when she's working a night shift or after she's gone to sleep.

In a true example of Rachel's love for all things police-related, she's the supervisor of our 911 emergency call center. Her usual hours are 7:00 a.m. to 4:00 p.m. But if someone calls in sick she has to cover their shift. Today she said she would only be there a few hours.

I send her a quick text. I THOUGHT YOU'D BE HOME FOR LUNCH.

While I wait for her reply, I'm already prepping my bedroom.

I close the door and shove a thick three-ring binder into the gap between the bottom of the door and the carpet. With the door secured, I roll my desk chair into the roomy walk-in closet. Then I stand on the chair to reach a small knot of rope that blends in with the murky old plaster ceiling.

Pulling gently on the rope releases a wide trapdoor, and a sturdy wooden stairway unfolds from the attic. My phone vibrates with Rachel's reply. GO AHEAD AND EAT. I'M STUCK HERE ANOTHER TWO HOURS.

Two whole hours!

Relieved, I fly up the wooden steps that emerge into the middle of a huge attic that spans both my bedroom and the guest bedroom next door.

It's pitch-dark up here even in the middle of the day because I've covered the small round window at the peak in the roof. Rachel never comes up here, but just to be on the safe side, I've staged it to look like I don't come up here, either. I shifted most of the boxes to the guest room side. Then along the stairs on my side, I've carefully arranged a pile of boxes, trunks, suitcases, tarps, and rolled-up rugs to act as a screen. If anyone sticks their head up here they'll think there's nothing to see on the other side of this pile but more junk and storage.

I tap my foot in an arch until I find the pedal switch. When I step on it, two lamps on the other side of the room blink on, bathing the area in a warm glow. I have separated the furniture and arranged it like a living room. There's a smooth, red leather sofa, a coffee table shaped like a kidney bean, and end tables and lamps. Some nights I just come up here to lay on the sofa and read, pretending like it's my own apartment. Other times I putter in the lab area I created from a desk and matching cabinet. But today, after everything that's happened, I *need* the box.

I keep it in a large wooden cabinet that I can secure with a padlock. I do this so often that my fingers spin quickly through the combination. I remove the lock and set it aside. I pause for a couple of seconds, inhaling deeply and then forcing air out through tight lips. No matter how stressed and anxious I am, I never rush this part. It's ritual. I want to feel it. Savor it. I need to make it part of me.

I sink to my knees and part the doors. On the bottom shelf is a simple white cardboard box, like the kind they use in offices to store files.

I take a pair of rubber gloves from the shelf and slip them on. Then I carefully slide the box out of the cabinet. I set it on the rug as gently as if it contained a baby.

In many ways it does. It contains baby me.

The day this box came into my life, it was as if the world cracked open and possibility was born. Today I worry where that will take us now.

▾ ▾ ▾

Last summer, Sydney offered us a short temp job at the police department. Three or four days archiving regular files like bills and things. Spam, Lysa, and I were happy to earn some extra cash. It was boring work, but we made it fun—shredding the old files to make room for new ones.

Almost immediately I keyed in on the fact that this huge storage area held *all* of the police department files. The work files were on one side but the evidence files were on the other. There was no reason for anyone to think that we would wander into the evidence side. There was also no one else in the storage room with us for long periods of time.

At first I just wanted to find my mother's evidence box, to know that it existed. So that one day, when I start my job as a forensic scientist, I can request the evidence and reopen her case. Evidence boxes are filed alphabetically by the name of the victim, so it only took me a few minutes to find the box labeled BLAKE, SARAH.

But it took two days to get up the nerve to actually open it.

Each night I would lie in bed and imagine what might be in that box. I hoped I might find something familiar, a memory or some link from me to her. What I actually found was . . . not that.

On top was a plastic sleeve containing clothing, stiff and stained with dried blood. *Her* blood.

That was more than I had bargained for. I closed the box and put it back on the shelf, vowing not to touch it again.

But when we got to our last day of work, with only two hours left on our shift, I realized my chance to go through the evidence from my mother's murder was about to expire. Shouldn't I take a look? Shouldn't I know what was in there? With only fifteen minutes left on the job, I decided to steal that box.

Getting it was easy. Sneaking it home was a huge challenge. You can have secrets when your transportation is a sky-blue vintage Vespa scooter, just not secrets the size of a file box.

What evolved was a weird no-plan plan.

Each step just became the next most logical thing to do. I took an empty box from the trash pile and dumped the contents of my mother's box into it. My stomach lurched when a huge knife in a plastic bag tumbled from one box to the other. I couldn't bring myself to look at it closely, but I knew the blade was coated with dark, dried blood.

I placed my mother's empty evidence box back on the shelf. No one was actively working her case, so it wasn't likely that anyone would look inside. But if the box went completely missing, that might get noticed.

I borrowed the keys to Lysa's car and, when no one was looking, I carried the box out and stashed it in her trunk. I didn't even tell my friends about it right away. I waited to confess until we were celebrating the end of the job with ice cream sundaes.

Lysa was horrified. "You've made me an accessory," she screeched.

Spam just thought it was an incredibly creepy thing to do.

They were both right, of course. But, like the great friends they are, neither of them turned me in or insisted we take it back.

My next problem was getting the box into my house. Rachel was taking a couple of days off from work that week, so Lysa had to drive around with my mother's murder box in her trunk until I could slip it into my house. When I brought it up to my room I realized how much it stuck out. It looked out of place on my shelves and wouldn't fit under my bed. I needed a secure place to stash it. One that Rachel wasn't likely to find.

That's how I discovered the secret space in the attic.

▾ ▾ ▾

"Hi, Mom." I lay my hands on the lid of the box, allowing narcotic tendrils of calm to work their way into my bones. After a few minutes, I move us over to the desk. Just having her near me is all I need.

On the desk I've arranged a microscope and the beginnings of a small lab from a box of things I found stored up here. I know this stuff belonged to my uncle Victor. Maybe someday I'll get to ask him about it.

For hair analysis, I only need to line both hairs up on a slide and look at them under the microscope. It will be easy to see if the hairs match each other, which is of course what Brianna is hoping. If they don't match, I'll have no way of knowing who the other hair might belong to, but at least Brianna will have some warning and she'll know to be careful about trusting Mark.

I place Brianna's hair at the top of the slide and the "tramp" hair at the bottom. I slap another slide over the top to hold them in place, then arrange the hair sandwich under the lens. A few tweaks bring them into perfect focus, giving me a view of the three main parts of these hairs. The part I'm most interested in is the medulla.

Hmmm.

I open my notebook to a clean page and draw a sketch of what I'm seeing.

Without the microscope, both hairs look identical in size, shape, and color. And yet the magnified versions could not be more different.

The outside layer of Brianna's hair is smooth and the middle is a long, dark, broken streak. The sample hair has a rough outside cuticle with little points that stick out, and the medulla isn't a streak at all, but made up of small, light, round shapes.

Once the sketches are complete, I put the hairs back in the bags and lock them and my mother's box back in the cabinet. I turn out the lights and head down the stairway, putting everything back as I go.

Since I'm unfamiliar with what round shapes in the medulla means, I go online to check it out, typing "medulla pearl shape" into a search engine.

The answer comes up immediately. I smile, because Brianna's going to love this. I send a quick text to Spam: CHECKED OUT HAIRS. TELL BRIANNA MARK'S COOL.

# 7

It's all about observation. Example: If a hair falls out, the root is going to have a little club shape to it. But if it's been yanked out it will be stretched and include small tags of skin. Now you've got evidence!

—VICTOR FLEMMING

According to Rachel I'm supposed to spend the weekend—well, as much time as I need, but at least the weekend—wrapping my brain around what happened to Miss P.

Both the reality *and* the finality of it.

I'd give anything to be able to create a different ending to that night. But I am clear that I didn't cause what happened to her . . . any more than my little baby self caused what happened to my mother.

Rachel wants to be sure I understand this so it doesn't become another survivor-guilt situation. It was just a wrong-time, wrong-place moment. And sometimes those things just happen.

I see her point, but accepting it is easier said than done.

So when Spam and Lysa drop by on Saturday to see if I can go to the mall, I'm not really feeling it. Rachel encourages me to go, though. She thinks it will do me good to get out.

Lysa drives and I take the backseat. No one says much on the ride over. But when Lysa parks in front of Battery Burger, I can tell this isn't a normal shopping excursion.

They've chosen our favorite restaurant. Also, Spam and Lysa look about as happy as the statues on Easter Island. I follow them to an outdoor table without protest. Spam makes it clear this isn't just about lunch.

"Time to spill," she says.

"Spill what?"

"Spill why you went to Miss P's house," Spam says.

I glance over my shoulder; the tables near us are becoming populated. "Not here. Okay?"

The waitress comes to take our orders. Spam orders pasta, I order a salad, and Lysa goes for the burger. We stay quiet until she leaves.

Lysa whispers, "My dad says they'll probably want to talk to us, too. We need to know what we can say."

"You weren't there. Just say that."

"That stupid box has changed you, Erin." Lysa leans in close to keep from being overheard by other diners. "Ever since we helped you take it, you've been . . . different."

"Guys, the box has nothing to do with this."

Spam pins me with a harsh glare. "Admit it. You thought you could find your mom's killer without our help."

"Wrong. I thought I could find my father." There, I said it. "Sue me for wanting to know the basic things about my life that you guys take for granted."

Spam and Lysa blink at each other.

"I did not see that coming," Spam says.

"Me neither," Lysa says. "But how?"

"Okay, it kinda did come from the box," I say. "In with all the police stuff was a report listing three guys the police talked to after my mother's murder."

"They only talked to three guys?" Lysa looks appalled.

"Well, no, they talked to a lot of people and, of course, they interviewed all of my mother's friends, like Rachel and Mr. Roberts. But these guys were special."

"They were suspects," Lysa guesses. "And they had motives."

"They were *boyfriends*." I drop that word like a bomb.

Lysa and Spam share a shocked look.

"Whaaat?" Lysa says. "The report called them *boyfriends*?"

"Actually, it just said she *might* have dated them." The notion of my mother doing something normal like dating brings a soft smile to my lips. "So I figured—you know—one of these guys could be my DNA dad and not even know it."

"Wow." Lysa and Spam say it at exactly the same time.

"I know, right?"

"How did you find them?" Lysa asks.

"Did you see them? Did you talk to them?" Spam clearly craves every detail, which is so funny, because I was sure she'd be against me trying to find my father. "Do any of them look like you?"

"I only saw tiny glimpses, and no, I don't think they look like me." I tear off a strip of my napkin and curl it around my finger. "Miss P thought I shouldn't get them involved unless we found a connection, but one was a boat captain who lives at the docks. Another was an artist who lives in that cute bungalow neighborhood on the south side. And the last one's an accountant who lives near Miss P."

"The boat captain would be great," Spam says. "He would probably be adventurous and brave."

I don't have the heart to tell her that when I spied on him, he was actually tired and a little drunk, which is how he ended up cutting his hand and I scored a bloody towel with his DNA.

"Yeah, but an artist," Lysa says. "Your mom was a photographer, so I could totally see you having an artist for a dad.

Think how awesome and romantic it would be to hang out in one of those bungalows."

I don't think Lysa would find the artist chain-smoking on his back porch to be very awesome or romantic, but I'll save sharing that image with her for another day.

"So how are you going to figure out which one is your dad?" Spam asks.

"IF. It might be none of them. The plan was to find out by comparing their DNA with mine. I went by their houses late that night, when the trash was out at the curb for collection, and pulled out something that would have DNA on it. Miss P was going to run the test. It was a long shot, but at least I'd know." I sit back in my chair, allowing the tension to drain out of me. It feels good to finally come clean about this with them. And for the first time in a couple of days, I'm hungry. The waitress brings our food and I steal some of Lysa's fries.

"That's a genius plan," Spam says, spreading her pasta around the plate to cool it off.

"It is," Lysa agrees. "Because taking things out of the trash at the curb isn't against the law. But why didn't you tell us what you were doing?"

"I didn't know how I was going to feel about the results. If there was a match—or if there wasn't. I was definitely planning to tell you the next day, but then the whole thing with Miss P happened." *Whole thing* doesn't even begin to describe the horror of that night or the realization that it will never be over. A glance at their sad faces tells me they don't need or want any more specific details, though. So I'm happy I let it go at that.

"What if one of them killed her?" Lysa says.

I gasp. It's not like I haven't thought about that. But the last thing I want is to be responsible for what happened to Miss P.

"That's impossible," Spam says. "If all Erin did was go through trash, then none of them even saw her."

I rest my elbows on the table and press my fingers against my eyelids. As much as I try to block them out, the gory kaleidoscope images from that night cut through. "I tried to be careful."

"See," Spam says. "She was careful."

"No. She said she *tried* to be careful," Lysa argues. She curls her hands into fists and rests them solidly on the table. "But look what happened anyway. This is why I keep saying we shouldn't be messing around with all this DNA, CSI crap."

"Hey, it's not like Erin killed Miss P," Spam argues.

"Maybe not," Lysa says. "But what if she led one of those guys there and he got upset over his DNA being stolen and did something? And it was all because she wanted to play criminal investigator instead of leaving that stuff to the professionals."

My voice is so small it's nearly buried by the sounds of the lunch crowd. If only I could bury my guilt, too. "Just so you know, Miss P wanted this DNA project as much as I did, and it couldn't have been one of the potential dads who hurt her because when I got there she was already . . ." I make a side slash with a shaky hand, which is easier than saying the actual words.

Spam crosses her arms over her chest. "So who killed her then?"

I shrug, palms up. "No clue."

"My dad always says the most obvious choice is probably the right one. Which means it must have been Journey," Lysa says.

"I'd go with that," Spam says.

I can't agree or disagree. I'm just not sure. "I-I don't know."

"It's okay that you like him," Spam says. "Serial killers are really popular. They get prison married and everything."

"Stop it. I don't even know him," I say.

"We know you like him, though," Lysa says, glancing at Spam.

I start to deny it but Spam gives me the hand. "Don't. Okay?"

"It's not like that. He's just—I don't know—a fantasy or something. I have no clue why he was there that night, but it didn't have anything to do with me. None of this has anything to do with me."

Just then Brianna and two friends stroll by our table.

Brianna opens her arms wide. "Erin," she calls out. "Thanks for the brilliant news about the hair. You always save the day."

Brianna is a perfect distraction.

The sketch I made of the hairs she gave us is in my notebook. I pull the book out of my bag and tear out the page with the sketch.

"Bri, hold up." I slide the paper across the table. "You've got to see this because it's so cool. You know how the two hairs you gave us looked identical?" I point to the top sketch. "Well, this is your hair under a microscope. See how it's all smooth on the outside, and inside there's a long dark broken streak?"

"Wait. They're different?" Brianna shifts a confused look to Spam.

"They're crazy different," I say.

Brianna frowns. "Spam said they were the same . . . that the hairs matched."

Now Spam looks upset. "That's what you told me to tell her."

Feathers are getting ruffled. Tensions are rising. Brianna is about to cry.

"Everybody just calm down." I fan them lightly with my

hands. "Spam, I told you to tell her Mark's cool. Because he is. Watch."

I hold the sketch out where they both can see it.

"The second one is a cat hair." I point to the bottom sketch. "That's why forensics is so amazing. See these round, pearl-like shapes? Well, only cat hair has that. I'm guessing it's an apricot Persian or some other long-haired cat." I press the sketch into Brianna's hand. "You can keep the drawing."

But big fat tears have replaced Brianna's smile. I take back the drawing and find a Kleenex in my purse. I press that into her hand instead.

"You heard what I said, right? Not blonde-girl hair but cat hair?"

"I heard you," she says, sniffing. "And I have an ex-best friend who owns that stupid Persian cat, too."

Oh. As Brianna rushes off in search of Mark, I'm starting to think the drama is piling up faster than I can process it.

# ► 8 ◄

Evidence is the engine of an investigation, but you still need the rest of the car in order for it all to make sense.

—VICTOR FLEMMING

I spend the rest of the weekend following Rachel's orders to rest and process.

By Monday, I'm ready to go back to school even though Rachel thinks it's still too soon. She runs me through a quick Q and A, just to make sure I'm not blaming myself, and I must pass because she agrees to let me go.

What she doesn't know is I've made a list of things to check out regarding Miss Peters's murder. And Journey Michaels is item number one.

I've always felt drawn to him, but never in a fearful way. Now I'm wondering if my instincts were telling me to look at him for another reason. Spam and Lysa think he's dangerous. But the police let him go, so how bad can he be?

If I can look straight into his eyes, I believe I'll see the truth.

It's early when I pull into the school parking lot, even though I don't need to be early to get a good spot. I'm allowed to park my scooter, which I affectionately call Vespy, in the green zone next to the flagpole and the administration building.

I'm not there three seconds before Principal Roberts is out the door and making his way toward me.

"Erin," he says. "It worries me to see you back so soon. Are you sure you're not rushing things? You need time to recover from your connection to this tragedy."

I give him my standard bland smile, but I honestly have no idea how I would know if I am rushing things or not. Why do the adults always think time will make a difference? Aren't I living proof that time doesn't heal anything?

Mr. Roberts must be fascinated with static electricity, because every time I take off my helmet he can't seem to curb the impulse to pat my hair back into place.

Today is no exception.

"This has been devastating for all of us," he says, patting right and then left.

Mr. Roberts has been my principal since kindergarten. When I moved on to middle school, he was promoted and became my principal there, too. Then, last year, when I headed to high school, he moved again. He likes to joke that he's growing up along with us.

This probably came from one of the shrinks I've seen along the way, but Rachel says it's important for me to have constants in my life, meaning things and people I can count on to be there every day. If nothing else, he's been constant.

"Thanks, Mr. Roberts, but I think I'm okay."

"You sure?" he asks. "If it gets to be too much, come see me. My door is always open."

"Thanks, I will."

"I'm here for you." His expression is somber but he still mimes a bowling move to send me off to class. It wouldn't be a Mr. Roberts encounter without a sporty farewell.

I keep my head down as I hurry toward the four-story building at the center of our campus and I steel myself for the whispers. *There she goes . . . that's her. The murder girl.*

Deep breath. Shoulders back. I'm about to step through the doors when a stray football drops out of the sky and makes direct contact with the top of my head. For a second, everything dims and sparks detonate behind my eyes.

Footsteps run past me. A guy's voice says, "Sorry," and then he's gone without a backward glance.

A lump swells under my hair. It feels huge.

Meanwhile, throngs of students stream past me, heading for lockers and classes. I realize they all have one thing in common: They don't know who I am, and they don't care, either.

Fine. I didn't want to be the murder freak anyway.

At the base of the stairs, a group of seniors huddle, talking in hushed tones. I slow up to listen.

"My parents are calling Principal Roberts," a blonde girl says. "They want to know how he's going to keep us safe."

"They're saying he'll get bumped from the team," a guy in a basketball jersey says.

"My dad says he's going straight to jail, so we can kiss the championship good-bye," says another.

"Who cares about a stupid championship; we lost Miss P."

"Not only that, but we'll always be remembered as the class with the killer!" The girl speaking glances over her shoulder and glares at me. I move off. I've heard enough anyway. It's pretty clear they're talking about Journey, and it sounds like they hate him now. I've just reached the top of the stairs when I hear one of the girls say, "Hey, wasn't that her?"

▼ ▼ ▼

Lunchtime. I bring my food to the cement steps. The sun is out and the weather is balmy. I shield my eyes and scan the grounds, looking for Journey. I usually have no trouble spotting him from up here. He always comes out of the cafeteria on the ground floor and high-fives about fifty people on the quad before hitting the courts.

But today I don't see him at all. It's weird.

There's a game on at the courts. But Journey's not playing. And the quad is nearly empty. I trace his normal route back to the cafeteria. No Journey.

My throat tightens. I nibble at my sandwich. It has no taste.

"Really?" There's an edge to Spam's voice, like a saw biting into an extra-thick block of wood. "Really?" she repeats.

Spam and Lysa are standing behind me. Lysa looks almost sunny, dressed in various shades of lemon. Meanwhile Spam's paired a cowboy hat with light-up disco-ball earrings.

"I am truly shocked to find you *here,*" Spam says.

I look to Lysa, who is usually our voice of reason.

"I'm with her," she admits. "Finding you up here looking for him is pathological."

"Not to mention creepy," Spam adds.

"I don't know what you're talking about." I feign ignorance.

Spam lifts her chin, indicating something down in the quad. I follow her gaze. I didn't notice him before but Journey's sitting on a bench, in the middle of the quad, directly across from my spot on the stairs. He's completely alone . . . and staring straight up at me.

"Oh man," I whisper.

"Stop it! Stop looking at him." Spam grabs my chin and turns my face.

"But he's looking at me," I say.

"He's trying to intimidate you." Lysa's using her calm voice.

"You think so?" I can't quite accept the notion of Journey as the complete opposite of who I thought he was.

Spam throws her hands in the air. "What is it with you? Are you just blinded by flashy white teeth? He's clearly trying to scare you so you won't tell what you saw." She glares down at him. "He's a shark in sheep's clothing." She pinches a spot on my jacket and twists it between her fingers. "Let's go."

"I'm not—"

"Oh, yeah you are."

I cram my lunch into my bag and roll my legs back over the ledge. I don't want to follow them, but they're not taking no for an answer.

"It's wolf," I say. "Wolf in sheep's clothing. Not shark."

"Trust me," Spam says. "That one down there is a shark." I'm at least a full five inches taller than Spam, but her glare is so intense I'm afraid my hair will burst into flames if I don't follow her.

"You guys, no one knows everything I saw that night. And I mean no one."

With a tight grip on my jacket, Spam hauls me down the stairs.

Lysa is right behind us. "Well, you must've seen something because even my dad says you're a witness."

Spam agrees. "And you're the one who dropped the dime on him."

"The what?" At the bottom of the stairs I stop and pull my sleeve away from Spam.

She turns to face me, one hand resting on her hip while the other flutters over her head. "Don't tell me you don't watch *Law & Order*. Dropped a dime . . . like, you know, *dropped* a *dime* in a pay phone and called the police."

I look from her to Lysa. "Just so you know, I used my cell phone and called 911, which is what any normal person would do."

# ▸ 9 ◂

What's really important about investigating a murder is finding
the truth. Sometimes it will seem like you're the only
one who cares about that part other than
the family of the victim.

—VICTOR FLEMMING

The area at the bottom of the cafeteria stairs gets a lot of foot traffic during lunch. The fact that Spam and I are engaged in a mild tug-of-war over the sleeve of my jacket in this spot attracts even more attention. She's trying to pull me away from the spotlight, while I want to walk straight over to the quad and confront Journey Michaels right where he sits.

Finally, I pull away from her and when I turn, there's Journey Michaels standing right in front of me. Towering over me, actually, with fists clenched and a murderous look on his face.

I have no words.

He stares into my eyes, long and hard, a twisted scowl marring his face. The crowd, hungry for a confrontation, closes in. I flinch as he brings up his fist and flings something right at me. A thin string of white and blue fabric hits me in the chest. "I think you dropped this," he says, nearly spitting his words.

A couple of friends from his team haul him away before he can say more.

It wouldn't matter. I'm too stunned to move or speak. My fingers close around the string. I open them and stare at it, trying to focus on the print. Small. Blue and white. It can't be, right? It just can't.

I'm barely aware of Spam and Lysa guiding me to the office because I'm silently freaking out. My ears buzz. My vision swims. Nothing makes any sense. Spam's prattling on, nonstop.

"Huh?" It's all I can think to say.

"You're not listening to me," Spam says. "I'm trying to tell you you're a witness and that's dangerous, mama."

Lysa squeezes my hand. "Go home and rest and try not to think about it."

But the fury on Journey Michaels's face and this stupid strip of fabric are all I can think about.

I wait out in the hall to see Mr. Roberts, nervously winding the strip of fabric around my fingers while he deals with irate parents. I try to listen through the door but I can't hear much, just raised voices.

As the parents leave his office, their wary eyes and stony faces broadcast their unhappiness. It's not hard to guess that they don't want their kids in the same class with a killer.

Several of the adults recognize me. I catch the nudges between them and clock how their expressions suddenly drip with pity.

When I finally get in to see Mr. Roberts, he overflows with concern. "What happened?" He comes around the desk and perches on the edge, hovering over me. He's so worried, I stop nervously fiddling with the fabric and shove it down into my purse. I need him to let me go home. I have to check this out. *Now.*

"You were right. It was too soon," I say.

"I'm sending you home." He scribbles out a pass. "I'd drive

you there myself but there's another group of vigilante parents on their way." He presses the pass into my hand and shoos me toward the door. I stop and look back. His face is etched with worry but he mimes a tight layup shot anyway. I offer a grim smile in response and slip out.

My mood is lighter as I leave the campus. For just one second I pretend that everything's okay and there is no more bad news coming and nothing terrible is about to happen. I turn down my street and make it almost to my driveway before I notice the police cars: two of them, parked on the lawn. A third one, a van, blocks the driveway.

Our front door, which Rachel and I never use, stands wide open at the top of the stairs. A team of officers goes in and out. The dead space inside me becomes an icy brick. I ramp the scooter over the curb and dump it at the edge of the yard, racing for the house.

A police officer comes down carrying a box. We meet mid-stairs. I move right, he blocks left. He jogs right, I move left.

"Hey. Whoa," he says.

"Excuse me. I need to get through."

Sydney appears above on the landing.

"Rachel?" My voice is barely human. I need to know and yet I'm terrified to know.

"She's fine," Sydney says, pointing toward the house. "She's in the kitchen."

The officer manages to get past me. I glance in the box. It's filled with my stuff: clothes and shoes. My laptop is sticking up. I whirl and follow him.

"Hey, that's mine!"

He holds the box out of my reach. I leap up, trying to grab it. "Step back, miss," he orders. "We have a warrant."

"That's my computer."

Sydney's fingers bite into my arm. "Erin. Stop."

"Why are you doing this? I told you everything."

"I know," she says. "Come inside, I'll explain."

Sydney holds me back. The officer steps around me and loads the box into the police van.

"Make him stop and I will."

"I can't do that. He's doing his job. And you need to let me do mine."

I break away and race toward the back door. It's the quickest route to the kitchen. I sprint up the stairs and turn the knob.

Rachel's at the table, clinging to a coffee mug like it's the last life preserver on the *Titanic*. Her eyes are rimmed red; dark shadows exaggerate the hollows of her cheekbones. Is this exhaustion or tear-streaked mascara? I can't tell.

I walk straight up to her, emotion bottled in my throat. I turn my palms up. How could she let this happen?

"Sit down," she says. "Sydney will explain."

I glare at the three police officers prowling our living room. They systematically open every drawer, fan through every stack of magazines, and inspect every pile of mail. Two more officers tromp down the stairs carrying more stuff from my bedroom. *My freaking room.*

I haven't done anything. How are they even allowed up there? Don't I have any rights?

I thump into the chair next to Rachel. My foot taps air, shaking the table. But I don't care. Sydney wanders in from the front door and heads in our direction. She stops to oversee the snooping officers along the way.

By the time she joins us at the table, I'm practically coming out of my skin.

"Syd, this is freaking me out. It's like you're looking for the murder weapon or something." I say it as a bad joke but Sydney and Rachel exchange the look of doom.

Sydney reaches into her bag.

"We have that." She removes a plastic evidence bag from her purse and carefully lays it on the table.

It's so thin, barely a mound where her fingers rest as she pushes the bag across the table at me. I expect to catch the glint of something sinister like a shiny metal scalpel or a flat hand-sharpened stake. My lungs practically collapse when Sydney lifts her fingers and I see it's . . . a nail file. This thing is eight inches long and three-quarters of an inch wide. It's made of hardened glass with a grinding surface that's guaranteed to last forever and a tip that tapers to a very wicked point. It's a completely stylish implement of ragged nail destruction. But I can see how it could also be a very deadly murder weapon.

I suck in a tattered breath. "My nail file?"

"So, you confirm that it is yours?" Sydney's eyes shift to Rachel. She sinks her teeth into her lower lip.

I look from one to the other. I couldn't deny it even if I wanted to. My name's painted on the handle in huge, purple letters, embellished with fairy wings. Not my taste but it was a party favor from Lysa's birthday. "Just because you found it in my room . . ."

"That's the problem, Erin, we didn't find it in your room," Sydney says, letting implication hang in her silence. "And you were there at Miss Peters's house."

"What about Journey Michaels? He was there, too."

"Erin, I believe you saw someone. I do," Sydney says. "I also believe you thought it was someone you knew. But we haven't found a speck of anything tying the Michaels kid to the crime scene."

My heart pauses for a moment, lurching awkwardly out of my chest like a baby bird leaving the nest for the very first time. "Wait. What?"

"The Michaels kid, we've got nothing on him."

"You're saying he's clear?"

"For the moment." Sydney's look seems to question whether it will stay that way.

"And I'm not?" Anger swells, crowding my rib cage.

"I'm sorry, I don't know what to think," Sydney says. "But so far, the only evidence we've found at the scene is yours."

"Of course my evidence is there, I found her, remember?"

Sydney makes a calming gesture. "I know you found her, I just think there are things you haven't told us yet."

Oh crap. The box!

"Is Erin a suspect?" Rachel asks, twining her fingers with mine. I squeeze back hard. If they found it, they haven't told Rachel yet. She's way too calm and sad. If she knew she'd be furious.

"It just happened so fast . . . I . . ." I start to explain.

"I'm sure everything about that night is a blur," Sydney says. "Which is why I do not want you to discuss any of this with anyone. Understand?"

"Fine," I say.

"Good. Now, tell me about the bag in the mailbox."

Oh my god . . . the stupid DNA samples! Here I'm worrying about the box and she's focused on things that don't matter.

"Syd, I can explain. It was just a bunch of random trash—DNA." I'm trying to focus on her, but I'm distracted by all three of the officers tromping down the stairs from my room.

"I hope you're telling the truth, because we're sending it off to be processed," Sydney says.

One of the officers leans in the door. He's got a white file box tucked under his arm. "We got it."

I stop breathing. Oh no. There it goes. No. No. It's way too soon.

Sydney looks from me to Rachel. "Don't worry, guys. I'll get this straightened out."

Me, worry? Ha! I'm a bottomless sinkhole of worry. And then I'm not, because, like the therapist always said, this is completely out of my control. They're taking my stuff and there's nothing I can do about it.

I stand up. "And then what?"

Sydney stops at the door and looks back. "Erin, I—"

"You got a search warrant, you're taking my stuff. That means you think I—I—" I can't say it. The words simply refuse to come out.

Sydney's speechless, too. She stares at me, her hand frozen on the doorknob. Rachel grabs my arm and pulls me back into my chair. "Erin, sit down," she hisses.

Syd leans against the door. "Is there something else you want to tell me?"

I shake my head, horrified we're even discussing this.

Syd exhales. "Look, this is the process we use to check out what we call persons of interest. I'd like to think the items we've collected from you will bring us closer to the truth."

Years with professionals have taught me to recognize psychobabble. "You're profiling me."

"Yes. But if you haven't done anything wrong, we won't find anything," Syd says.

That wasn't what I wanted to hear. I've done things. Many things. There's no way of knowing what she knows.

Stung, I sit perfectly still and stare at the table. After a few seconds, and without another word, Syd leaves quietly, closing the door behind her.

Usually, Syd and Rachel hug good-bye and exchange last-minute thoughts. Sometimes, Rachel even walks all the way down to her car with her.

This time Rachel sits, allowing the quiet to swallow us.

# 10

If you haven't done anything wrong, we won't find anything.

FAMOUS LAST WORDS
—DETECTIVE SYDNEY

As soon as Sydney's car leaves our driveway I bolt from the table, knocking over my chair.

"Erin?" Rachel gasps.

"Sorry. I need to go to my room."

She ferries her cup to the sink. "I'm coming with you."

I don't want her to come, but I can't exactly say that.

My room is the first door at the top of the stairs and it's open wide. The view stops me like a punch in the face. I'm not the neatest housekeeper in the world. But this . . .

Every shelf, drawer, and basket has been searched. While they tried to be neat about it, there are piles of stuff everywhere, sliding and tumbling into one another. Loose beads and bracelets are like the pox, dotting everything with color. There are haphazard paths of scattered CDs. Photos of my friends stare up from the gray carpet. I pick up one of Spam mugging and slide it into my back pocket. My sheets, blanket, and mattress are separated from one another. I can't believe Sydney would let them do this.

Ironically, my closet—the only thing I actually care about—

is closed up tight. I hop mini-islands of stuff to get there and swing the door open.

*Holy crap!*

The closet's bare. Not a slip of ribbon or scrap of cloth; only bare walls, bare poles, empty shelves. To my eye the knot in the ceiling that pulls down the ladder is glaringly obvious. I slam the door and lean against it, my breath coming in ragged gasps.

Anxiously I scan the piles of clothes, shoes, papers, and makeup stacked around the room. The cops didn't miss so much as a safety pin. But what I don't see down here is anything from the attic.

Is it possible?

Rachel trudges over to the mattress and tugs on it. "Help me with this."

I get on the other side and we lift it back onto the bed frame. Then we work together to put the sheets and blankets back on.

"I'm sorry," she says, gesturing to the mess. "When Syd said she had a search warrant I didn't know what to say. I had no idea. Maybe I should have consulted a lawyer first. I just—" She looks lost and I feel so guilty.

"This is my fault, Rachel. I'm the one who's sorry." So so so sorry—

She hurries around the bed, pulling me into a tight hug. "Shhhh. Don't think like that. Remember, you did not cause this. I don't know why terrible things happen to good people, but sometimes they just do." She lets me go, taking in the state of the room again. "I'll help you clean this up after dinner."

"I can do it. It's not that bad." I twine my fingers with hers and squeeze.

She squeezes back. "Dinner will be ready soon."

"Sounds good."

I should throw myself straight into picking up all this stuff. But I can't concentrate. I almost can't even breathe. It's risky, but I have to know.

I grab the strip of fabric from my purse and head up into the attic. My insides curl and slide like melting Jell-O. I scramble past all the junk, bracing myself for the worst.

But the attic is exactly the way I left it.

Padlock in place . . . everything. The police never came up here.

I go straight to the cabinet, do the padlock thing, and swing the doors open.

Her box is there, on the bottom shelf, right where it's supposed to be. That box the officer was holding . . . it wasn't my mom's. The relief that floods through me could fill this room.

I know the contents of this box by heart but in order to be completely sure I go through each thing, one piece at a time.

Eight-inch chef's knife. Police reports. Paperwork and my mom's photo albums. Everything is here and intact. I save the plastic sleeve containing her shirt for last. I don't even need to remove it from the plastic. Just laying the string that Journey threw at me on top tells me it's a perfect match to the blue-and-white peasant print. What does this mean? Are there two shirts exactly the same? Is someone trying to re-create my mother's murder with me as the victim this time?

It's a chilling thought.

Rachel is expecting me downstairs but I have to fully check this out. I have to know what I'm dealing with.

Wearing rubber gloves and only touching a small spot on the neckline, I gingerly pull the shirt completely out of the plastic sleeve and open it up. The style has no collar but a deep,

*V*-like split in the front that's designed to have a long string or tie on each side of the split so it can be tied closed.

One tie is attached and caked with blood.

The other is missing.

I examine the wad of fabric Journey threw at me. Realization drips into me like acid. This strip of fabric is not from a top *like* my mother's. It's from her actual shirt.

A hot, nauseating chill rolls through me.

There's only one person who could have kept this tie for all this time, and that is the person who killed her. Journey would have been a baby back then, like me.

So it couldn't have been him.

Maybe the killer gave it to Journey . . . and sent him here to taunt me with it.

No. That makes no sense. No one knows I have this box. Without the box, the tie doesn't match anything.

I slide the shirt back into the sleeve and place the extra tie on top. Then I return the box to the wooden cabinet and lock it up.

So much for Rachel's assurances. I'm clearly more responsible for Miss Peters's death than anyone knows.

I return to my room and throw myself into a cleaning frenzy.

While I'm at it, I track everything the police took. They left the printer, but took my laptop and my MP3 player. Sydney even made me hand over my cell phone. I'm basically banished to the '70s that Rachel is so fond of carrying on about. She grew up just fine without all of this technology.

Spare me.

Once my room is back together, I head down to set the table for dinner. It's some kind of stew, delicious and filling. Rachel's not very talkative and neither am I. But we make it through. She cooked, so I handle the cleanup. While I work, she stays and reads. Normally, I'd hang out for a while, too. But since I don't have my computer, it's easy to say I'm going to bed early. Besides, after everything that's gone down today, I'm exhausted.

Despite a headful of fitful thoughts, I actually do drift off to sleep.

▾ ▾ ▾

Hours later, I bolt awake, caught between some crazy dream and thinking a strange noise woke me up. I fumble for the light on my nightstand. It blinks on, casting a reassuring glow. Something nags at me but I can't seem to grasp it.

Then I spot the slash of white splayed across the carpet in front of the French doors that enter my bedroom from the balcony. It's the English report I left on my nightstand. Except now it's on the floor, and there's a very large shoe print stamped onto the back of it.

A man's shoe print.

Other black smudges stain the light gray carpet in several areas, but the print on the back of the paper is clear and distinct. I crouch low, my nose literally an inch away from the crisp outline of the heel of a shoe with rays that cut through a wavy circular tread at the top and a familiar logo stamped clearly in the middle.

I rock back on my heels. While I was sleeping, someone came in through my balcony doors and stamped the bottom of his shoe in black grime on the back of my report.

Someone was in my room.

Bold, terrifying images of Miss Peters, floating on her back in a pool of blood, and the police photos of my mother, in the same position, wearing that blue and white shirt.

Rachel!

I have to get to her.

I quietly make my way downstairs, jumping at the crazy tall shadows that suddenly dance along the wall before realizing it's only me, sneaking past the night-light. I duck into the kitchen and collect a small knife from the drawer. Then I proceed slowly to Rachel's bedroom at the back of the house. Where my balcony overlooks the street, Rachel's overlooks the backyard.

Her door is closed, no light shining from under the crack. I press my ear to the wood. At first it's silent, like a tomb. And then I hear rustling and creaking floorboards. The hinge on her balcony door howls.

I fling her door open wide in time to catch a tall shadow lurking on her balcony.

I scream, and the shadow clatters down the stairs.

Rachel leaps out of bed and grabs me.

"There's a man on your balcony. Right there. Right there." I'm pointing frantically.

Rachel barely glances outside. Instead she pulls me into the hall, even though I resist. "Rachel, you're not listening to me."

She takes me by the shoulders and steers me to the kitchen.

"Shhhh. Calm down." She's using her soothing voice. "There's no one out there. It's just a nightmare. Is that a knife? Give me that. Now sit down; I'll make some hot chocolate."

"It wasn't a nightmare. I'm fully awake. Seriously, Rachel, call Sydney. Get the police out here. I saw someone. I know it."

She empties a couple of chocolate packets into cups and waits for the water to boil. "Just breathe," she says. "What you've been through would give anyone nightmares. Everything's okay. I promise."

"There's a man's footprint in my bedroom, on the back of my English report."

"I'm not surprised," she says calmly. "How many police officers were up there today?"

She's being aggravatingly logical.

"It happened after they left," I insist.

"How can you be sure?" she says.

"Because." Because I am sure. Because that report came home from school with me. And I have no clue how Journey ended up with a strip of fabric that matches my mom's shirt, so how can I be sure of anything?

I am sure I saw someone on Rachel's balcony, though. And yet she's so calm I'm even starting to doubt that. I make it through about half of my cocoa and then I'm ready to go back to bed. Really, I just want to be alone so I can think this through.

Back in my room, I remember a line from one of Uncle Victor's books: *Evidence is about facts, not emotion.*

I run the logic test.

Is the footprint from the police?

No, because I cleaned up *after* they left and this report was not in my room when they were here. These pages were in my messenger bag that I brought home from school. I didn't take them out until after the police were gone.

Someone was definitely in my room. So who was it? Journey Michaels? One of the potential dads? My mother's killer?

None of these choices are good.

I shove every binder I have under the French doors. They work like doorstops. Three on each side ought to do it. Then I set about preserving the print.

If someone is tracking me, the smartest thing I can do is track them right back. I make a copy of the print by setting the resolution on my printer to high. Then I stash the original up in the attic cabinet.

▾ ▾ ▾

I managed a few hours of sleep, but it's not enough. Getting ready this morning is like trying to jog through glue. I throw on a clean pair of jeans and a midnight-blue T-shirt, rake a comb through my hair. Add a little mascara and some blush, and I'm done.

I grab my bag and head downstairs. Rachel's already gone. There's a simple note on the table. "E—" with a scrawled heart . . . signed "R." I smile and tuck that into my bag before I head out the door.

I'm all for clues, but I'll admit the strip of fabric from Journey has me completely baffled. What would my mother's killer have to do with Journey?

My brain throbs from overthinking.

I make it to school early, but move fast when I see Mr. Roberts heading my way. He takes a shortcut across a planter to intercept me but gets waylaid when he steps on something stringy, probably gum. He hops on one foot while scraping the other on the planter rim.

Once I'm sure he won't make it to me in time to pat my hair back into place, I toss him a sweet wave. He sends me off to class with an imaginary field-goal kick. Clearly, sports are his life. But I'm on a mission.

It's time for Journey Michaels and me to have this out face-to-face.

# 11

Getting to the truth is almost always a combination of observation, psychology, and quick thinking.

—VICTOR FLEMMING

Instead of staking out my spot on the stairs, I anxiously pace in front of the entrance to the quad, scanning every face that comes toward me. Journey's easy to spot. He's head and shoulders taller than everyone else.

I step directly into his path. "Why were you in my room last night?"

"What?" When he realizes it's me he jumps to the side. "Stay away from me."

I move back in front of him, blocking his path. "Where did that strip of fabric come from?"

He rears back. "Screw off!" He moves angrily around me.

"Tell me where you got it and I will," I say, intercepting him for a third time.

"Fine." He throws his arms out in frustration. "I guess it came from you, when you stole my van. Now leave me alone."

"Wait. What? I never stole your van." I'm trying to walk next to him, but it's not easy. I have to take four steps to his one.

"Really?" He stops. "Because somebody did that night. And

when I got it back, that strip of fabric was on the floor. So you tell me." He shifts his weight and moves away from me again, then he turns, walking backward. "It didn't come off any of *my* clothes." He tugs at the collar of his T-shirt for emphasis. "Dudes don't wear little strings."

I can't keep up with his pace and, for a minute, I stop trying. "I know where it came from," I call after him. "I need you to tell me how *you* got it."

"And I need you to forget that I even exist." Without slowing down he turns around and keeps walking in that unique, boulder-busting way of his. I scramble after him like a mini dog desperately trying to catch up.

He slows for a couple of high fives with some of his basketball pals and a fist bump with the yearbook photographer. For her he pauses and strikes a casual pose. She complies by shooting his photo. I hang back, waiting until the last second to lunge forward so I don't photobomb him.

I'm ready to beg.

"I get it. I seriously do. I don't know how that strip of fabric got in your van, but I can tell you it came from a very dangerous person. It's really important for us to talk. It's probably even a matter of life and death. And I promise, no setup. Nothing bad."

He bites the corner of his lip and glances at the basketball court. "After school?"

"Now."

He shakes his head. "I don't know what game you're running—"

"No game." I raise my hand and cross my heart. I'd stick my finger and make it bleed if that would convince him. "Please. Five minutes. That's all I need."

"Fine." Journey's jaw is tight. "My van." He lightly touches my lower back to guide me through the crush of approaching students.

I don't know what I'm doing or what I'm going to say. I haven't thought this far ahead. And now I can't even think straight because I can *feel* Journey Michaels's fingers on my back, even through the fabric of my shirt, and they are warm.

I'm surprised that Journey's van is an old, hulking commercial vehicle the color of rust. I squint at it. Or maybe it's not the color, it's the condition. The passenger door squeals in protest when he opens it for me. It's also high off the ground so getting in is a struggle. But I manage it.

While he moves around the outside, I take in the inside. This vehicle is easily ten years older than we are. There are only the two front seats, and the whole back is empty. The floor has been repaired with slats of wood that appear dry and splintery. Light streams in from small, square windows on the double back doors. The gap between my seat and the driver's seat is huge. If the giant stick-shift column jutting out of the floor wasn't in the way, I could fit a table in here between us.

After a second, Journey opens the driver's door and gets in. He turns sideways on the seat, sliding his feet and legs into the area where the gearshift is located. I shift sideways in my seat, too. Now we're facing each other, our knees only a few inches apart. The combined smell of his soap and sweat wafts toward me as he leans forward, resting his elbows on his knees. I inhale deeply without trying to be obvious.

"Okay," he says. "Get to it."

"I'm going to ask you again, just tell me the truth. Okay? I won't freak out."

He keeps a wary gaze on me. "This better not have anything to do with *me* going to jail."

"Did you sneak into my bedroom last night?"

He scrambles for the door handle. "That's it. I'm not down for some crazy setup." I grab his arm to keep him from bailing out of the van.

"Just answer me. Yes or no!"

"No!" He practically screams it. "What do you think? I don't want to be anywhere near you right now. And I certainly wouldn't risk going into your bedroom. I don't even know you. Are you insane?" He yanks his arm out of my grasp.

"Fine. I believe you. Don't go."

He pauses but keeps his hand on the door handle.

"What were you doing at Miss Peters's?" I ask.

He throws his head back. "I want to hear your side of things first."

Just the two of us in this intimate space is intense. I struggle to get my thoughts in order. But I'm distracted by things I didn't know. Like how his lashes and eyebrows form a dark frame around light gray eyes which are the color of steel.

"Right. Okay. That's fair." I grope for words. "I went there to drop something off. She knew I was coming."

"Me, too." I can tell from his tone that he finds this odd.

"What were you dropping off?"

"You first," he says.

I shake my head. "No, you this time."

"A toothbrush. Okay? I was dropping off a toothbrush." He indicates that it's my turn.

"Cigarette butts, coffee cup, and a bloody towel."

At exactly the same time, we point at each other and say, "DNA."

"Geez, was Miss Peters trying to make a career out of DNA, or what?"

"She didn't tell you her plan? She has . . . well, had a degree in forensic chemistry. She was trying to get the school and the police department to pool their resources and share a forensics lab to handle both classes and crime." There's no mistaking Journey's sadness. He misses her as much as I do.

"I only knew about the class."

Journey shrugs. He leans forward, resting his elbows on his knees. "She wanted to teach high school science classes and run a crime lab part-time."

"I'm pretty sure that not having a crime lab is the whole reason my mother's murder has never been solved." I cringe as soon as the words leave my mouth. I usually like to get to know someone a little before dumping my notorious past into their lap. Journey surprises me by not having the typical reaction.

"I hear ya. My dad probably wouldn't be a convicted murderer right now, either." He gives me a sheepish look.

"Wait. What?" I study his face.

"You didn't know?" He squares his shoulders. "I don't talk about it much, but yeah, my dad's in prison for murdering a sixteen-year-old runaway."

"You're kidding!"

"He was sentenced when I was four. So far he's refused to let me visit until I turn eighteen, which means I barely remember what he looked like then and I have no clue what he looks like now."

"Man. That's tough."

"Especially since my mom completely lives for the day she can get him a new trial. That's what the toothbrush was for. Miss Peters was going to try to grab some of his DNA from it."

"But your dad's still alive. Why don't you collect a fresh sample straight from him?" I ask.

"Yeah." Journey's gaze becomes distant, as if he's looking straight through me. "Here's the thing, there are only two ways for my father to get a new trial. One of those ways is if his DNA doesn't match what was collected at the crime scene."

"And?" From the defeated sag in Journey's shoulders I know there's more to this story.

"And the attorney and my mom don't want to try for the DNA defense."

"Why?" This makes no sense.

"Because." Journey looks away again. "What if his DNA does match? Then there's no hope for anything else. At least if they try for a procedural error in the first trial there's a glimmer of hope."

"Wow. That's a tough situation."

"Yeah. It's not like you see on TV where everything goes in order and the good guys win in the end. This game has a lot of rules that make no sense."

"But you're worried that his DNA would match the crime scene?"

"No." Journey sets his jaw. "I'm one hundred percent certain that it won't. Testing the toothbrush was Miss Peters's idea. She said we would just go slow and take it one step at a time."

"She was amazing," I say.

Journey offers a wide shrug. "I don't know about you, but my dad is screwed without her."

Screwed doesn't begin to describe the loss. It's a bottomless sensation, as if there's nothing that will ever stop the sadness pouring out of me.

Grief radiates off of Journey, too. He pretends to stare at the hair on the back of his hand; not exactly depraved killer behavior.

"Couldn't Miss P have taken DNA from both you and your mom . . ."

"And then subtracted hers to figure out his?" Journey says.

"Long story. He's my dad, just not my *biological* dad. And besides, my mom's backing the lawyer's position of not wanting to get his DNA on file. I was risking a lot going along with Miss P. But I trusted her."

I always had a sense that Journey and I shared things in common. It's weird to discover how right I was.

"Anyway," Journey says, snapping back to earth. "What was so life and death that you had to tell me?"

I study his face for a long moment. What I'm about to do requires a huge leap of faith and trust that I haven't given to anyone. I ignore the tardy bell ringing in the distance. "Actually I need to show it to you . . . at my house."

"Now?" he asks.

"This is more important than class. Trust me."

"It better be, because for the record, I don't trust anybody." He sticks the key in the ignition and cranks it. The van sputters and wheezes through a couple of tries until it finally catches.

"Yeah. That makes two of us," I say.

# 12

A crime-scene tech must process each layer methodically or he risks contaminating the entire scene.

—VICTOR FLEMMING

Journey guides the van toward the nearest parking lot exit.

"Turn right," I say, offering directions to my house.

He flashes a brilliant, if slightly embarrassed, smile. "This is going to sound sketchy, but I actually do know where you live."

"You do?" I slide down in my seat and wrap my hoodie tighter around me. "I didn't think you even knew who I was."

"Well, after you had me handcuffed and questioned for killing Miss Peters I figured I'd better check you out. You know, *The Art of War,* 'know your enemy.' By the way, that whole thing with your mom really sucks."

"Wait, I'm your enemy?" I'm surprised by the deep ache that creates in me.

"You were that night for sure." He shrugs. "At the moment the jury's still out."

"Okay, but seriously. You were in my room last night? Right?"

"I said no. Why do you keep asking?"

"Because someone was."

"Someone in your family, maybe?" he asks.

"No. Trust me. It was much creepier."

"Creepy, huh?" Journey gives me a sideways look. "Glad I've made such a good impression on you."

As tense as this is, Journey couldn't be more charming if he tried.

"Why do you think we were at Miss P's at exactly the same time? Was it an accident or are we being played by some mastermind?" I ask.

"I don't know about a mastermind," Journey says. "Normally, I would have gone earlier. But my mom worked a double. I always pick her up when she works late." He shrugs. "She works late a lot because we need the extra money."

"I had to wait until Rachel went to sleep before I could sneak out." He pulls up in front of my house and parks on the street. We get out of the van and walk up the driveway. He's strolling casually, with his hands in his pockets, and I'm clinging to my messenger bag like it's a floatation device.

"Wow. You snuck out and got caught?" He playfully nudges my shoulder with his. "Things must be tense around your house these days."

Stunned, I stop in my tracks. *Holy crap.* Journey Michaels just did the playful shoulder nudge to *ME*.

He keeps walking a few steps but I'm in shock, still processing what just happened.

"What?" he says looking back.

"Nothing. Just . . . yeah. Things have been kind of tense."

"At least you're not under suspicion for murder."

"Actually, I'm not completely clear, either." I lead him around to the back of the house, up the stairs, and inside. Then, he follows me up to my bedroom. I toss my bag onto my bed.

"They came in here with a search warrant and went through everything."

"Harsh," Journey says.

"You have no idea—unless they went through your room, too."

He shakes his head. "Not yet."

Miss Peters's support meant everything to me, and what I'm hearing from Journey is that she meant the same to him. I edge toward the closet and take in a deep breath. "Miss Peters trusted you, so I'm going to trust you, too. Don't make me regret it, okay?"

"I may not look like it, but I am totally trustworthy." Journey follows me into the closet.

"You need to see this to understand it." I lower the stairs and pause for a minute, debating. If I go up first, he's going to be looking straight up at my butt. But I'm pretty sure it would be weird for me to make him go first.

"Wait down here until I turn on the lights." I scramble up the ladder, slide past all the stuff, and find the foot switch. In a second, the attic is bathed in a warm glow.

Journey grins as he pops around the pile of junk and surveys my setup. "Wow. You have your own little apartment up here."

"Yeah, sort of. Except no one knows I use this space."

"I do," he says.

"You can't tell anyone about this. And I mean anyone. Promise?"

He crosses his fingers and lays them against his chest. "Cross my heart."

I step over to the cabinet and start to open the lock. Journey moves in close, hovering behind my left shoulder. I don't want him to see the combination. I point across the room. "Go sit over there." My trust only goes so far.

He moves to the other side of the attic and sits down on the sofa. He runs his hand over the red leather. "This is nice. Where do you get something like this?"

"It's from Italy. Same place my scooter comes from."

"Your scooter is sick."

"Thanks. It belonged to my mother. All of this stuff up here was hers. She was a fashion photographer and Italy was her favorite assignment."

I snap on the gloves, remove my mother's box from the cabinet, and ferry it to the center of the room.

"What's that?" Journey joins me on the floor.

"It's the evidence from my mother's murder."

He raises one eyebrow. "How'd you get that?"

"You don't want to know." My expression sends a message that sometimes you do what you have to do.

Tight-lipped, he nods in agreement. It's like he understands me in a way no one has before.

I remove the top of the box. The tie that came from Journey lies on the top. I hand it to him. "This is the string you found on the floor of your van the night Miss Peters was murdered."

Next, I remove the plastic evidence bag containing the shirt. I partially pull it out of the plastic; just enough for Journey to see where the missing tie was supposed to be attached. He leans forward, a frown wrinkling the area above his eyes.

He glances up, locking his gaze with mine. "It's a match."

"Yeah." I refold the shirt and slip it back into the bag. I press the bag back into the box. "My mother was wearing that top when she was murdered. Which means that tie you're holding has been missing for fourteen years."

Deep concern clouds his face. "So it could be the same person?"

"It has to be," I say.

"But why leave it in my van?"

"That's what we need to figure out." I motion to the stairs. "C'mon. We should get back to class. I don't know about you, but I've never cut before."

"Me neither, actually."

Journey waits by the stairs while I lock everything, including the extra tie, back into the cabinet.

We step out of the closet. I close the door and I'm just picking up my bag when my bedroom door is kicked open with a loud bang.

Instinctively, Journey shields me behind him. "Whoa!" He throws his hands into the air. "Don't shoot."

I look around him, expecting to put a face to the shadowy visitor I saw leaving Rachel's bedroom the other night. But instead, I see Rachel and Sydney.

Sydney gives a commanding gesture with her gun. "Step away from her."

"Erin, what the hell is going on?" Rachel's voice is shrill.

I jump in front of Journey, waving my arms. "Everything's fine. Nothing's going on. Syd, put the gun away."

Sydney reluctantly lowers her gun.

Rachel motions to the door. "Everybody downstairs."

Journey and I exchange defeated expressions. He waits for me to go first. Rachel and Sydney follow us into the kitchen.

Rachel puts one hand on her hip. The other becomes a sinister, pointy finger. "I want to know what was going on up there and I want to know now." Her jaw is so tight it's a wonder the words can still leak out.

It looks bad: cutting school *and* getting caught with a

boy in my bedroom. "It's not what you think, Rachel. We weren't—"

"You weren't what—kidnapped? Murdered?" She looms in my direction. "Because when your principal calls to tell me you left campus with the same boy you identified running from a murder scene, *that's* what I'm thinking." She swivels, aiming a final angry glare at Journey.

I hang my head. This is really messed up. "He didn't kidnap me, or hurt me or anything. We just came here because we needed to talk about what happened that night."

Sydney's back goes rigid and now she's waving a pointy finger, too. "That is exactly what I did not want the two of you to do." Her frustration resonates in the emphasis she places on each word. But at least she returns the gun to her holster. "Did I not expressly tell both of you: *Do not* talk about this with anyone?"

Journey and I glance at each other, then stare at the floor.

I weigh the odds and decide it might be worth it to come partially clean. "Syd, what if we know something you don't?"

"That's a huge red flag to me. I do not want a couple of teenagers thinking they know more about this than I do." Sydney gestures between Journey and me. "I especially do not want you two comparing notes or having anything to do with this investigation."

"But—" I say.

Sydney slices an angry finger through the air. "Hear this: As of this moment, you two are the closest things I have to suspects." She begins to pace. "The only reason you're not locked up, Erin, is because I know you." Sydney gets right up in my face. Then she leans toward Journey. "As for you, I don't have enough evidence to hold you . . . yet! But that doesn't mean I'm going to stop looking." She steps back and appraises us with hands on her hips. "This behavior is way out of line. Trust me. If you two had anything to do with that murder, I will find out." She looks up at Journey. "Are you a deranged kidnapper?"

"No, ma'am."

"Then hit it." She motions to the door. Journey takes off. I listen while his steps fade down the stairs and across the driveway. I hear the van engine crank a few times, then catch. With a thunk of his transmission he's gone.

Rachel takes a seat at the table and props her forehead against her hands. I'm rooted to the floor, afraid to move.

Sydney nudges Rachel's shoulder. "I'm going to take off." Rachel flutters her hand in a slight wave. Sydney moves past me, keeping an icy stare on my face for an extra-long moment. And then she's gone.

I drop into the chair next to Rachel. Her head is down and she might even be crying. "I'm sorry I worried you . . . I'm . . ."

She puts up the palm of her hand. "Not now."

I suck the inside of my cheek in between my teeth and clamp down. Things have never looked worse. We know things they don't know and no one wants to listen to us.

# 13

You must combine physical evidence with witness statements and known facts in order to get a complete picture of what happened.

—VICTOR FLEMMING

Rachel's furious. Instead of letting me go back to school, she sends me to my room. I spend the day reading and doing homework and putting away things that were moved during the police search. I stay there until she calls me down for dinner.

I smell meatloaf before I even hit the bottom of the stairs. I'm in for the lecture from hell, as well as some evil punishment, all of which I rightly deserve.

If it hadn't been for friggin' Principal Roberts being a snoop and calling Rachel, Journey and I would have been back in class before the end of first period. Our worst fate might have been a late slip.

Rachel has already set the table, which is another sign of the level of trouble I'm in since setting the table is usually my job. I can't believe I got caught with Journey in my bedroom. So embarrassing. Even though what she thinks was going on wasn't, I'd rather shave my head than have to explain it.

I slide quietly into my seat.

Rachel remains tight-lipped as she delivers plates of food

and glasses of water to the table. When she finally sits down I begin to worry that we might go through the whole meal without speaking a word.

She pauses briefly, shifting a tired expression in my general direction. "Don't ever let that happen again."

"I won't. I promise."

"I expect you to do detention for cutting," she adds.

I agree enthusiastically. "I will. No problem."

"If you continue to act out we *will* be going back to the therapist. Do you understand?"

"Yes, ma'am."

"That's all I have to say." With a sweep of her hand she places her napkin on her lap. And then we eat our entire meal in complete silence.

My guilt and worry transforms her delicious meatloaf into a glop of sawdust that sticks in my throat. There's still one orange left in the fruit bowl. I stop eating, take it out of the bowl, and press it to my nose. I never actually told Miss P about stealing the box. But I did tell her about finding my mother's things in the attic and about the men my mother might have dated. If she were still here would I be able to tell her about discovering the missing tie?

Rachel gives me a funny look but doesn't say anything. I set the fruit back in the bowl and try to choke down a few more bites.

In the heat of the moment, when Rachel and Sydney were bearing down on us, I almost fessed up about the box and the tie from my mother's shirt. Isn't this exactly what Rachel has always warned me about—my mother's killer staying close and watching me? Doesn't the reappearance of the tie from that shirt prove that he's close?

Given the way they acted, though, I'm glad I didn't tell

them. After catching me with Journey, Sydney wasn't going to believe anything I said. And the box—the only source of comfort I have left—would be gone.

When we're done eating, Rachel carries her plate to the sink. "Good night," she says before leaving quietly and going to her room. I clean up the kitchen and head upstairs to mine. With another long night ahead of me, I gather my notebook and pen.

My goal? A list of questions that need answers.

I crawl into bed without washing my face or putting on pajamas and bury my head in the covers. Just when I had convinced myself that I didn't have anything to do with what happened to Miss P there's new evidence to suggest the opposite.

At first, I was willing to believe that finding her body was an unlucky coincidence and I just needed to grieve for her and find a way to go on. But that strip of fabric clearly binds her story to mine.

▾ ▾ ▾

My morning classes are a blur. I move from one to the next, turning in papers and taking notes. Brain = not engaged. Instead, I turn to my personal notebook and jot down a step-by-step list for investigating Miss Peters's murder. One: What she was working on that caused someone to take her life. Two: What is the connection to my mother. Three: Who left a shoe print in my bedroom.

I grab lunch and head outside to my spot at the top of the stairs. Instead of settling in like I usually do, I wait for Spam and Lysa. When they show up I suggest a remote outdoor table around the back of the cafeteria, where we can talk.

Their attitudes are a little frosty. The rumors are already flying about Journey and me cutting school together yesterday.

To Spam and Lysa this is another instance of me going off and doing something on my own.

"You could have at least let us know you weren't coming to school yesterday," Lysa says. "You were so upset the day before. We were really worried and then you didn't return any calls or texts."

I recount how I arrived home to find the police searching my room. Then I run down the list of all the things they took, including my cell phone. I even tell Spam and Lysa about the shoe print in my bedroom and the man on Rachel's balcony. And before they can lecture me, I also describe how I begged Rachel to call the police on the spot, but she refused. The only thing I left out was how the tie that Journey threw at me matched my mother's shirt. It's too scary for me to think about, let alone discuss.

Even without that detail their worry is palpable.

"What are you going to do?" Lysa asks. "You've got to do something."

"First thing, I'm going to try to ID that shoe," I say. "Who wants to go to Shoe Haven after school?"

Spam can't make it because she has to do a computer setup for her father's electronics store. But Lysa's delighted. We drop my scooter off at my house and take her car.

Shoe Haven could be the largest shoe store in the world, and it's clearly Lysa's favorite spot on earth. The room is lined with narrow tables from one side to the other, laid out in rows like a cornfield. But instead of golden veggies, it's a view of every shoe imaginable.

The moment we step inside, Lysa totters, zombielike, toward a group of women around the sale section. Meanwhile, I drift toward the men's athletic shoes. I brought the copy of the shoe print with me.

What I have to go on is the Nike logo in the middle of the sole and the top part of the tread which has horizontal rays piercing a circular design. I move quickly along the row, turning shoes over and inspecting the bottoms until I find what I'm looking for. The print exactly matches the Michael Jordan classic AJ1, a mid-top basketball shoe made by Nike. A white size eight is on display, but it's clearly too small. From the boxes stacked below, I find a size nine. Also too small. Further down, a size eleven is a perfect match. That's it. My intruder wears size-eleven Michael Jordan classics. I rummage in my bag for my cell phone to take a picture of the shoe. Then I remember Sydney took my phone. Grrr.

I spot Lysa wandering toward me, her arms full of shoes. I borrow her phone and take a quick photo of the top and bottom of the shoe lined up next to the print. I e-mail the photos to both myself and to Spam. I add a quick message asking her to save it for me, since I don't have my computer at the moment.

I'm done. But to get Lysa to leave Shoe Haven, I have to get her to stop vacillating between three different pairs and to settle on the open-toe pumps in her favorite color of royal blue, which will look great with everything she owns. In exchange, she forces me to buy strappy silver high heels which will look fantastic with absolutely nothing I own. I did save 70 percent off the price. Which means I got a fantastic deal on a pair of shoes I will never wear.

▼ ▼ ▼

Lysa drops me off at home and I leave my new shoes sitting out on the kitchen table. By the time Rachel comes home, I'm almost done with my homework. She looks surprised at my new shoes. I can tell she loves them, but she's probably thinking they're so not me. How great would it be if my current troubles could be managed by a pair of strappy silver heels instead of a pair of size-eleven Michael Jordan's?

"You're going to need a computer for your school work, and I'm pretty sure mine is too old to do you any good," Rachel says.

"Spam can probably hook me up with something refurbished from her dad's store."

"Good idea," Rachel says.

The words are barely out of her mouth when a knock sounds on the back door. And there's Spam. She wanders in wearing a pair of short denim shorts, red striped soccer kneesocks, pink paisley rain boots, a red T-shirt, and a black TechNext baseball cap. Her hair is slicked back in a ponytail. She drops a heavy red canvas tool bag on the chair and gives Rachel a hug.

"Hey *mamacita,* how you doin'?" she asks.

Rachel hugs her back. "I'm fine, Spam. What are you up to?"

"Not much, just making a little house call." Spam opens her tool bag and pulls out a laptop, a cell phone, and a wireless modem, stacking them on the table.

"Wow. Do you have our house bugged or something?" I ask.

Spam gives me a wide-eyed look. "I could totally do that and you would never even know. But why would I need to? You already tell me everything. Right?" Her look is more warning than question.

Spam turns to Rachel. "If you want to know something, don't ask her. Ask me."

Rachel laughs. "You two scare me."

Spam throws an arm around my shoulders. "What's scary is my girl being out of touch. I can't have that."

"That's very nice of you, Spam. How much do I owe you?" Rachel asks.

Spam shakes her head. "No worries. These are trade-outs for repair. She can keep them for as long as she needs. I can help you set them up now if it won't mess with your dinner."

"Sydney and I are going out, but you guys can order Thai, if you want," Rachel offers.

"Ah, thanks. I can't stay. I promised my dad I'd make empanadas," Spam says.

"Yum. What time should we be there?" Rachel asks with a laugh.

Spam laughs, too. "Yeah, you don't want to do that. You'd be lucky to get a crumb with the little monsters at the table. And their manners are disgusting."

"Come on, Spam. Your little brothers are adorable and you know it," I say.

Spam rummages in her bag and pulls out some cables and a small plastic box of mini tools. "They're adorable, but they're still little monsters."

"How old are they now?" Rachel asks.

Spam fills us in on her brothers' ages—eight, ten, eleven, thirteen, and fifteen—and their various antics. She's the oldest. We bonded in fourth grade over the fact that I didn't have my mother and neither did she. Though hers just walked out one day and never came back.

When we were young, we used to pretend our mothers had very important jobs as princesses. They couldn't just go to work in the morning and come home at night. A princess had to work the whole time and they had to do it for a lot of years. One day our moms would be promoted to queens. Then they would come back and take us to live with them and we would become the new princesses.

Around sixth grade, we grew out of the princess stage. Since then, Spam has refused to talk about our mothers at all. "Live in the now" is her motto.

I wish I could.

A light tap comes from the back door. It's Sydney. Instead of inviting her in, Rachel grabs her purse and blows me a kiss, saying she won't be late.

I can't help thinking Rachel is intentionally keeping Syd and me apart—not a good sign.

# 14

Written documentation is so critical that my personal notebook is part of the official evidence in every case I work on.

—VICTOR FLEMMING

Spam scoops up the new equipment and charges up the stairs toward my room. I follow, even though my mind is still focused on what's up with Rachel and Sydney.

Spam sits at my desk and silently plugs in cables and powers up the laptop. Tapping keys, she focuses on linking everything together. The silent treatment combined with the tight pinch to her mouth suggests she's in a bad mood.

I perch on the edge of the desk.

"Spam, what's wrong?"

"I'm going to ask you the same question." She swivels the chair to pin me with a hard look. "I looked at the print you sent me. You do realize the love of your life was stalking you in your own bedroom."

"I never said he was the love of my life."

"Yeah. But you act like it." She goes back to pecking at the keys. "And it's affecting your judgment."

"Just because the print is a basketball shoe doesn't mean it's Journey's. And, for the record, I'm not in love with him. . . . I just find him interesting."

She reaches into her pocket, pulls out a folded piece of paper, and slams it on the desk. "Then maybe you'll be interested in this."

I unfold the paper. It's an order form from the athletic department of Copper South High School—our school—for forty pairs of white Michael Jordan classic AJ1 basketball shoes, in various sizes. I scan down the list and see it: *Journey Michaels, size 11.*

"How did you get this?"

Spam's gaze is drawn to an imaginary spot on my ceiling. "You remember when my dad's store donated a bunch of computers to the school, right?"

"Of course. The library would still be in the dark ages if it wasn't for your dad's store."

"Yeah, so we set up the system over there and part of the maintenance agreement is that he checks it every now and then. To make sure they don't have any viruses or anything."

I happen to know that Spam's been hacking her father's computer security walls since she was ten. I gasp. "You can spy on everything our school does on computer?"

She gives me puppy dog eyes. "I don't. I wouldn't. I only did this to save your life," she adds, reacting to my widening gaze.

I roll my eyes because what I know is that in third place—right behind Spam's dream jobs of hacker and professional gamer—is working for *TMZ,* the online gossip site. She's addicted to drama. "Saving my life is a little extreme, even for you."

"Okay. Fine. Don't focus on that," she says. "The point is he and his shoes were in your bedroom."

"Wrong. Anyone on the team could've been in here, or even anyone with the same shoes. We don't know every person in

Iron Rain who owns these shoes." I scan down the order form. "Look. The school ordered four pairs in size eleven. One of them was Principal Roberts. Why don't you accuse *him* of being in my room?"

Spam pushes a few keys on the keyboard, bringing up Skype. Melodic beeps signal she's calling someone. Within a few seconds, Lysa's face appears on my screen.

"Did she listen?" Lysa leans into the camera.

"What do you think?" Spam shakes her head.

"You guys were talking about me?"

"Yes," Lysa says. "And now we're trying to talk some sense into you."

I flop down on the end of my bed. Spam adjusts the angle of the laptop so that we're both visible on Lysa's monitor.

"What I need is your support and help finding Miss P's killer."

"Whoa. See? Right there. That's the crazy train," Spam says.

Lysa agrees emphatically. "Right. You are not a police officer or a detective. You need to stand down."

My face twitches. "Stand down? Lysa, you're not a hostage negotiator, either, but you're trying to sound like one."

"I'm trying to talk some sense into you." She makes a grumpy face.

"Here's some sense. We're really good at this stuff and we do it for silly things like Cheater Checks. Why would we not give our best for Miss P?"

Spam shakes her head, stands up from my desk, and gives me a quick hug. "I have to go. Hungry monsters await." Spam moves toward the camera and her face fills the screen. "Make her listen."

While Spam packs up her tools, Lysa knits her fingers together and straightens her shoulders. "Here's the problem,

Erin. When you get like this, we're not sure if you need stern words or facts."

I choke on her words. "Get like what? What are you talking about?"

Lysa leans close to the camera, her hands imitating the shape of a small box. "I think you know what I'm talking about."

I glance over at Spam, who suddenly refuses to make eye contact. "Is this about the box, Journey Michaels, or investigating the murder?" I refuse to hide my irritation.

"It's about all of it and keeping you safe," Lysa insists. "That box got you into this, and as for Journey, well, Spam has already given you sufficient information—"

Oh my god. Really? *Sufficient information?* Lysa is channeling her mother.

"Lighten up with the psychobabble," I say.

Lysa huffs. "It's not psychobabble."

"Maybe not when your mom says it. She's a trained therapist. But you're just . . . nosy and butting in."

As Spam grabs her bag and heads for the door, I slam the laptop closed and go after her. "Spam, wait."

She stops at the top of the stairs and tosses me a loaner cell phone. "I'm speed dial numero uno," she says.

I follow her. "Yeah? I hope you keyed your name in as *Loca* because that's what I look up when I want to call you." With a grin, she flips me off over her shoulder. I follow her into the kitchen. She pauses at the back door.

"What do you guys want me to do?" I ask.

"Tell Rachel everything so they'll lock Journey Michaels up and you'll be safe," she says.

"But—"

"Just do it," she says.

“I’ll think about it.” She gives me a hug and slips out the back door. But I’ve already made my decision. They don’t know about that strip of fabric, and how all of this circles back to my mother’s murder. I’m not saying anything until I figure out what the connection is.

# ▸ 15 ◂

Every murderer has a tell, and where it usually shows up is in their unorganized behaviors.

—VICTOR FLEMMING

I roll through morning classes on autopilot because all I can think about is how everything has changed. Before I know it, it's time for lunch.

When Spam and Lysa arrive to hijack me from my spot on the cafeteria stairs, I'm waiting for them . . . with Journey Michaels in tow.

Spam gives me a half laugh, but poor Lysa's eyes are about to fall out of her head.

I get it. Journey looks especially cute today. His snug sweater shows off his abs, and the dark gray color sets his eyes to *stun.*

"We need to talk." Let them try and say this is all about Journey with him sitting right there.

Spam doesn't look happy about my surprise lunch guest, but she turns and heads down the stairs with a motion for us to follow. She leads us to what is becoming our favorite table behind the cafeteria.

Clearly I didn't think this through in advance. With only two sides to the table, I'm not sure where to sit. I busy myself brushing leaves and dirt off the benches to avoid picking a side. Spam and Lysa settle it by sliding in next to each other.

I offer Journey a shy smile and take a seat opposite them. Then he sits down next to me. We leave a noticeable space between us.

"So, the rumor must be true, huh?" Spam says.

Confused, I glance at Journey.

Spam waves her index finger between us. "That you two are now . . ." She wraps two fingers tightly together.

Journey and I squirm.

"No," he says.

"Nothing like that," I say at the same time.

"Really. Did you not cut class together earlier this week?" Spam's mouth twists into a smirk. I forgot how addicted she is to gossip. Inquiring minds definitely want to know.

"We did. But it's not what you think," I say.

"I hope so," Lysa says. "Because you two getting together after Miss Peters's murder is creepy." Lysa retrieves a sandwich from her bag and nibbles on one corner of it.

"We actually only met two days ago." I glance at Journey.

"Really, only two days ago?" A slow, simmering fury builds up in Spam. "Should I mark that on my love calendar? Because yesterday you let us lecture you on what a lurker he is and never told us you were seeing him."

"Who says I'm a lurker?" Journey says.

"We're not seeing each other," I say at the same time. "But we have figured out that together we have information we didn't have separately."

I'm relieved that Spam is dressed sedately. I need Journey to take her seriously. She's her usual impatient self, though, patting her hand on the table for me to get to the point. "Like what?" she says.

I need to lead into this delicately. "The kind of information that says we have to investigate Miss Peters's murder."

Spam opens her bag and pulls out an orange. She digs her fingernails deep into the skin, releasing the citrusy scent. It immediately brings up a flood of memories. I picture Miss P in lecture mode—which she liked to call inspire mode—telling us how in science, like everything else, we have to *dig deep* to get to the truth.

"Nope. Disagree," Spam says. "I'm not in favor. Cheater Checks is one thing. Murder is a whole new level. I vote we leave it to the police." Spam proceeds to peel her orange.

I realize that I didn't bring any lunch and it looks like Journey didn't either. Spam notices and sets a few segments of orange in front of each of us.

He looks at Spam. "Hi. I don't know your name. Let me just say that I don't trust the police." He pops a piece of orange in his mouth. I'm content to hold my piece and inhale the fragrance.

"The problem is the police don't know what we know," I say.

"Then maybe you should tell them," Spam says. "Miss P obviously didn't do that and look what happened to her."

"Okay. We don't know what Miss P knew," I say. "But I am worried that what happened to her could happen to us. Or, me at least." I go around the table making eye contact with each one of them. "I'm not going to lie. This is serious."

"Have you received a threat?" Lysa asks.

"Not directly. But indirectly, yeah, I think I have." I look to Journey. "These two are the best people to help us figure this out." I gesture across from me. "Spam's a tech rat: computers, cell phones, servers, flash drives, spy cams, anything electronic. She can hack it, and if she can't, she knows who can."

Spam shoots me a bug-eyed "WTF" look.

"No worries," I say, attempting to soothe her. "He's cool."

She and Lysa exchange some wary side-eye.

"Lysa's father is a lawyer and her mother's a psychologist. So she's great for legal stuff or anything having to do with human nature."

Lysa holds her hands up like balancing a scale. "I try to be the voice of reason, but these two almost never listen to me."

Journey smiles politely.

"Evidence is my thing: fingerprints, hair, ink, lipstick. Anything forensic. We're like the Three Musketeers."

"Yeah. We're exactly like them," Spam says, tossing her hair and sounding chipper. "Except, oh right, when you decide to go off on your own."

I give her a harsh glare. "Not now."

"Look, I get it. You guys are all organized and into this." Journey rakes his fingers through his hair and clasps his hands around his neck. "So, no offense. But none of your tricks or techniques can compare to investigating a murder."

His words are like a giant thud in the middle of the table. "What?"

"I'm not trying to be demeaning or anything," he says, reacting to my crushed expression. "But you can't compare nailing a cheating boyfriend with catching a killer."

Lysa narrows her eyes at him. "Maybe you're afraid of what we'll find. Hmmm?"

I put my hand up. "Easy, Prosecutor. He's innocent."

"So, who called this meeting?" Spam asks, her face devoid of all emotion.

"I did." Journey and I say it at the same time and then look at each other like *Did you really just say that?*

"Dude, I thought we were on the same page," I say.

Lysa and Spam exchange a look.

"I thought so, too," he says. "But you're ignoring that I've been doing my own *investigations* for five years now trying to clear my dad. I don't do forensics . . ." He sweeps his hand toward me. "Or computer stuff . . ." He gestures toward Spam. He looks Lysa straight in the eye for a long moment.

"What?" she asks.

"Truthfully, lawyers creep me out." Journey looks around the table at us. "I don't care how good you are, there's only so much we can do."

After a long silence, Spam looks from me to Journey and back to me again. Her eyes are cold, dark embers.

"Erin, you're my best friend," she says. "I'd give you a kidney if you needed it. I'd give you both kidneys. But I think he's right, you should leave this one for the police."

"Tried. Giant fail! I practically handed this evidence over to Sydney and she shut me down."

"You didn't practically hand it to her," Journey says, correcting me. "You hypothetically asked, if you had evidence, would she want to see it."

"Right. And she said no."

"I'm dying to know. What is this earthshaking evidence?" Spam crosses her arms over her chest.

I glance over my shoulders, right then left. "I don't want to get into the details here. But trust me, it changes everything."

"Is it from the box?" Lysa asks.

I don't need to answer. My pinched expression says it all.

"I just want to slap you and call you Pandora." She squeezes the sides of her face and moans. "We never should have helped you steal that thing."

"You say that, but the things in the box give us an advantage." I glance at Journey. "Do you think the police would have ever matched up what you found with what I have?"

To his credit, Journey doesn't even blink. "Of course not. All they want to do is pin the crime on the first person they can. Which, if that detective has her way, will be one or both of us. She even said so."

Lysa and Spam share concerned looks.

"Yeah, someone's trying to make it look like Erin and I murdered Miss P . . . together."

"It gets worse." I reach my hands across the table to Lysa and Spam. "What we found links Miss Peters's murder to my mom's."

Spam sits forward. "Define linked?"

"As in the same person," Journey says.

Spam shakes her head. "That's impossible. It's been . . ."

"Fourteen years." And every single one of them feels like a scar on my heart. "The killer—man or woman, we don't know—who left my mother lying in a pool of blood did the exact same thing to Miss Peters."

Lysa gnaws at a cuticle. Even Spam and Journey take a minute to stare at the scratches and chipped paint on the table.

I get it, we're all hurting for Miss P and she's the only person who would be willing to help us unravel this. But I also forget how uncomfortable it is for normal people to talk about these things. I've been dealing with words like blood, murder, and dead for so long I have a callus on that part of my soul.

"Alright. What do you need?" Spam asks, her voice thick with emotion.

"More information, for starters," I say.

"Fine," Spam agrees.

"I'm there," Lysa says.

Lunch bell rings. Perfect timing.

"Let's meet here after school to plan this out," I say.

Everyone mumbles their agreement as we get up from the table. Lysa and Spam head off in one direction. Journey and I stand there for a minute, then he hands me a torn-off slip of notebook paper. "Here's my cell phone number and e-mail address." He shrugs. "I just thought, you know. In case you need to get in touch with me."

"Great. Perfect." I fumble with my bag. "I should give you my contact info, too."

He shoves his hands into his pockets and turns, calling back over his shoulder, "Just text me . . . or e-mail," he says. "Then I'll have it."

I watch him move off and blend into the crowd heading for their classes.

I tingle at the sight of the scrap of paper in my hand. Journey Michaels just gave me his phone number.

It takes an extreme amount of restraint not to Snoopy dance on the spot, because that would be a complete dork move. Instead, I toss my hair back off of my face, turn, and head to class.

It doesn't help that I momentarily forgot which class I'm supposed to be heading to and so I'm walking in the opposite direction. I keep walking until I'm sure that Journey is out of sight before turning back and hustling to beat the tardy bell.

# 16

Chain of custody is critical to insure that the evidence of a crime is true and hasn't been tampered with.

—VICTOR FLEMMING

The last bell rings and I race to the student store to pick up some drinks and snacks before heading to our meeting place. I sent Journey a text, as he instructed. It was just a brief *"see ya later."* As I pass the basketball courts I catch sight of him hanging out with a couple of his teammates. A cheerleader is listening intently to what he's saying and rubbing his shoulder in a consoling way.

So I guess I didn't turn him into a pariah, after all. And for that I'm a mix of happy and some other emotion I'd rather not inspect too closely.

Spam and Lysa are waiting at the table. But instead of their usual nonstop chatting, they look like strangers waiting for a bus. The only signs of life are Lysa's eyeballs, nervously sliding between Spam and the basketball courts, and Spam's thumbs, scrolling and clicking through her phone.

I slide onto the bench opposite them and deposit the snacks and drinks in the middle of the table.

My phone pings. I pull it out of my pocket. A shiver races through me at the sight of Journey's name. "He's on his way."

There Spam and Lysa go again.

Lately, they share a secret look over everything I say.

I get it. *Me* getting a text from Journey Michaels is a pretty big deal. At another time this would have been cause for much squealing and flailing arms. They don't seem particularly happy, though.

Lysa looks at Journey. "He's trying to tear himself away from some cheerleaders."

I glance over. The one cheerleader has multiplied into three. It's practically a pageant. They're each giving him a parting hug. I turn back to smile at Spam and Lysa. We used to laugh about this stuff all the time. Now it looks like I'm facing a firing squad.

Journey arrives, taking the seat next to me. "Did you get my text?"

The way he asks is so casual it flusters me. My face burns with embarrassment, so I skip over his question and dive right in. "Let's go over the night Miss Peters was murdered just to get everybody straight on what happened."

"We'll go first." Spam glowers at me across the table. "Oh right. Lysa and I weren't there. Is that straight enough?"

"I'd give anything to not have been there," Journey snaps. "No one wants that." His arm accidentally brushes mine and we quickly jerk away from each other.

"It's interesting that you're willing to tell us everything now that you need our help," Spam says, still sulking. "How do we know you won't go rogue again?" She tears open a bag of chips and drags one of the drinks over to her.

"I won't. I promise." I look to Journey for confirmation. "We'll work together. Like a team." He agrees, also taking a drink for himself.

"Awesome. Kumbaya all around," Lysa says with a sarcastic edge. "Can we get on with this? I have a ton of homework."

I tip my hand toward Journey. "You start."

He clears his throat and leans forward, resting his elbows on the table. "Miss Peters knew I was coming that night, too. I was dropping off a toothbrush that belonged to my father to see if she could get his DNA off of it."

"So you can try to get him a new trial," Lysa says.

This surprises all of us, but no one is more surprised than Journey.

"How'd you know?" he asks.

Lysa smiles. "My father was your father's attorney. It was his first murder trial."

Journey's lips tighten. "That means he's my attorney, too. I mean, I'm hoping I won't actually need one. But at the moment."

I thought I was the only one keeping secrets but wow, Lysa knew Journey's father was in prison and never told us. Now Spam and I exchange side-eyes.

Lysa scowls. "You know, there's a rule of law called attorney-client privilege. Just because I accidentally hear something around my house doesn't mean I can go blabbing it all over. You guys understand that, right?"

Spam and I nod. Journey pauses, taking it all in.

"Anyway." He shakes his head and continues. "Miss P's house is on a corner. I pulled up and parked along the side, not the front. Erin can tell you, my van is stupid hard to start and I didn't want to get stranded. The neighborhood was completely deserted, so I left it running while I ran up to her porch."

At the mention of Miss Peters's porch, I fade out a little. The images are still too fresh.

"All I had on me was the toothbrush, no bag or anything. I

didn't want to just—you know—leave it on the porch." Journey glances at me. "It didn't occur to me to put it in the mailbox. My brilliant idea was to use the drawstring from my hoodie and tie the toothbrush to her doorknob. But instead of taking my sweatshirt off, I tried to pull the string out while I was still wearing it. The hood got all closed and wrapped around my head. While I was dealing with that, I heard someone jump into my van and start to drive it away."

I can tell by the way Spam and Lysa are paying attention that Journey's goofy charm is having a good effect on them.

He acts out the next part. "I'm trying to rip off my hoodie and run after my van."

I stifle a laugh at his depiction. He snaps a serious look in my direction.

"Hey. It wasn't funny. I seriously had to chase *my own* van."

"I know. I'm sorry," I say.

"Anyway, I ran five blocks before I found it! Sitting in the middle of Pine Lookout. The driver's door was open and the keys were on the hood."

Spam frowns. "How weird is it for a car thief to leave both the van and the keys?"

"At the time I figured it was just someone punking the idiot who left his car running," Journey says. "But after I found out about Miss P, the motive definitely seemed more sinister."

"At this point he didn't know anything was wrong with Miss P," I say.

"Right," Journey agrees. "After I got my van back I drove around a little looking for the creep who stole it. Usually when someone steals a car it's because they don't have one. I'm coming down the block when I see Erin walking up to Miss

P's mailbox. I was going to drive up and talk to her. Maybe she saw who took my van. But one second she's walking up to the door and the next she's on the ground, screaming."

I hold up my hand. "Miss Peters was already—you know." My eyes well up as I remember that awful sequence of events and how nothing I could have done would have changed things for her.

Journey pauses to take a sip of his drink. "I freaked out. I didn't know what was going down but I didn't want any part of it." He glances over at me with an apologetic look and reaches out to swipe the veil of hair off of my face.

I'm so stunned at his hand coming toward me that I rear back, making me look kind of crazy. "Sorry," I say, tucking my hair behind my ear.

Journey shifts back to telling the story. "Anyway, I started to feel terrible for driving away. I mean, there was something obviously wrong with this poor girl. I had to go back and check on her."

Holy cow. I didn't even know *this* part. Journey's charming description of coming back to rescue me is really sweet. A glance at the smiles on Spam and Lysa suggests they think so, too.

"Awww," I say.

Journey looks a little guilty. "Well, I also realized that I had dropped my hoodie and the toothbrush somewhere in the yard. So, this time, I pulled around back and parked in the alley. I wanted a clear view of the street and yard. As I walked around the side toward the front, my hoodie and toothbrush were still in the grass where I had dropped them. When I bent over to pick them up, I triggered the motion light. The light popped on and I saw everything: Erin and Miss Peters covered in blood. I just ran. I didn't notice the strip of fabric on the floor of my van until I got home."

I raise my finger to interject again. "A strip of fabric that came from the shirt my mother was wearing when she was killed."

"That's impossible," Spam says.

"I know," I say. "But it's true. I have that shirt, in the box at my house."

"Why would the person who murdered your mom want to hurt Miss P?" Lysa asks, her voice thick with sadness.

They all look to me as if I have the answer. I wish.

"That's what we have to figure out," Journey says.

"What's weird is how the tie binds you together," Lysa says. "Without it you two wouldn't have any connection at all."

My stomach flip-flops. The situation sucks rocks, but having a connection to Journey is a definite plus. "We were there at the same time," I say. "Which I'll admit is also weird."

"What's the next move?" Spam asks.

"Right now we're going to Journey's house so I can thoroughly go through his van. I'll be looking for fingerprints, hair, fibers, anything I can find."

Spam squints. "Didn't the police already do that?"

"They did," Journey says. "But they were basically looking for evidence they could use against me. I'm counting on our little Sherlock here to find something they missed."

He gently nudges my shoulder, sending my nerve endings into a frenzy. Is it my imagination or is he flirting with me? The table goes silent as they all look to me. Meanwhile, I'm geeking out over a stupid shoulder nudge.

"I . . . um, it looked like they only dusted the door handle and the steering wheel. I'm planning to go over it more carefully."

"What do you want us to do?" Lysa asks.

"We need to pull together a view of everything Miss P was doing and everyone she talked to before she was killed. Spam, can you get her phone records?"

She shrugs. "Most people are pretty lame about passwords. I'm guessing I can hack her account. Cell phone, right?"

"Yes. I'll text you her number," I say.

Spam gives me a mock salute. "I'm on it."

"What about me?" Lysa asks.

"Your dad told me not to worry," Journey says. "But he said that to my father, too. And I know how that turned out. If you think there's something I should worry about, will you tell me? I don't want to get blindsided."

Lysa flutters her hands nervously. "I can't mess with my father's files. There are all kinds of laws about that, and if I got caught it would make things a lot worse for you."

"You don't need to touch his files or take anything," Journey says. "Just listen, snoop around, and report back."

Lysa smiles. "I'm an awesome snoop."

"Anything else?" Spam asks.

I catch a glimpse of Principal Roberts. He's standing in his usual post by the parking lot, but instead of watching students leave, he's staring at us.

"Yeah. We need to keep all of this away from Mr. Roberts. . . . I know he cares and he's trying to look out for me, but he's a direct narc line to Rachel. So this has to stay between us."

"Got it," Spam says.

"I'll send everyone an e-mail tonight to let you know what we find in the van."

"Okay."

Spam and Lysa gather their stuff while I clean up the trash from the table. Journey is waiting for me to finish. "Text me your address and I'll meet you at your place," I say.

He hedges, shifting from one foot to the other. "It'll be better if I drive you."

We pretend not to notice the look Spam and Lysa share.

# 17

This won't sound very scientific, but you should never overlook the importance of being yourself in high school.

—MISS P

"I don't mind riding with you," I say while nervously torturing the strap on my bag. "But I have my scooter." *I'm also freaked out about being alone in a car with you because my hands will sweat like a kitchen sponge and my throat will close like a clogged drain—but of course I'm not going to tell you that.*

"I can fit your scooter in the back of the van," Journey says. "I'll pick you up in front at the Green Area." He lopes off toward the parking lot.

"Okay." I hope he doesn't live too far away. And it's not like this is a date or anything, but I fail at keeping one-on-one conversations going with boys, and my best friends know this. Spam and Lysa walk me to the Green Area.

"So, you and Journey, huh . . ." Lysa says slyly.

"I know. Crazy, right? I mean, we're just trying to figure all of this out." A tingling sweeps up the back of my neck and spreads across my cheeks. I flip my hair from behind my ear. I can't say any more but Spam and Lysa know. The look they exchange this time is a little warmer.

"Just be careful," Lysa says.

"Keep your head on straight, chica," Spam adds.

I nod. Their advice is good. I feel comfortable with Journey but I get it, there's still a lot we don't know.

At the Green Area we hug, then Spam and Lysa continue on toward the parking lot. I barely have my bag stashed in the seat compartment of my scooter before I spot Mr. Roberts ambling my way.

"Erin, do you have a minute?" He parks his reading glasses on his giant, bald forehead and mimes a batting warm-up move.

I try to look busy, but he doesn't take the hint. "How is your schoolwork?" he asks. "Are you managing to keep up? I can speak to your teachers if you need extra time for any of your assignments."

"Thanks, Mr. Roberts. But everything's fine." My panic meter starts to rise; Journey will be pulling up in his van any second. Mr. Roberts will immediately alert Rachel if he sees me leaving with him. Out of the corner of my eye I see Lysa and Spam hurrying back from the parking lot.

"Hey, Mr. Roberts." Lysa shoots me a tiny smile over his shoulder. When he turns, I give her a grateful look and mime begging.

Mr. Roberts scowls. "Excuse me, Alyssa. I'm with another student." He turns back to me. "Erin, I'm worried about you. Why don't you come to my office and we can talk about it?"

"I can't right now, Mr. Roberts," I say, tugging on my helmet. "I have to get home. Can we do it tomorrow?"

"I need something, Mr. Roberts." Lysa taps him on the shoulder. "Can we go to your office?" When he continues to ignore her, Lysa regards him with wide, frustrated eyes.

For some reason Mr. Roberts is laser-focused on me and I'm getting desperate. Off to the side, Spam is typing furiously into her phone. Suddenly, nearly every cell phone in the vicinity pings, including my own.

I check my phone. It's an SOS blast text, something Spam devised to promote pop-up school functions. It reads: "HEY CS'ERS, ANYONE STILL ON CAMPUS REPORT IMMEDIATELY TO THE GREEN AREA FOR FREE STUFF."

I gape at Spam.

"It'll just take a minute," Mr. Roberts says, still trying to get my attention.

"I'm sorry. I really can't." I'm looking past him at the stream of students trickling into the Green Area from all points within the school. Spam's amazing. She gives me a small shrug and a wink before sauntering off to the parking lot.

Mr. Roberts's eyes widen at the throngs of students showing up. "What's going on here? Excuse me. There's no loitering on campus. What . . . free?! There's nothing free here."

I decide to leave before Journey pulls up and our plan is blown. "Bye, Lysa. Bye, Mr. Roberts." I ease the scooter away from the curb and drive toward the nearest exit. In a show of perfect timing, Journey's van rumbles up behind me.

Meanwhile, the crowd around Mr. Roberts continues to grow. He might suspect we were up to something, but he'll never be able to prove it.

With Journey tailing me, I drive around the block to a neighborhood where no one at school can see us. Then I pull over. Journey gets out and comes around to the curb.

"Sorry about that. I had to ditch Principal Roberts." I slide my helmet off and the static makes my hair stand straight out around my head.

He stifles a laugh. "With your hair sticking up like that and the sun shining through it you look like a Tesla coil." His voice catches on a shred of emotion.

"Oh. Sorry." I quickly try to pat my hair back into place.

"Don't apologize." Journey takes ahold of Vespy's handlebars and rolls her toward the back of the van, where he hoists her carefully inside. He even covers her with a tarp and secures her with bungee cords. Then he proceeds around to the passenger side to open the door for me.

I wipe my sweaty palms on my jeans and hope I can think of something non-dorky to say. But as Journey pulls away from the curb, he launches into a detailed story about a series of mystery novels he likes where the main character is a reluctant detective who wants nothing to do with solving a crime. Clues and evidence give him an actual rash. But he keeps stumbling over corpses and suffers from a strong moral obligation to get it right.

Journey glances at me with a somber expression. "I kind of think we're like that. We want to make sure no one decides we had anything to do with this . . . but at the same time we want to get it right for Miss Peters."

"Yes. For Miss Peters," I agree.

While Journey drives, we exchange bursts of conversation, here and there. But there are long bouts of silence, too. The normal state of my brain is a crazy cycle where I'm always trying to stay one step ahead of every situation. But for some reason the air between us just feels easy and comfortable. When I'm with Journey, I can actually breathe and relax. He knows about my past, my investigations. He even knows about the attic . . . all huge secrets I've kept from the people I love the most. It's hard to believe my fantasy crush has turned out to be the one person I can trust with *all* of my secrets.

I stretch my legs out, settle back, and actually relax a little while he drives. I don't think anything of the few unexpected turns he makes until my familiar neighborhood starts to give way to strip malls and shopping centers and then to run-down industrial areas. At that point, I sit up straighter in my seat and begin tracking the changing landscape. My surroundings are becoming increasingly remote and deserted.

Relaxed? Did I just think I was relaxed? Because I'm suddenly tense again. Very tense. My fear is threatening to become full-blown panic. I can't think of a single good reason he would have for bringing me all the way out here. And now I feel stupid. Deadly freaking stupid. What was I thinking, trusting him? I don't really know anything about him. And I especially don't know where in the hell he's taking me. Spam and Lysa know where I am, but they don't think I'm in any trouble.

Journey glances over, as if reading my thoughts. "You're the first friend from school that I've brought here."

"I thought we were going to your house." Rachel calls me a cool customer because I usually appear calm on the outside, but my voice comes out shaky and Journey definitely notices.

"Don't let the neighborhood scare you. It's not as bad as it looks."

I blink at the trash-strewn curbs, the abandoned sofas, the wrecked car parts. It's a rusted-out ghost town. I've heard stories about this place but I've never been here. Iron Rain includes a wedge of Oregon coastline bordered by the Pacific Ocean on one side and the Columbia River on the other. A long time ago, this whole area was one fish-canning operation after another. But as the salmon dwindled, so did the industry. Only one broken-down skeleton of a cannery still remains. The urban legend is that the ghost of an old sea captain haunts the place.

When Journey turns off the main road, it's clear that's where he's headed.

A scorpion tail of fear wriggles inside me. "The Calistoga cannery's been closed for years," I say.

"I know it looks bad, but we can't afford to fix it up," Journey says.

No lie. The cannery is a condemned hot mess. There's no way that someone actually lives there. I know Journey didn't kill my mom or Miss Peters . . . but what if he knows who did? Aren't there stories about serial killers working with young protégés? What if Journey is the messenger, bringing me to the real killer, like a gift? My body might never be found.

I squirm, wondering if I can dial 911 without looking at my phone.

Obviously Spam could. She'd be all like, *Hey everybody, come on down,* and she'd include a GPS link, all while holding her phone behind her back. I'd have to muddle around in my bag for at least five minutes just to even find my phone.

"We?" I manage to get out, my voice barely a squeak.

"My father bought the place cheap. He was going to apply for a grant and turn it into a historic site with a hotel, shops, and a restaurant. But he wound up in prison instead."

I gaze at the weathered, boarded-up hulk of a building looming at the end of the deserted road. It looks like the set for the latest *Saw* movie.

"You live in *that*?"

"We're not insane." He attempts to soothe me with his warm gaze. "It's nice. You'll see."

He reacts to my incredulous look.

"I know. But my mother refuses to let it go. She wants my father to have something to come home to." There's a sad shadow of a smile on his lips. "She's been trying to get his case reopened for ten years. All those legal fees don't leave any room for renovation."

He's so warm and sincere I can't help being drawn in. Gazing into his eyes quiets my brain enough to slow my panicked breathing. Clearly we should have talked more before I agreed to do this. How did I not know he lived way out here? I need to get my head straight and be more careful. But, for the moment, I sense I am safe.

Journey puts the van in neutral and sets the emergency brake. He gets out and unlocks a massive, ten-foot-high, chain-link gate. He slides it open and motions for me to move to the driver's seat. I unbuckle my seat belt and move over. Then realize there's no way I can drive this thing.

I gesture, palms up, and shake my head.

He jogs back and sticks his head in the open window. "Don't tell me you're one of those wimpy girls who can't handle a stick," he teases.

"You got me," I admit. "Completely lame." I start to move back to the passenger seat, but he reaches in and touches my shoulder. The warmth of his fingers spreads like an electric current through the fabric of my T-shirt.

"It's easy. I'll teach you." He leans in through the window until we're almost cheek to cheek. He has an errant lock of hair that frequently falls over his forehead and frames his jaw. At this particular moment, he's close enough for that chunk of hair to tickle my cheek. Goose bumps chase one another down my back and arms as his breath plays over my neck. His right arm slides around the back of my seat and I can barely breathe with him this close.

Oh my god. He is seriously flirting with me.

He reaches his left arm through the window and calmly points. "The pedal on the left is the clutch. It releases the gears. Press it all the way to the floor with your left foot."

With a robotic movement, I mash the pedal hard.

"Keep your right foot on the brake, too," he says quickly.

I mash the brake, too.

"Now, look at the diagram on the gearshift. Up and to the left is first. That's all you need to get through the gate."

I put my hand over the gearshift and rock it lightly from side to side.

"When you're ready, push the clutch in and move the stick into first gear."

The clutch is in, but when I try to push the stick into gear it makes a horrible grinding noise. I stop and give Journey a worried look.

"Push hard. As long as the clutch is in you won't hurt anything."

I try again with a hard push and it drops into first with a thunk.

"Great!" He almost cheers. I feel invincible. He pulls his head out of the window. "Okay. You're good to go. Release the emergency brake and slowly ease your left foot off the clutch while, at the same time, pressing slowly down on the gas with your right foot." He demonstrates with his hands—left up, right down. "Once you get through the gate just push in both the brake and clutch to stop."

Easy to say . . . but so hard to do. Not to mention that my insides are super thumpy because I don't want to screw this up. I try, but just letting my foot off the clutch a tiny bit sends the van bucking forward. It shudders, wheezes, and gives a long drawn-out mechanical death rattle. The engine dies, leaving the van only halfway through the gate.

Embarrassed, I flee the driver's seat.

Journey climbs into the van. "Not bad for your first attempt," he says.

He turns the key and the starter *rrrrr-rrrrr-rrrrr*s for a minute.

He lets it rest and then tries again. The stubborn van doesn't catch on the second, third, or even the fourth try. "This starting thing is getting worse," Journey says. Finally, on the fifth try, it kicks over. He smiles at me. "Ready to try again?"

Embarrassment creeps up my neck. "No freakin' way."

"Okay." He surrenders. "I won't make you."

My cheeks blaze. My reaction might have been a little over the top.

Journey drives through the gate, then stops and gets out to close it behind us. The clang of the massive gate being closed and locked in place clears the fizzy romantic notions from my brain. He might have been a little flirty with me, but we're here for one reason and one reason only—to collect evidence.

Journey climbs back in, puts the van in gear, and angles to the side of the creepy building, which is so huge that it blots out everything else, including the horizon.

As we leave the asphalt parking area, Journey slows and drives us onto a flat area lined with old, wooden planks. It's a bumpy ride. He flashes me one of his megawatt smiles. "Won't be long now," he promises, completing the drive around the building to the front, which faces the water. All I can think is *Holy wow.*

The front of the old cannery building is still a mess and a half. But angled off to one side is a small cottage, shaded by a giant redwood and set in a tiny patch of grass and flowers. It's quaint and charming and looks like something out of *Snow White*. Nestled here, in this setting, it's breathtakingly beautiful.

The cottage sits up on a slight slope, no more than twenty feet from the water's edge. It's a simple, two-story, Cape Cod design, white with deep red shutters and a rolled roof. The building looks stoic and strong. But the most amazing thing is its spectacular view of a lighthouse way in the distance. "Is that . . . ?"

"Yep, Cape Disappointment. It's one of our most romantic landmarks. Our house was the guard shack for the cannery before my parents got ahold of it."

"I can't believe you live here," I say.

"I call it Cape Disappointment, but my mother calls it Cape Can-do. Guess which one of us is the optimist?"

"It's lovely." My fear melts away. "How could you be disappointed here?"

"It beats calling it the Cape of Broken Dreams." A hollow bitterness creeps into his voice. "Because that's what this place is really: a pit for my family's broken dreams. Miss P's DNA experiment was my last shot to help my father. Not only did it not help him at all, but now I'm in almost the same trouble and I've lost Miss P. Like I said, just a giant heap of broken dreams."

All this time I've been wallowing in my own self-pity without giving a single thought to anyone else. Suddenly, I get it. This is why my Uncle Victor does what he does, because nothing soothes a grieving family member like information and facts.

I turn sideways in my seat and lay my hand over his on the gearshift. It's a bold move but I want him to feel the fierceness of my determination. The warmth of his skin surprises me, though, and I pull my hand back, folding it into my lap.

"I promise you we will get through this. We will completely clear both of our names. And then I will help you find the evidence you need for your dad."

Journey takes my hand from my lap, cradling it in both of his. He leans toward me. I lean toward him, too. It's like a magnet is pulling us together. I'm powerless to resist—not that I want to. It's crazy, but the more he leans toward me, the more I want to melt into him.

My vision turns bright, microscopic, illuminating things I've never noticed before, like the sprinkling of freckles over the bridge of his nose. His thick, strong eyebrows. When I see the tip of his tongue dart out and wet his upper lip, my eyes flutter closed. I'm almost certain that Journey Michaels—the boy I thought would never even know my name—is about to kiss me.

# 18

A latent fingerprint occurs when the body's natural oils
and sweat are deposited onto another surface . . .
which could even include another body.

—VICTOR FLEMMING

It's not that I've never kissed a boy before.

I have. Many times.

Well, okay, not many.

Maybe a few.

What I've never done is kiss the boy who puts my heart into a drum solo with just his smile; the boy who makes my knees tremble and my hands shake. Sure, I've fantasized about kissing Journey Michaels, but I never thought it would really happen. I definitely never pictured it here . . . like this. And yet, here we are. I swallow hard.

My eyes flutter closed and my exposed heart dangles perilously. Then, just as there is the lightest brush of lips—before I can fully sink into the feeling—there's a sudden loud *splat*. We jerk apart. I shriek. Journey cracks his elbow on the dash, cursing under his breath.

I blink at the windshield.

Why is there a large fish sliding down the glass? Its cold, round eye is frozen in a disapproving stare.

"Holy— What the—?"

"Damn bald eagles," Journey says. "If you're going to catch the stupid thing, eat it." Journey opens his door and stands on the running board. He grabs the fish by the tail and flings it toward the water. Then he sniffs his hands and wrinkles his nose. "Ew."

I can imagine.

He looks back at me from the doorway of the van, soft and a little wistful. We both know the moment has passed.

"I have to wash the fish smell off of my hands." There's a tightness to his voice that wasn't there before. "But first I'll park down by all that crap in front of the cannery. The light's better down there and we can use those pallets to stand on if we need to."

As he rumbles the van over the rough terrain, I take in the full spectacle of this location. A low stone wall and a ring of trees separates the two properties. The beauty of the cottage is a direct contrast to the decay of the cannery, which sprawls even farther down this finger of land to a rickety boat dock littered with pallets and rusted machinery.

Journey eases the van between piles of junk into the spot with the best light.

We both get out and I wait while he removes Vespy and sets her on the ground. As he walks back to his house to wash the fish yuck off his hands, I roll Vespy over to the wall and park her in the shade.

First I'll check for fingerprints, and then I'll see what else I can find. I retrieve a pair of rubber gloves from my toolbox. Rachel buys them by the box for coloring her hair, so I always have an ample supply.

My fingerprint kit resides in the small makeup pouch I carry with me at all times. This seems appropriate since my first kit actually *was* makeup: a blush brush, crushed smoky eye shadow, and teeth-whitening strips.

I'm not the kind of girl to ever have a problem choosing evidence over white teeth and eyes that pop.

I've since moved on to the real thing. My setup is ritual. Black fingerprint cards go in my back right pocket. Small packet of lifting strips, front left. The jar of red fluorescent fingerprint powder—which glows a neon red under ultraviolet light—gets tucked into my back left pocket. I usually slip the pen-sized ultraviolet flashlight into the front of my bra, but that feels too flirty to do in front of Journey. I stick it in my back pocket with the fingerprint powder. I'm just unpacking my fingerprint brush from its plastic sleeve when Journey slides up next to me.

"I had no idea searching for evidence required makeup," he says.

"This?" I ask, offering a smug smile. "This is an original Zephyr fingerprint brush. It's what the pro crime-scene guys use."

"The pros? Really?" Journey's skeptical. "Because I have a paintbrush that looks just like that and it only cost five bucks."

"Wow. A whole five bucks?" I expertly roll the slender handle between my fingers. The shimmery bristles fan out until it looks like a supermodel dandelion on steroids. "Well, *my* brush is made up of a whole bunch of little fiber bundles."

Journey's eyes widen with mock interest. "A whole bunch? Really? Is that a scientific term? Exactly how many is in a whole bunch?"

"Yes. It's a scientific term." I hold my arms out wide. "A whole bunch is thousands of bundles. Each bundle is hundreds of individual treated-glass filaments." Now I'm reciting the description off the Zephyr package from memory. As I walk slowly toward him I continue to twirl the brush at eye level.

Journey chuckles and backs away, inching closer to the van.

"And each one of these filaments is a fraction of the thickness of a hair."

"Okay. You got me," he says, throwing his hands up.

"Not yet," I caution. "I scored *my* brush online for the low price of eleven dollars and four cents, plus shipping." I shake the brush at him like a pom-pom. "*Now* I got you."

Journey leans back against the van and looks down on me with a crooked smile that adds tiny crinkles to the outsides of his eyes. "I don't know if I've got you," he whispers. "But I think I *get* you."

"You do?" I sound stunned but I'm not really. There is an overall easiness when I'm with Journey that I've never felt before. I don't know what it means but it's like nothing in my whole life has ever felt this right. I look off in the direction of the lighthouse, silently praying it will protect me from a disaster. "The light's not going to last long," I say.

"You're right. I should let you get to work," he says.

I know they're just words, but that thick, wistful tone is back and it seems to say so much more.

From the traces of black powder the police left behind, I can tell they only dusted the driver's door and the steering wheel. No doubt these are the best spots where someone might leave their prints, but I'm hoping some creative thinking will find some the police missed. As I make a tour around the van, I try to recall everything about that night. It was late and the air was frigid. I remember how it burned as I sucked it into my lungs.

Journey says he parked on the side of Miss Peters's house and left the engine running while he stepped across the grass to the porch. Someone—he didn't see who—jumped in and took off.

I walk around the van and try to imagine how I would approach it if I wanted to steal it and not be seen. I'd stay low and come up from the back, hugging the shadows near the bumpers. I would first peer around and locate Journey before trying to take his van. With my right hand I would steady myself against the bumper, at about the spot where it curves toward the front of the vehicle.

So this is where I start.

Kneeling next to the bumper, I load the superfine, florescent powder onto the brush and let it lightly sprinkle onto the paint. I work the brush over the area by twirling it right and left between my fingers. I work several inches in each direction, but no prints emerge. I get up and slowly move around the back of the car, toward the driver's side. I scan close. Any spot that looks even a little smudgy to my eye gets the powder treatment from my brush. Sometimes I check myself by using the ultraviolet penlight to reveal telltale finger marks.

I continue to work my way around the outside of the vehicle, keeping my face only an inch or two away from the surface. I check low and then high. Journey shadows me, looking over my shoulder, trying to see what I see.

I don't see any prints . . . until I reach the side view mirror. There I discover the mother lode: all four fingertips plus the thumb of a left hand.

"When was the last time you adjusted this mirror?" I ask.

Journey shrugs. "I have no idea."

Fortunately, I brought the large size lifting tape that's designed to capture a whole handprint. I powder the mirror, apply the tape, and peel off the prints. Journey holds the index card flat while I tape the prints onto the card.

"Wow. You made that look easy," Journey says.

"Lifting prints isn't hard; it just takes a lot of practice to keep the tape from sticking to itself."

"What's next?" he asks.

"The inside."

I open the door and look for any and all smooth surfaces where fingerprints might show up. There's not much. The dash is old and the paint is chipping off so it's not a good candidate for maintaining fingerprints. The seats are worn and rough. Still trying to put myself into the mind of the person who took the van, I pretend like I'm getting in for the very first time.

Being mindful of every action I would have taken, late at night, in an unfamiliar van, I decide I would look into the back and make sure there was no one else in the van with me. I carefully tip the driver's seat forward using only one gloved finger. The back of the seat is smooth black plastic that is not worn like the front. At the very top, I can see four clear fingerprints before I even dust the area with powder. It looks like someone gripped the back of the seat and turned around to peer deep into the van.

Journey and I exchange a look. "I touched the back of the seat earlier," he says. "Remember?"

"We'll eliminate your fingerprints if they show up," I explain. "We're just hoping to find the prints of someone who never should have been in your van to begin with."

After we've taken care of the fingerprints, I give the whole inside of the van a detailed inspection. Only one other thing stands out: a shred of notebook paper wedged in the driver's seat-belt clip.

I retrieve tweezers from my kit to remove the crumpled scrap. I smooth it out. It's about one inch long and half an inch wide. It's part of a note, written in blue ink. The top line reads: "ur DNA" and below that are the letters "ked" and "Pre". But I can't decipher that.

Grasping the corner of the note with tweezers, I hold it up for Journey's inspection. "Is this yours?"

He shakes his head. "Seriously, chimpanzees have better handwriting than I do."

"Okay. I think we've done all we can do here. I'll save this anyway. It could be a clue or it could be nothing."

I get out of the van and carry everything over to the wall where I parked Vespy. I take a seat on the ground and open the cargo area. I have to enter every piece of evidence into my notebook and organize it before I can stow it. The scrap of paper goes into a small Ziploc bag and back into the toolbox. The fingerprint cards slip into an outside pocket of my messenger bag. I jot down everything we found and where we found it.

Behind me, there's a rusty creak as Journey opens the door to the van. "Cross your fingers that this piece of junk will actually start," he calls out.

I raise my hand over my head, fingers crossed. I make a conscious choice not to turn and gaze at him because it would be easy to get all distracted. Journey Michaels almost freakin' kissed me. That's huge. *Huge.* My lips tingle a little.

He'll try it again. Right?

The van engine rumbles to life and I smile. Sure, I could get home on my scooter, but it would mean going it alone.

"We're good to go." Journey strides past me and hops the wall on his way to the house. "Want a soda for the ride home?" He walks backward for a couple of steps and nearly trips. I shoo him on and go back to organizing my notes. Damn, he's adorable.

Behind me the van engine revs high—our chariot is warmed

up and ready. Strangely, the engine continues to rev until it becomes a scream. I glance over my shoulder at the exact moment that something snaps and the van rockets forward on a straight path toward me.

Literal deer in headlights.

I'm gripped with fear; nothing moves right. I untangle my legs and struggle to my feet. The van thunders toward me. My brain tries to decide—right or left?

Vespy!

I grab her handlebars and tug. She doesn't budge.

Her foot peg is snagged on the wall.

I tug harder as the van screams toward me.

# 19

An investigator's first step, before collecting any evidence, is to develop a theory regarding the type of offense that occurred.

—VICTOR FLEMMING

A thousand thoughts collide all at once: the missed kiss, moon, Rachel, Mom, peaches, Miss P, oranges.

Nearly on top of me, the van appears monstrous.

I cringe and brace for the impact, frozen where I stand. Journey looms over me from the other side of the wall. He's right in my face: his eyes huge, his jaw muscles bulging. His fingers gouge the soft flesh of my armpits. He yanks me toward him.

"Erin!" he bellows.

I go limp, and with one massive effort he falls back. My head slams the top edge of stones as he hauls me over the wall. At the last second my right foot tangles in Vespy's handlebars.

"My foot," I gasp.

Journey rolls to free me from the scooter, winding up on top of me. He hunkers down, forming a protective shield against everything but the screech of metal compacting metal and the huge cloud of dust. Finally, with a choke and shudder, the van dies, it's quiet again, and we're still alive.

"What the—?"

Journey leaps off of me, his expression a twist of horror. "You're bleeding."

I sit up, even though I'm woozy. My fingers explore my forehead, finding a large, tender lump and some fresh blood. "Is it bad?"

Hopping nervously from one foot to the other, he puts his hands out, afraid to touch me. "We have to get you to the emergency room." He gingerly lifts me up and sets me on my feet. Then he stands back as if he's afraid to be too close.

I brush myself off, checking for spots that hurt more than others, since basically everything hurts. I dab at the blood streaming into my eyes.

"Your freaking van nearly killed us," I say.

"Sorry. Sorry. So sorry. The emergency brake must've slipped. I can't believe I got to you in time." Journey looks over the wall and grimaces. Then he wraps his arms around my shoulders and turns me away.

"Don't look, okay?" he says. He tries to use his shirt to wipe away some of the blood.

Hearing "don't look" makes me snap my head around.

The front of the van is wedged against the wall. If it's dented or scratched at all from the impact, it barely shows.

What I don't see is Vespy.

I rise onto my tiptoes and peer straight down. Now I see her. My poor scooter lies mangled between the brick wall and the van. A low moan escapes my lips.

Journey hops the wall and opens the driver's door, peering in. His expression ratchets from worry to shock. "I'm calling 911." He pulls out his phone.

"No!" I stagger to the wall but it's too high for me to simply hop over. Plus, I have to keep one hand pressed to my forehead to hold back the blood. "Seriously, don't." It would be really bad for a call about me to come in while Rachel's on duty.

Journey stares helplessly into his van.

I manage to slide my hip onto the top of the wall and swing my legs over. I join him at the door of his van. Now I see it.

A brick is holding down the gas pedal.

He looks at me like *What should we do?*

"Don't touch anything." I pull out my phone. This'll go down better if I make the call.

▼ ▼ ▼

First one police car shows up, then two more, along with a sergeant. Paramedics treat the lump and gash on my forehead at the scene. Then Journey and I are transported back to the police station in separate cars. Once we arrive, we are placed in separate rooms.

I'm in the room they use for briefings. It's large, with several tables, a bunch of chairs, and a huge whiteboard. I take the seat farthest from the door, at an angle that allows me to see everyone who walks past.

Not long after I arrive, Rachel storms in and walks up to the table. She simply glares, her arms crossed over her chest and her foot tapping angrily.

"What?" I ask.

"You better have a damn good reason for ignoring my rules," she says.

I'm almost killed, Vespy is wrecked, and all she can think about are her stupid rules? I stack my fists one on top of the other and rest my chin on them.

She turns on her heel and storms out, slamming the door. Every couple of minutes a new group barges in. They stand over by the door, talking in hushed tones, and then leave.

Everyone seems to be talking to everybody . . . except me.

I wonder what they're doing to poor Journey. The first cop who arrived on the scene saw the brick on the gas pedal, but acted like we were trying to pull something. Not that he came right out and said that, but I could tell. I think they even put Journey in handcuffs again when they took him.

I'm exploring the huge bandage on my forehead with my fingers when the door opens again. Out of the corner of my eye I see a man walk in. He's wearing a rumpled suit. I place him somewhere in his forties, but there's a kind of hipster air about him. For one thing, he's wearing sunglasses indoors. Another is the hair: It's short, but mussed in a way that looks cool, not sloppy.

Based on his confident swagger, I conclude he must be a new shrink that Rachel's hired to check me out. She thinks I'm acting out over what happened to Miss Peters. Fine. I'll show her acting out. I take my sunglasses out of my bag and put them on. Two can play this game. I slouch in my seat and wait. Mystery Man strolls over to the opposite side of the table and takes a seat.

I concentrate on reading text messages on my phone.

Pretty soon the door opens again. Sydney leads Rachel and Principal Roberts inside and shuts the door behind them.

Principal Roberts glances over at me with a tepid smile as he explains, in hushed tones, how worried he was when he saw *that boy* following me out of the school parking lot.

Rachel shoots me an angry look. Yeah, okay; I'm supposed to call her if I go somewhere after school.

Mystery Man leans forward. "Maybe you should take off your sunglasses if you don't want to piss her off even more."

"What about your sunglasses?"

"It won't make her less angry with you, but if you insist, I'll go first." He takes his sunglasses off and slips them into his pocket. "Now your turn."

I slide my sunglasses off and look directly at him. "Oh my god. You're—"

He extends his hand across the table. "Victor. Nice to finally meet you."

Holy crap. It's *Uncle* Victor.

"I brought this for you," he says, handing me a small shopping bag. Inside is a tiny white ceramic unicorn wrapped in tissue paper. I give him a puzzled look.

He shrugs. "I guessed at what girls your age like and I obviously guessed too low. But, in my experience, you'll appreciate stuff like that again in about twenty years."

I smile. It was sweet of him to bring me something. "It's cute. Thanks. You picked kind of a sucky day to arrive, though. Rachel's acting like I'm all Mallory Knox or something."

Victor sits back in his chair and sticks his feet out. "It sounds like she thinks you're okay but your boyfriend might be Mickey Knox."

I grin. "Ha! A Tarantino fan. Me, too."

"Actually, I'm an Oliver Stone man," Victor says. "But you're not old enough to know *Natural Born Killers,* are you?"

"Netflix plus insomnia. You'd be surprised. And for the record, he's not my boyfriend." I'm telling the truth, but wish I were lying.

Victor rests his elbows on the table. "But is he Mickey Knox? That's the question."

I get caught in his hard stare. Sitting up straight, I give him a direct look right back. "He's not Mickey Knox. Not at all."

Victor nods. "I hope you're right, because from where I sit, this is about to turn into a major cluster."

As if on cue, the door opens and Police Chief Culson sweeps

in all official-like. He wears a cloud of concern around him like a superhero cape. After a taut hello to Sydney and Rachel and a nod to Principal Roberts, he heads straight to me.

"Erin, dear. Let's have a look at you?" He rolls his hip onto the table, turning his back to everyone in the room, including Victor. He inspects my forehead. "Stitches?"

I touch the bandage. "No. Just a bump. I'm okay."

"You can't be too okay, you're in a police station."

"What I mean is, physically I'm fine, but I do think someone tried to, um, kill me." I look to Victor, then to the chief. This is the first time I've actually put it into words, but that's what it boils down to. Someone snuck up on us and tried to turn Journey's van into a killing machine. It's time to admit that I'm scared.

I expect them to mull over the question of who did this, but the chief pulls a small notebook and a stylish pen from the inside pocket of his jacket. "Do you know of any reason why that boy would want to harm you?"

"Journey? What? No. He saved me." I stand up. "Where is he? I need to see him. Let us explain."

The chief puts out his hands to calm me. "So, you believe it was just a bizarre accident? Mechanical failure, groundhogs or something like that?" he asks.

"Groundhogs?! It was sabotage."

"So you saw someone else in the area?" he asks.

"No. But—" I glance around the room. Rachel, Sydney, and Principal Roberts are in the corner, arguing. Chief Culson is concerned, but skeptical. I turn my pleading gaze to Victor; he's my last hope. "Please. I need to see Journey. Make them let me."

The chief purses his lips. "PTSD is pretty common in situations like this, Erin. That stands for post-traumatic stress disorder. In other words, your fear and anxiety could be affecting your ability to accurately process what happened."

"Dude, I think I know what PTSD is, my mom was murdered when I was a baby," I snap. I sit back down and slouch even lower in my seat. Nobody's listening to me.

"This must be a technique I'm not familiar with." Victor kicks back in his chair and props his right ankle on his left knee. "Is it more efficient to tell the victim what happened rather than take her statement?"

The chief's eyes darken, like storm clouds over the ocean, but his smile gets wider and appears to fill with even more teeth. After a brief, awkward moment, he twists his body to greet Victor, as if he's just realized he's sitting there.

"Ahh, yes," Chief Culson says with a chuckle. "You Feds are such sticklers on technique." He stands and thrusts his hand across the table. "Nice to see you back, Vic. I'm sure Rachel loves having the family together again."

Victor gets to his feet and accepts Culson's hand. "It's good to be back and comforting to see that so little has changed."

I watch in amazement as the two men try to polite each other to death. Victor's comment sounds innocent enough, but I can't miss the fact that Chief Culson's face looks like he just smelled a fart.

The two men drop the handshake, but retain the polite veneer. Victor shoves his hands into his front pockets and rocks back on his heels. Chief Culson rolls his fancy pen around between his fingers. "Change is overrated. We small-town guys have learned the value of status quo. So, any official reason you're—?"

"Vacation," Victor answers before the question is even fully on the table. I'm not sure what the story is between them, but Victor seems to have lost a little of his laid-back hipster shine.

And Chief Culson suddenly has twice as many teeth. If I had to guess, I'd say these two hate each other.

"Well, our girls couldn't be in better hands," Culson says. He lays his pen on the table in front of me. "Take my pen, hon. And use a couple of pages from your notebook there. Just write down everything that happened today. Make it as long or as short as you like. Anything and everything you think we need to know to get to the bottom of this, because I promise you, we *will* get to the bottom of this." He glances at Victor.

I slide his pen back across the table. "Thanks, Chief. I have a pen."

He closes his hand over mine, sealing the pen inside. "Please, Erin, I insist. This is a Conway Stewart. I have an aunt who lives in London and she used to work for the factory. Every year she would send me a whole box of these pens *for free,* because she knew they were my favorite. You can consider it a gift from me to you. After what you've been through, you could use a little something. Don't you think?"

Before I can even answer, Sydney strides up. She gives me a little half smile, but otherwise she's all business. "Here's where we're at, Chief. We're all in agreement that we want him held on probable cause regardless of whether she makes a statement against him or not."

I erupt out of my chair. "You can't do that. He saved my life. Why can't you people get that through your heads? That's it. I want to see him. Now. I'm not saying another word until you let me."

Rachel joins the conversation. "Sit *down,* Erin. You're in no position to demand anything. Chief, every time she's with that boy something bad happens."

I plop down into my chair and aim a frustrated, helpless

gesture to Victor. As the others wander back over to the door to continue plotting against Journey, Victor nudges the notebook and pen in front of me.

"Sketch me the layout. Where was the van, where were you, where was Journey?" he says.

Finally, someone is asking questions that make sense.

I quickly make a few marks on the page. I sketch a rectangle labeled *van* near the bottom, surrounded by some squiggles labeled *junk* and *pallets.* A line across the page is labeled *stone wall.* An X labeled *house* on the other side of the wall. A stick figure next to a scooter, labeled *me,* on the van side of the wall and finally, a stick figure *Journey* on the house side of the wall. Then I spin the notebook back to Victor.

He cracks his knuckles and looks it over for a couple of seconds. "How high is the wall?" I hold my hand up about hip height. He nods. "And this distance here?" He points to the space between the van and my stick figure. "About the same as the width of our yard?"

I agree.

He presses the pen into my hand. "Hold on to your socks," he says.

Victor walks over to the whiteboard and erases what was on there. On one side of the board he quickly reproduces my sketch in bold black marker. He curls his lower lip in and whistles for attention.

The room goes silent as everyone stops talking and turns toward Victor.

"Here's the question, folks." At the top of the whiteboard he pens the key words as he says them. "Is it possible for a *teenage boy* to apply a *brick* to the gas pedal of a rickety *van* launching a deadly trajectory . . . then run, vault a four-foot-high wall, and drag an average-sized teenage girl to safety before the van can reach her?"

"Just so you know, Vic, that boy is a star athlete," Principal Roberts says.

"Okay." Victor scribbles the word "athletic" above the words "teenage boy." "Any other qualifiers I need to factor in?" No one responds. Victor looks to me. "This is the layout, right?"

I nod.

"Okay. Let's break this down. A Tesla Roadster Sport accelerates zero to sixty in three point seven seconds." He draws a rocket on wheels. "I'll assume Journey's van has almost nothing in common with a Tesla Roadster?"

I shake my head and stifle a giggle.

"Then it's probably fair to say the van would take at least ten seconds to achieve sixty miles per hour, giving it an acceleration of approximately eight point eight feet per second per second. I didn't just stutter. I know it sounds weird, but that's how you say it."

I sneak a look at Rachel and the rest of the adults. While Victor is clearly enjoying the hell out of this, their enthusiasm for blaming Journey is sinking fast.

He continues. "Since we know the van traveled a distance of approximately eighty feet, we can use a basic physics formula and determine that it probably took the van about four seconds to hit the wall with a final velocity of twenty-five point eight miles per hour."

Chief Culson interjects. "Okay. We've heard enough, Vic. You can stop there."

Rachel, Sydney, and Principal Roberts head for the door. I don't know what they're going to do and they show no intention of including me in their plans.

"Wait. Don't you want to hear how it's technically possible?" Victor asks.

Sydney walks back to the whiteboard. "Are you saying he did it?"

"I'm saying Usain Bolt—the fastest man in the world, with a top sprint speed of twenty-seven point seventy-nine miles per hour—could've done it." Victor writes this number on the board and underlines it. "Which means it's technically possible . . . but highly improbable. I don't see how holding this boy will generate the outcome you desire."

Rachel takes Sydney by the arm and guides her toward the door. "Sorry. My brother's always been an a-hole," she mutters.

Meanwhile, I'm elated. Mini fist pump.

That. Was. Amazing.

# ▸ 20 ◂

Arches, loops, and whorls might sound like hot roller coaster moves
but really they are how we distinguish between the
three common fingerprint patterns.

—VICTOR FLEMMING

An hour later we're back home, sitting around the kitchen.

My head is throbbing, but I'm relaxed knowing that at least Journey isn't spending the night in jail. Rachel and Sydney weren't happy with the way Victor cleared him, but they had to agree it didn't make any sense to hold him.

Victor is totally my hero.

The whole incident feels fuzzy. But a brick on the gas pedal can only mean one thing, right? Someone really is trying to kill me.

Rachel combines ingredients for her famous spaghetti sauce while Victor and I hang out around the dining room table. Victor's sleeves are pushed up and he rolls Chief Culson's fancy pen between his fingers.

"I can't believe he's still handing out the hoity-toity pens from England," Victor says with a snort. "Who cares? It's so juvenile."

Rachel slips a lid onto the sauce pot. "What's juvenile is how you and Charles continue to cling to your grudge after all these years. It was high school, Victor. Let it go."

"I'm not holding on to a grudge." He passes the pen back to me. "These are seconds, you know; damaged in some way. That's why she sent them to him for *free*." Victor uses air quotes as a mocking gesture.

Rachel throws her hands in the air. "Honestly, who cares?" she says. "I'm going to change."

Once Rachel leaves, I grab my messenger bag to take my stuff up to my room. The bag tilts, spilling the fingerprint cards I lifted from Journey's van. I make a quick swipe to scoop them up, but I'm not quick enough for Victor.

"Hey, fingerprint cards," he says. "Let me see those."

I hand the cards over, excited to see what he'll say but also a little nervous. If Rachel spots these cards, she'll know what we were up to at Journey's house, and that won't go over well. "I was just messing around," I say.

Victor studies the cards. "Are you in one of those special forensic classes? I think they're using one of my cases for classroom instruction."

"Really? Which one? I've read all of your books—several times. I'm kind of a fan so I'm sure I'd know all the details."

"A fan, huh?" Victor smiles. "These fingerprints look more like an apprentice."

My eyes grow huge. "Really? You think so?"

"I do," Victor says. "Your technique is good. You've almost captured the fingertips of two complete hands. A right and a left. They're not from the same person, though."

"They're not? How can you tell?" I peer at the cards, trying not to fangirl freak out over getting to see them through Victor's eyes.

"Well, there are three main patterns to fingerprints—" he says.

I jump in. "Arches, loops, and whorls."

He chuckles, pointing at one card with his little finger. "Good. But are you aware that arches are only found in about 5 percent of the patterns we see?" He gestures to the card in my other hand. "While we see loops in 60 to 70 percent of the patterns. So yeah, my guess is these are not the same person."

"Wow." I'm in complete awe. I make a mental note to check Journey's fingertips next time I see him. Is he a whorl or an arch?

"But you're not in one of those classes, huh?" Victor asks, handing the cards back to me.

"I wish." I stash the cards more securely in my bag.

Victor frowns. "Too bad. I keep hoping I'll come across a classroom that's doing it. But not having kids, you know, I'm not around that many classrooms."

Suddenly, "Poker Face" by Lady Gaga blasts out loud and clear.

Victor and I lock eyes, momentarily baffled, until I realize it's the ringtone on my new cell phone—the one Spam gave me. She *would* set her ringtone to Lady Gaga.

I grab the phone and answer, "Hi, hold on." Then I give Victor a quick wave as I exit the kitchen and take the stairs, two at a time, up to my bedroom. Once inside, I close the door and lean my back against it.

"You're not going to believe this." I'm breathless with excitement.

"What? That someone tried to kill you?" Spam sounds upset.

"Oh. You heard."

"I just got off the phone with Lysa. What the eff happened at Journey's house?"

"Someone put a brick on the gas pedal of Journey's van and

sent it speeding toward me." I drop my messenger bag on the floor and slide under the comforter on my bed. The sheets are cool and soothing.

"It wasn't Journey?" she asks.

"No. He was behind me."

"And you're sure it wasn't an accident?" demands Spam.

"How could a brick on the gas pedal be an accident?"

"I'm coming over," she says.

"Great. Then you can meet my uncle." I pause dramatically. "Because he's here."

"Wait. Your uncle? The FBI dude?"

"Yeah. Crazy, huh? I've wanted to meet him my whole life. He's a-mazing. Like the god of evidence. You won't believe what he did to keep Journey from being arrested."

"On my way," she says.

I throw back the covers and attempt to stand up. It's a lot more difficult than it should be. The aftereffects of nearly getting killed have settled into my muscles and joints. This calls for a hot shower before dinner.

By the time I make my way downstairs, Spam has arrived and is setting the table while regaling Victor with stories of her online gaming escapades. She throws out words like "MMOG," "first-person shooter," "mezz," "caster," "noobs." I shake my head. She's wearing a black short jumper with the sleeves rolled up, and red-and-black-striped leggings that stop above the knee.

I worry that Victor will think she's silly. But that's not how he's treating her. He's talking to her the same way I saw him talk to Sydney.

"Okay. So then what's an M-M-O-R-P-G?" he asks.

Spam goes to the cupboard where we keep the bowls, pulls out four, and ferries them over to the stove for Rachel to ladle out the food. "Massive multiplayer online role-playing game," she says.

"The first *M* stands for massive?" he asks.

"Right," she answers.

"Okay. And how is that different from a first-person shooter game?"

Spam brings a couple of bowls of steaming pasta drenched in a rich sauce to the table. She sets one in front of Victor and one in front of me. Then she takes the chair opposite Victor and waits while Rachel brings two more bowls of food.

"Well, a *massive* is a virtual online playing field where a huge number of players come together and play all at once. You see all the characters, like watching television. And one of those characters is yours to move around and do things with."

Victor looks like he's really interested in what Spam has to say. "And?" he says.

"And in a first-person shooter all you see of yourself is your hand and your weapon. Everything else is your prey."

"Okay. I get it," Victor says.

Rachel sets Spam's dish in front of her and another in front of her own chair. Then she takes her seat, pausing to give me a quiet, simmering look. She hasn't said much since she found out I left school with Journey. I'm pretty sure if Victor and Spam weren't here right now, I'd be getting an earful.

"With whom do you play these online games? Friends from school?" Victor asks.

"Some are from school. But they could be from anywhere. It's kind of cool, I've played with people from all over the world," Spam says.

Victor frowns. "How do you know who you're playing with?"

Spam shrugs. "Because it's online, you never know exactly,

I guess. The cool wizard dude could be some forty-year-old perv, which is why I never give out any personal info online."

"Good. That's what I was trying to find out. Smart girl," Victor says. Then he turns to me. "Are you into this online gaming stuff, too?"

"No. Spam tried but I'm not that much of a dork." I give Spam a smirk and she responds with a poisoned grin.

Victor looks pleased. "Perfect. Don't suddenly get interested, okay?"

"I won't. But why?"

Victor lays down his fork and looks at each of us as if considering what to say.

"It's okay. You can tell them," Rachel urges.

Victor leans forward, clasping his hands in front of him. "There are obvious reasons why I want to keep this between us. But the truth is, I'm not actually here on vacation. Rachel asked me to come to look into what happened to your teacher. She wanted to be sure it didn't have anything to do with you. After today's incident, well, let's just say it's a good thing I'm here."

I gasp. Even though I know it's probably true, hearing the words spill out of his mouth pretty much scares the crap out of me.

Rachel adds, "We're not telling you this to worry you. I contacted Victor after Miss Peters's murder because I was concerned. At the time, I thought I was just being my crazy, overprotective self. But now I'm not so sure. I don't want to take any risks."

"I'm glad you called him, Rachel. Journey and I need someone on our side." My heart soars. Having Victor help us with the investigation will be the greatest thing that has ever happened to me.

Rachel pauses, gnawing on her lip. "Let me be clear, Erin. This isn't about sides. And it isn't about you and Journey or even you versus Journey. . . ."

I get a sinking feeling that I know where this is going and I don't like it.

"He's already dealing with a troubling family situation," she says.

"That doesn't have anything to do with him," I exclaim.

Rachel puts out her hand to calm the conversation. "I'm not saying it does . . . or doesn't. I'm just saying that for now, this boy is off-limits outside of school. I don't want you seeing him."

Wow. She can't be serious. Just when there might actually be a me and Journey, she wants me to stop seeing him. Separating me from him won't solve anything, especially not Miss Peters's murder.

Instead of answering her, I pick up my fork and begin pushing sauce and noodles around my plate. I can sense everyone's gaze on me.

Spam reaches over and grabs my free hand, giving it a squeeze. "No sweat, Rachel. We don't really hang out with him anyway, right, Erin?"

I can't lie straight to Rachel's face, so I just nod.

"Good. Then we're on the same page," she says.

I swirl some pasta onto my fork and manage to deliver it to my mouth. Rachel doesn't get it. There's no such thing as no Journey. The person who killed my mother and Miss Peters might not have intended to bring us together, but he did. Together we know things no one else knows, and together we will survive this.

Rachel's edict about Journey leaves a prickly edge to the air in the room. Everyone is waiting for me to say something so they'll know that I agree with Rachel's rule. But I just can't. My throat's so tight I can hardly swallow my mouthful of food. Finally, after a very long silence, I manage a compliment. "The sauce is good, Rachel."

Just letting my voice out in the room and keeping it steady and strong is enough to break the spell. Everyone digs in.

Victor slurps up sauce and then makes a big display of eyeing Rachel. "Wow, Erin's right. This sauce even beats Mom's."

Rachel softens and returns Victor's smile. Before long, they're telling stories about when they were kids. I'm hanging on every word as Victor launches into a story about Rachel and my mother when they were young. But Rachel cuts him off. What she says sounds innocent enough: "I'm sure the girls have had enough of our ancient stories." But I know I'm not imagining the look of warning she flashes him. Victor seems to understand her code, and switches the topic to basketball and the old hoop that used to hang out on the front of the garage. Victor inquires if Spam and I would be interested in shooting some afternoon hoops if he put up a new one. Too bad. If Journey weren't banished from around here, Victor would have a real shot at a pickup game.

The way Rachel was able to curb Victor's conversation about my mom makes me realize that getting his help on the investigation is probably pretty unlikely. And without the piece of information that Journey and I have on Miss Peters's killer, the fabric that connects her to my mom, I don't expect he'll get very far on his own.

I call this an impasse.

# - 21 -

When collecting evidence, the state that evidence is found in must not be altered at all. . . . Remember that: not at all.

—VICTOR FLEMMING

The next morning, a car horn out front signals that Spam and Lysa are here to pick me up for school. I asked them to show up a half hour early because I had something I needed to do in the library. But the library isn't where we're going.

I race down the stairs and through the kitchen and offer a quick wave to Victor, who is sitting at the table having coffee and toast. "See you later."

"Yeah, later," he mumbles, hoisting his cup in lieu of a wave.

Spam is waiting with the passenger door open and the front seat pulled forward to let me in. Lysa has the top down on the car. As I squeeze past Spam to land in the backseat, I bark out a few basic directions. "We have a quick stop to make. Go past the school and get on highway 30 for about five miles."

Lysa backs out of the driveway. "I'll drive as far as you want as long as coffee's involved."

I think for a minute, picturing the intersection where we're headed. "Not only is there coffee, but it's donut-shop coffee. And I'm buying."

Spam squeals, but Lysa is quiet. "Where are we going?" she asks.

"It's no big deal; just a quick stop to pick something up."

"That's all the way across town. What do you have to pick up over there?" she wonders.

"You'll see when we get there. Trust me."

I can tell she's not convinced, because she remains quiet on the ride over. That's not a problem this morning, though, because Spam is talking enough for all of us. She's right in the middle of jabbering about how Chelsea caught her boyfriend making out with Sarah when I see him, walking toward the corner, in that style that's all his own.

"Stop!" I yell.

With a loud squeal of brakes, Lysa slams the car to a halt right in the middle of the street, sending Spam and me forward against our seat belts. She whips her head right and left, looking for something that's about to hit us. When she sees nothing, she turns to glare at me. "What?"

"Oh, um. We're here." I hardly need to point out the donut shop on the corner, since the smell of old grease hangs heavy in the morning air. A little unsure of me and the neighborhood, Lysa eases the car into the parking lot, but hesitates to pull into a space. "Why are we stopping here again?" she asks.

"Just park and let me out. I'll get our coffees."

Lysa parks, but neither she nor Spam hurry to open the doors. They both turn toward me in the backseat.

"What's going on?" Spam asks.

"Yeah, why did you make me bring you all the way out here?" Lysa asks.

I don't answer.

At first, Journey looks a little confused as he walks toward

Lysa's car. But once he's sure it really is me, his smile beams as brightly as the sun coming out from behind clouds. He strides toward us. "Hey guys."

My plan should be pretty obvious from this point on. Journey's van was towed to the police impound lot last night, along with my munched scooter, so I texted him last night that we'd give him a ride to school.

He texted back that this was a good place to meet.

I should hide my extreme euphoria at hearing his voice, but I can't. "Hey guys. Look, it's Journey." I flash him my most inviting smile. "Need a ride? Hop in."

Lysa turns around in her seat. "Why didn't you just tell us you wanted to pick him up?"

"I was afraid you'd say no," I say.

"That's right, because Rachel doesn't want you around him," Spam says.

"What are you, my parent?"

Lysa shrugs. "I'm not supposed to be around him, either."

I rise out of my seat and throw one leg over, ready to climb out of the car. "Fine. I'll ride the bus with him."

Journey stands by the car, his gaze shifting back and forth between our faces. He's a little baffled. "What's going on?"

Spam and I glare at each other for a long minute. I shift my weight toward the outside of the car. She snaps the door handle, opening her door and getting out. Pulling her seat forward, she gestures Journey toward the backseat. "Get in."

"Erin?" he asks.

"It's okay. Come on." I bring my leg back inside.

He climbs into the back and slides over to sit behind Lysa.

"Who wants coffee?" I ask.

Lysa waves her hand in the air. "I'm good."

Spam sinks back into her seat. "Me, too," she says, buckling her seat belt.

"Okay. On to school, I guess." I slide down in my seat and buckle in. Journey watches me with a puzzled look. "What?" I smile. "We're a team now."

"You better hope my dad isn't monitoring my GPS this morning," Lysa says as she guides the car out of the parking lot and drives toward school. "Or I will be seriously grounded."

Journey snakes his hand across the seat and pats my hand. I pat his hand in reply, but when I sense Spam eyeing me over her shoulder, I move my hand and replace it with my messenger bag.

"You're not supposed to see me anymore?" he whispers.

"Don't worry. Rachel's just a little freaked out about the whole van-munching-Vespy thing."

Spam turns in her seat. "Maybe she has a reason to be freaked out."

"How can you say that?" I'm feeling attacked from every side.

"Because every time something bad happens, he's there, too." Spam crosses her arms over her chest.

"Don't get all Judge Judy. Journey saved my life. And besides, we agreed we're a team."

"How are we a team when you promised Rachel you wouldn't see him outside of school?"

My finger comes up, right in her face. "I didn't promise her that . . . *you* did."

Journey puts his arm up between Spam and me. "Hey, whoa. This isn't getting us anywhere."

I sit back and gaze at the business neighborhood whizzing past; we're a couple of blocks from school. "We need a homework session . . . tonight, my house. Six o'clock, okay?"

"Are you including him?" Spam asks.

"Of course I'm including him."

Spam starts to open her mouth to argue, but I read her mind.

"Rachel's covering three to midnight again tonight. She won't be home."

Lysa pulls into a parking space at school and there's complete silence in the car.

Journey speaks first. "I'll be there."

"Me, too," adds Lysa.

Spam is quiet for a long minute. "Fine," she says.

We get out of the car, slam the doors, and each head toward class separately.

Picking Journey up this morning must've pushed Spam and Lysa pretty hard because even though I stop by all of our usual spots I don't see either of them during lunch. Instead I find a quiet table and try to figure out our next steps.

I refer back to the list in my notebook. Item one: What was Miss P working on. Spam's already agreed to check out the phone records. Miss P's house is the crime scene, so I'll never get in there, but I do know another place that might help us.

I need to get us into the lab at school.

# 22

> There's always right and wrong. And then there's what your gut tells you to do. My gut has never steered me wrong.
>
> —VICTOR FLEMMING

I slide into biology class as the echo of the tardy bell fades. Of course, we have a substitute teacher again today, and we will continue to have them for some time to come.

This one, an older grandmother type, offers me a patient smile before scrawling her name on the board: Mrs. Henderson.

I give her two days.

She announces we'll be watching a movie. My guess is we'll be watching a lot of movies over the coming weeks, until they sort out who's going to take over the class.

To follow through on finding out what Miss P was up to during her final days, I need to get into the lab and snoop around, but without a qualified biology teacher on hand, that's not going to happen. If I want in there today I'm going to have to be creative.

I'm wearing a navy blue hoodie over a white tank with thin straps. I slip my hand inside my hoodie, grasp the strap, and pull hard. It takes a couple of tries, but I manage to break the strap. I rummage in my purse for my mini sewing kit.

While the TA sets up the equipment for the movie, Mrs. Henderson moves her papers to the back of the room. Just beyond her is the door to the lab. Holding my strap in my hand, I make my way over to stand in front of her. In a low whisper, I explain that my shirt ripped and ask for permission to slip into the next room to fix it.

"Oh dear," she says sincerely. "Maybe you should go to the nurse instead."

"Huh? No. I mean, uh, I can't. Because . . . um, well I'm not hurt, and what if someone else was really sick and the nurse ignored them because she was fixing my strap? That would be awful, right?" I add a pleading-puppy look to seal the deal.

Mrs. Henderson is grandmotherly and kind, not stupid. She narrows her eyes. "Calm down, dear. What I meant to say is that the nurse can probably hand you a safety pin, which shouldn't prevent her from providing care to others."

Great. Since when are subs such devoted problem solvers? I shake my head. "Oh, yeah, but see, a safety pin will show, and look, I have this sewing kit and everything. My friend can help me fix it quickly." I motion to Spam, who responds with a scowl.

Mrs. Henderson glances from me to Spam and back to me again. I try to look hopeful and trustworthy. Reluctantly, she agrees. I motion for Spam to follow me. But she shakes her head.

What? Like I have time for this.

I grab Spam's sleeve and tug. She either comes with me or her favorite pink sweater is going to have one arm longer than the other. She frowns, but follows. We slip into the lab and I lock the door behind us.

The lab is a large room, about the same size as the classroom, but designed with tables in the middle and room for activity stations along the counters against each wall. A certain amount of clutter is normal for this space. But today things look particularly disorganized.

Spam slouches. "I was planning to sleep through the movie."

I guide her straight over to Miss Peters's desk. "No time for naps. Boot up her computer and copy all of her files to your cloud drive."

Spam starts clicking keys. "We shouldn't be in here," she says.

"Maybe not, but I'm guessing we'll only get one shot at this, and we owe it to Miss Peters to do our best. Besides, we know what the lab looked like before. The police won't have a clue if something is missing . . . or new."

Next to Miss Peters's computer is a holder containing pens and pencils, and I remember the scrap of paper we found in Journey's van. It had the word DNA on it.

I know it's a long shot but if I could prove that scrap came from a note written by Miss P, it might actually be a real clue. I scoop up all the pens and jam them into my pocket. Next, I open the sewing kit and find a tiny safety pin. I slip my arm out of my top and reattach my strap. Then I take a closer look around.

"Whoa. Somebody trashed this place," I say.

"It looks the same to me." Spam glances up from the keyboard and shrugs.

"Not really." I gaze at the chaotic mess of papers covering the entire top of Miss P's desk. Along the walls, all of the activity stations have been shoved to one end of the counter. Instead of being spaced out to accommodate two or three students, the microscopes are shoved together and toppled over. The cupboard doors are ajar.

There isn't stuff thrown all over the floor, but otherwise, the status of the lab isn't that different from my bedroom after the police executed their search warrant. "Someone's been in here looking for something."

"Probably the police," Spam says.

"Maybe," I say, but I'm thinking, *Not really.* The mess they left in my room was methodical. This is haphazard.

I wander toward the back of the room. "This stuff is new."

Stuck in a big jumble with everything else is a small centrifuge and a plain box made of clear acrylic with a black and red electrical wire coming out of it. There are also bottles of gels and dyes, gel trays, and a small light box.

Bam! "Here it is. A motive for Miss Peters's murder."

Spam's head snaps up. "What?"

"This is everything she needed to run DNA."

Spam shakes her head. "But she was killed before she could actually do it, right?"

"Maybe. Maybe not." I inspect the bottles. "These bottles have been opened." Neither Journey nor I knew Miss Peters was looking to run DNA for anyone else. And this makes me wonder: What else didn't we know? "She told me she was keeping her plan under wraps until the right time. But if she ran DNA on the wrong person, it could definitely be a motive for them to kill her."

"Maybe you should show all of this stuff to the police," Spam says.

"The equipment doesn't prove anything, though. We need to know if she actually ran any tests."

Since I'm standing next to the lab refrigerator, I open the freezer. It's empty except for a large, white plastic tub with a bold black label that reads: LIVE BACTERIA. I smile. This was my favorite Miss P joke. There's no live bacteria in here. This is where Miss P used to hide her Popsicles and candy bars.

I take out the tub and pry off the top, expecting to find a couple of fruit pops and a Snickers bar. What's there instead is a plastic box about the size of an iPhone. Inside are four small vials. I inspect the box and the labels on the side of each vial. It's a kind of code. I'm in the process of deciding what to do with this discovery when there's a light tap on the door. The knob turns, but it's locked.

"Ladies, I need you to come rejoin the class." It's Principal Roberts.

I glance at Spam, my expression full of questions. She gives me a thumbs-up and shuts down the computer.

"Erin?"

I make a snap decision and shove the box into the front pocket of my hoodie. "Okay, we're coming." With Spam behind me, I open the door. Principal Roberts is all smiles. He steps aside, allowing Spam and I to move past him into the classroom. "Is everything squared away?" he asks.

I pat my strap.

"That's what I like to hear." He mocks a golf swing to motion us through the door and into the classroom.

I'm stunned to see Sydney and a couple of uniformed officers standing by. Spam's face fills with fear as she slips out ahead of me.

"The lab is all yours, Detective. Please let us know if you need anything else," Principal Roberts says.

"I'll do that," Sydney says, snapping on a pair of rubber gloves. She gives me a wink as she files past me into the lab.

The cold lump of the frozen box in my pocket is nothing compared with one that's twice its size in the pit of my stomach. Should I hand this box over to Sydney? If it's what I think it is, it shouldn't fall into the wrong hands. I'm afraid if I give it to her it will wind up in a file box on a storage-room shelf, and fourteen years from now no one will have even looked at it, let alone figured out what it was.

I glance at Spam. She doesn't know I took anything. But if she did, she would expect me to turn it over. I could probably even get out of trouble with a little explaining, but something in my gut holds me back.

In every one of Victor's cases, outlined in his books, he described a point where there was obviously the right thing to do and for some reason his gut told him not to do it. And in every case, his gut proved him right. This DNA might not have anything to do with what happened. But for some reason I don't want to give up this evidence. Not yet. So I'm going to hang in there with my gut, too.

After class, I wait in the hallway for Spam. She joins me and we start walking toward the parking lot. "I hope you're not getting in over your head with this investigation," she says.

"I'm not." I hesitate at the door to the nurse's office. "But if we don't check this stuff out, no one will."

Spam frowns. "Why are you going to the nurse?"

"I need an ice pack." When she tilts her head to one side, I flash just the corner of the box in my pocket.

She gasps. "You took that from the lab? Erin, you can't do that."

"We need to know what it is. Don't freak out. We'll go over everything tonight."

I slip into the nurse's office, feign a sprained wrist, and pick up an ice pack, which I wrap around the box in my pocket. I hurry to the parking lot, hoping to catch a glimpse of Journey.

"Need a lift?" The voice comes from behind me.

Ugh, Principal Roberts.

I pause, mouth open, not really knowing what to say. "I-I . . ."

He smiles. "I'm on my way to your house anyway. Your uncle and I are going to relive our old high school glories by shooting hoops in your driveway." He raises a couple of gym bags bulging with balls and shoes.

How is it even possible for cool, insightful Victor and clueless, dorky Principal Roberts to exist in the same universe, let alone be friends?

I blink. "But we don't even have a basketball hoop."

"You do now." He flashes his phone at me for confirmation. There's a photo of our driveway with a shiny new basketball hoop hanging above the garage door. The text reads: IT'S ON. "I'll let him know I'm bringing you home." He dials the phone but keeps talking to me. "Damn shame about your scooter. That was a classic. Oh, hey, Vic. I'm on my way and I'm giving your niece a ride home, too. Okay. See you soon, buddy."

I follow Mr. Roberts to his car, which is parked right by the office. I hope no one sees me leaving school with the principal. Talk about sketchy.

▾ ▾ ▾

Victor's out in the driveway as we pull in, gesturing proudly to his new installation. He's wearing a faded T-shirt and an ugly pair of sweats. I really can't bear to see my idol reduced to this level of mortal humiliation, so I leave them to do their thing while I head upstairs into the house.

First order of business is to find a place to stash Miss Peters's samples. Hiding things in plain sight was easier before Victor showed up. I could always just tell Rachel it's one of my experiments and she wouldn't ask any more questions, but I can't take the chance that Victor won't recognize DNA samples.

I rummage through the frozen food. Popsicles? No, Rachel eats those sometimes. Buffalo wings, potpies, those get eaten pretty regularly, too. Hmmmm . . . I dig out a tattered bag of frozen peas from the very back. Neither Rachel nor I like peas. We never eat them. But Rachel's idea of the perfect ice pack is a bag of frozen peas, so there's always at least one in the freezer.

I lay the bag on the counter with the seam side up. Lifting the seam, I carefully slit open the bag a few inches along the underside. I dump out some of the peas and slip the small box into the bag, then fold the flap of the seam back to hide the slit and stash the bag in the very back of the refrigerator.

I step back and give the freezer a discerning look. As long as Victor doesn't love peas, Miss Peters's samples should be safe.

# 23

Tracking Internet activity is one of the easiest forms of forensic surveillance. Every mouse click and key press can be traced by a computer specialist.

—VICTOR FLEMMING

Rachel is already at work and Lysa and Spam are allowed to come over anytime, but getting the forbidden Journey past Victor could be a problem.

I finish my homework around five-thirty and head downstairs. Victor and Principal Roberts are collapsed around the kitchen table guzzling neon sports drinks.

Sweat streams down Victor's neck and his T-shirt clings to his torso in damp patches. "Man, I'm at the gym four days a week, but you killed it out there," he gasps. "Who do you play with to stay in that kind of shape?"

Mr. Roberts is damp, too, but he appears less exhausted than Victor. He blots his forehead with a small towel. "It's high school, those guys can play for days," he says. "Seriously, our team went all-state last year. I try to hang out with them once or twice a week." He grins as I enter. "Hey, there's the little lady. Grab a seat."

I try not to think about the fact that my high school principal is in our house and just focus on how long I've known him . . . basically, since I started kindergarten. He called me "little lady" back then, too.

I slip into my chair and curl my foot up under me. "Should I even ask who won?"

"No," Victor says. He slips off his shoes and pretends like he's going to toss one at Principal Roberts. "This guy here totally humiliated me. It was like being time-warped back to high school."

"Hey, wasn't me dishing out the humiliation back then. It was Chuckles. And, if you recall, he smoked both of us."

Victor snorts. "I saw him yesterday. He's the same pompous bag of crap he always was." Victor glances at me. "Sorry, you didn't hear that."

I shrug. "No worries." He must mean Chief Culson, whose real name happens to be Charles.

Victor stuffs the basketball shoes into the gym bag and nudges it toward Roberts with his toe. "Thanks for the loan of the shoes, that was fun."

Principal Roberts nudges the bag back to Victor. "Keep them here, at least until you leave. Maybe we'll have the chance to do it again. They're my old pair anyway."

"If you insist. I'm entitled to a rematch." Victor picks up the bag and takes a few steps to the hallway outside the kitchen. He opens the closet door, which is built into the space under the stairs, and stashes the gym bag inside. At first it seems weird that he would make himself so at home. Then I remember that he and Rachel grew up in this house.

I glance at the clock. It's a quarter to six, and the girls will be here soon. I send Journey a text asking him to hold off. First I need to figure out what Victor has planned.

"So you know Rachel won't be home for dinner tonight, right?"

Victor nods. "She called a little while ago. I'm going to run through the shower and then Carl's taking me out on the town."

Mr. Roberts grins. "I promised to show him the Iron Rain nightlife."

"That'll take fifteen minutes," I joke. It gets a laugh out of both of them. I hope they don't notice how relieved I am that I'll have the house to myself for a couple of hours.

Victor plucks a twenty-dollar bill out of his wallet. "Rachel told me to buy you a pizza. Will this cover it?"

"Yep." Normally, I'd mention that Spam and Lysa are coming over, but with our principal sitting right here, I pass. He already knows more than enough about us.

Instead, I stuff the bill into my pocket. "Have fun, you guys." I'm smiling as I head back to my room to send Journey another text.

About thirty minutes later, Victor and Principal Roberts are gone, and the pizzas and Lysa and Spam have arrived. I lead them upstairs to my bedroom.

"Where's Journey?" Spam asks. "Did he bail?"

"No. He's on his way." An awkward silence develops between the three of us as we just stand there in my bedroom. Finally, I clasp my hands together and take a deep breath. "Okay, I'm going to show you something and I don't want you to freak out."

Spam slides her tongue over her teeth and exchanges a heavy eyebrow look with Lysa. I'm getting a little sick of all the meaningful looks going on around here.

"It's nothing bad. In fact, it's actually really cool. It's just something I haven't told you about yet." I open the door to my closet and perform the ritual of moving in the desk chair, standing up on it, and pulling down the stairs. I don't tell them, but I've left the balcony doors unlocked for Journey.

"You want us to see your attic?" Lysa asks.

Bringing the pizzas, paper plates, and napkins with me, I head up the ladder. "Yes. C'mon."

First Spam and then Lysa tromp up the ladder behind me. Balancing the pizzas over my head, I slide through the narrow opening at the top and switch on the light. I motion them past the decoy pile of junk and into the open area. I'm slightly breathless at what they'll think of my makeshift lounge/lab.

Their faces are a mix of confusion and awe.

"Where did all this stuff come from?" Spam asks.

"It's my mom's. Take a seat." I gesture to the stylish red leather sofa.

Lysa thumps down on the sofa and bounces a little, trying it out. But Spam slowly stalks around the space, taking everything in.

"How did it get up here?" Spam wonders.

"Rachel must've put it up here. I found it when I needed a place to stash the box. Remember how weird it was that I didn't have anything of hers? Well, now I do. It's all up here. And not just her furniture."

"How do you know all this stuff belonged to your mom?" Spam is cautious and skeptical. "It could be Rachel's, right?"

"I found pictures. Whole photo albums." I pull a binder from a box. "Wait 'til you see this." I hold the album out to Spam. Instead of taking it, she crosses her arms over her chest.

I move in close so she can't avoid looking at it. On the front is a photo of a pastel-colored beach cottage. "My mom inherited this cottage from her parents . . . my grandparents. Look what she wrote: 'It is important to feel tethered to somewhere.' " I flip through the pages and stop on a downward picture of her bare feet on wet sand, each toe painted a different color. "And here she wrote: 'Ready to put down roots.' It's so cute, her toes all painted . . ."

Spam presses her lips together and glances at Lysa. "Erin . . ."

"Wait. Wait. This is the best one," I say as I flip to a photograph of just my mother's flat belly. In pen, she had drawn an arrow pointing to a spot below her belly button. In her spidery handwriting she scribbled: "Eric? Or Erin?" "My name could have been Eric. How weird is that?"

Lysa turns away. "Erin." Her voice is gentle. "All of this stuff is your past, and it worries me that you're living so deeply in it."

"This is not my past. Don't you see? It's my beginning." I snap the album closed. "I was loved and wanted. My mom had a dream for the two of us to be a family, and someone took that dream away."

"You're still loved and wanted," Lysa says.

Spam looks down. "What's that?" She has noticed the edge of a chalk design on the floor, most of it covered by a rug.

I start to say it's nothing. But Spam bends down and peels back the rug, revealing an outline of a body on the floor. An outline that exactly matches the crime-scene photos I found in the evidence box.

"Oh my God, you drew that?" whispers Lysa, covering her mouth with her hand.

Spam steps back, her face a mask of shock. "I'm guessing you didn't find this layout in a photo album."

# 24

Evidence, at its most basic level, is simply visible proof that something happened.

—VICTOR FLEMMING

Spam looks at me like I'm the prized panda who just devoured her newborn cub. Lysa seems less judgy, but her eyes are huge and sad. A few tears stain her cheeks.

"Erin, you realize this isn't normal, right?" Lysa says. "You've re-created the scene of your mother's murder."

"But—" I try to interject.

Lysa holds up her hand, quieting me. "Your feelings about your mom were always in there. They had to be. And I can imagine the things in that box set you off on a river of rage and sadness. But instead of dealing with those emotions, you're standing here saying, hey, check out this cool secret life I've created. . . ." She trails off, gesturing helplessly in every direction.

I get it, they're afraid for me . . . or maybe *of* me. But they still don't see the *real* me.

"You have the privilege of knowing who your parents are. Yes, your mom walked out on you, Spam. But if you passed her on the street tomorrow you would still know who she is. I grew up knowing *nothing*. Every photo and stick of furniture that you see up here is a brand-new link to my past. I'm learning what my mother thought about things, that her favorite color was red, that she wanted to be a mom more than anything." I touch the chalk outline lightly. "Even this comforts me."

A voice comes from behind me. "It comforts you because it makes her real."

I turn around. Journey is standing just inside the attic, next to the pile of junk. His voice unleashes a slight flutter of anticipation in my chest.

He ducks to clear a low beam and moves toward us. "Otherwise, your mother would just be another one of those things we are taught to believe in—like Santa Claus, the Easter Bunny . . . God." He shrugs. "My dad."

There's a long moment when no one speaks.

Spam unfreezes first. "Seriously? *He* knew about your secret attic-slash-reenacted-crime-scene before we did?" I add hurt to the array of looks on her face.

"This is freaking me out," Lysa whispers.

Spam goes to sit on the sofa next to her. Journey and I take seats on the floor.

"Erin, I'm concerned about your mental health," Lysa says.

"My mental health is fine," I insist. "It's my physical health you should be worried about."

Spam and Lysa exchange an ominous look.

I tick the points off on my fingers. "Fact: The person who killed my mother is definitely still out there. Fact: He *killed* Miss Peters. Fact: I need your help so I'm not next."

"The second one is not a fact yet." Spam sits forward. "Before we go any further I want to see every piece of evidence you have. No holding anything back."

"Agreed." They wait quietly while I go to the cupboard,

remove the lock, and bring out my mother's murder box, along with a small paper bag. I set everything on the floor in front of me while I slip into my gloves. Once I'm ready, I level a probing look at each of them before lifting the lid. I'm not sure if it's the knowledge we've acquired or the danger we're in, but we're not the same as we were. We're different.

The tie Journey found in his van is on top. I pull it out.

Journey takes it and stretches it between his hands. "I found this on the floor of my van *after* Miss P was killed," Journey says.

Next I hold up the plastic sleeve containing my mother's shirt. "My mother's shirt has been in this box for fourteen years. It's missing a tie exactly like that one."

Lysa curls into a ball, hugging her knees. "Wow."

Spam snaps her fingers and points at me. "Motive? Why would someone do that? Why now? Why leave behind a trophy he kept for fourteen years?"

I gently pack the shirt and the tie back in the box. Not sure I have an answer for her.

"Come on," Spam says. "You always say motive first."

"He didn't mean to leave it. He screwed up," Journey says.

"But why now?" Spam says.

No one says anything for a long moment.

"I agree with Journey. I think it was an accident. A fluke."

"Too many flukes and we have a problem." Spam shakes her head. "Is there anything that actually makes a case?"

I put the lid back on the box and dump out the contents of the paper bag.

"Not sure yet. I found fingerprints on the van that the police missed. According to Victor, they're from two different people, but I haven't had a chance to run them yet. I'm pretty sure the box I took from the lab freezer will turn out to be DNA samples. But I have no clue how to verify that or how to read them."

"What do the police have?" Spam asks. "Anyone know?"

"They have a glass nail file with my name on it, which they say is the murder weapon." I hate admitting this, because it's another thing in a long list that I can't explain.

"What?" Spam looks wary.

"The nail file from my party was the murder weapon?" Lysa says.

"Unfortunately, yes." I add a sigh. "I don't know what it means, but I'm pretty sure it's the reason Rachel keeps looking at me like I'm a ticking time bomb."

"Well, that proves for sure it couldn't have been me." Journey inspects his fingernails. "Anyone who's seen my nails knows I have no use for a nail file. That's what teeth are for."

I flash him a quick smile. "Besides, where would you get my nail file unless I gave it to you?"

"Where would anyone get your nail file unless you gave it to them?" Spam wonders.

"Good question," I say.

Lysa raises her hand. "Oh. I overheard there was a partial footprint in blood at Miss Peters's house, but Journey's shoes came back clean. I was in the hall when my father took that call from the detective."

Journey looks relieved. "Sweet. Maybe I'll get my Nikes back."

"Is that all?" Spam looks at me.

"There's the size-eleven Nike footprint I found in my bedroom."

Spam and Lysa silently shift their gaze to Journey's feet. He says, offended, "Yes, I wear a size eleven and I have a pair of Nikes, but did you not just hear Lysa? The police have had those shoes since the first night. It couldn't have been me."

Spam offers Journey a small wink. "Way to rock an alibi."

Journey smiles. "I try."

"Good point," I say. "Lysa, Spam, you guys have been suspicious of Journey this whole time. Well, Lysa just confirmed that the police have had his shoes since that first night. Can we finally agree that Journey is no longer creepy or a suspect and accept him as part of the team?"

Spam and Lysa exchange a nod. "Yes. Okay," Spam says.

"He's in. No more weird looks," Lysa agrees.

"Thanks," he says. "And I mean that." Then he turns toward me. "No one has been in your bedroom since that night though, right?"

"Not that I know of." I paw through the evidence in the small bag. I isolate a small Ziploc bag and hold it up. "Oh. There is one last thing, a torn scrap of paper I found stuck in the seat-belt clip on Journey's van. There's some writing on it and Journey says it's not his. Chromatography doesn't tell us much but I'm going to run a test on it anyway. And that's it. That's the extent of our evidence."

Now that I say it out loud . . . it's not much. But I know from Victor's books that even the smallest, most unlikely piece of evidence can tell you something.

"Okay. Here's what I've got." Spam pulls some folded sheets of paper out of her back pocket and curls her foot up under her on the sofa. "Miss P's cell phone account was, as I predicted, extremely easy to hack. I've checked out all the calls to and from her cell for the last three months. There was only one number that looked sketchy."

"Whose was it?"

"I can't tell." Spam gives me a shrug. "It's an old landline: 555-8446. I tried calling it but it just rings, no voice mail."

"Wait." I blink a couple of times, training my gaze on the

ceiling. "Why is that number so familiar?" I pretend to dial it on my phone. "It's two numbers off from Rachel's work number."

"Where does she work?" Journey asks.

"The police station. She's the 911 unit supervisor." Spam answers Journey's question because my brain is busy trying to figure out what a number close to Rachel's could mean.

"Are you saying the calls were to someone at the police station?" Journey asks.

"It's possible," Spam says. "They often link business phone numbers in sequence like that."

"But wouldn't there be voice mail?" Lysa asks.

I'm wondering the same thing. My paranoia kicks in. "How many calls were there?" Did Miss Peters discuss my DNA hunt with Rachel? No. If Rachel knew about that, she would have been all over me. Besides, the number isn't Rachel's, it's just close to it.

Spam scans the printout. "The calls went both ways, to Miss Peters and from her. There were one or two last month, but more than ten right before . . ." She trails off with a sigh. A quiet moment follows while we all reflect on what we've lost.

No question, we are truly and irrevocably changed.

When the silence threatens to pin us to the floor, I get to my feet. "Be right back." I lightly skim down the ladder and bound through my bedroom, down the stairs, and into the kitchen. There's a drawer where Rachel keeps all the weird things that don't belong anywhere else, like take-out menus, rubber bands, and her collection of little screwdrivers. Underneath all the junk is an old address book from before she put everything on her cell phone. I bring it back upstairs.

The three of them are still sitting there, silent and sad.

I curl onto the floor and slide up close to Journey. We're not touching, but I can feel the warmth radiating off of him. Just being near him makes me feel better. He gets me. He even said so. I flip through the pages of Rachel's phone book. The usual veil of hair slides across my forehead and into my eyes. Journey rescues it and tucks it behind my ear. The warmth of his fingers as they linger on my neck summons a minor blush. I'm hoping Spam won't notice, but a quick glance up at her face finds a silly smirk plastered there. I'm so busted.

"Okay. I'm looking up Sydney in Rachel's book. Her direct line is 555-8442."

Spam checks the list. "That's not it."

"Who else?" I flip to *C*, looking for Chief Culson's name. I find the name Charles and a notation for a private line. "What about this one: 555-8446?"

Spam sits forward. "That's it. Whose is it?"

I gnaw on my lip, not sure how these things hook up. "According to Rachel's book, it's Chief Culson's *private* line."

"That could explain why I couldn't track it down," Spam says. "Private lines are different from direct lines. They're supposed to be—well, private. Off the books."

"Makes sense for the chief of police, I guess. Right?" I say.

"Maybe Miss Peters called him because she was being threatened," Journey offers.

"But why would she call his private line and not the main line?" Spam wonders.

"Besides, the chief doesn't investigate problems, he's responsible for overseeing the entire unit," Lysa says. "If Miss Peters had a complaint she would talk to an officer or a detective, like Sydney."

"Plus, if she was afraid of someone, the police would have a record of that and they wouldn't be looking at us," Journey says.

Spam shakes her head. "I doubt that they're seriously looking at you."

Lysa picks at a ragged cuticle. "Actually, I heard my parents talking. First it was just Journey they were looking at. But now that the two of you are hanging out, well, people are starting to wonder."

I glance over at Journey, but he just stares straight ahead. "Screw what they think. The only way for Erin and I to stay safe and out of trouble is for us to stick together," he says.

I inch my fingers across the floor until just the tips of mine meet just the tips of his. He slides his hand forward.

"He's right," I agree.

We're not holding hands exactly, but it is a touch of support. Maybe even solidarity.

"Fine. Just don't get so caught up in your lovefest that you miss something." Spam gets to her feet. "Anyway, I need to go. I'm helping my dad tomorrow and it's going to be a long day."

The rest of us stand up, too. "I can't get to the fingerprints until Monday after school, but I will get to the chroma test over the weekend. I'll also research the box from the lab freezer. You need to go through Miss Peters's computer files."

Spam gives me a quick hug. "I'll get to the files over the weekend, too. But the minute we find something concrete, we're taking it to Sydney. Agreed?" Spam says.

"Agreed."

"I want you safe," she says.

Journey slides his arm around my waist. "Don't worry. I've got her back." He squeezes my waist, sending a flush of goose bumps across my body in all directions. I'm kind of speechless. Spam's eyebrows rise and Lysa's mouth falls open.

"Roger that," Spam murmurs, as she shoots a serious side-eye toward Lysa.

There's an awkward silence.

They can't really expect me to talk when my brain is exploding from the whole Journey-just-put-his-arm-around-me thing. Then I realize that this is the first time one of us has brought a sort-of boyfriend into our group and how much it might look to Spam and Lysa like Journey and I are squaring off against them.

"No matter what, we're still a *team,* right?" I say.

Journey drops his hand from my waist and quietly studies his shoes.

"Yeah!" Lysa finally says. "A killer team." She gives a weak arm pump. "Oh. Bad choice of words."

I was trying to bring them together, but my team comment fell flat. There's definitely a feeling of my side with Journey and their side with Spam and Lysa.

Journey clears his throat. "Do I need to slip out through the balcony like I came in?"

Spam and Lysa go all heavy eyebrows to each other again. I know what they're thinking. That he's been hanging out in my bedroom. But they're wrong.

"It's only nine-thirty; Rachel won't be home for a couple of hours yet, and I'm pretty sure Victor's still out." We troop together out of the attic, down the stairs, and out the back through the kitchen. Spam and Lysa wave good-bye and continue on down the driveway. Journey hangs back. He takes my hand, massaging it with both of his.

"We're going to figure this out," he says. "You know that, right?"

I press my forehead into his shoulder. It's solid, like a wall. He lightly circles his arms around me and pulls me close. His fingers play with the tips of my hair. I breathe out a long, pent-up sigh. I want to say something, but my throat is so tight a pea couldn't slip through.

"Okay, yeah. Got it. I'll get back to you in a day or so," a low male voice promises, but it isn't Journey. It's coming from deep in my backyard.

I jump away from Journey and squint into the darkness. There's a cement patio located behind a flower bed toward the back of our garage. Rachel and I never use this area. In the dim light, I can barely make out Victor sitting at an old table out there, talking into his cell phone. He clicks the phone off, rises, and comes toward us, shuffling through the dried leaves.

I panic but don't know what to do. It would be obvious if Journey took off running mere seconds before Victor reaches us. Our backyard isn't that big. There's no way Victor hasn't seen him. Instead we both just stand there with blank, guilty expressions.

Victor stops in front of us, looking from me to Journey and back to me.

"I assume this is Journey," he says.

I avoid making direct eye contact.

Journey thrusts his hand forward. "Nice to meet you, sir."

"Nice to meet you, too." Victor takes his hand and they shake. Victor continues to the bottom of the stairs before pausing. "You coming up?"

Journey and I exchange a look. "I better go," he says. "See you Monday?"

"Yeah. Monday," I say.

Journey turns and lopes off down the driveway. I head up the stairs even though it feels like he's taking a part of me with him.

Once inside the kitchen, Victor takes a seat at the table. I head for the refrigerator and pretend to check out the contents. "There's some leftover pizza, if you're hungry."

"I'm good," Victor says.

I close the door and stand at the table for a few seconds. I don't want to sit down and discuss what Journey was doing here. I fake a yawn. "Well, I think I'm going up to bed."

"So early?" Victor asks. He sounds disappointed.

"Yeah, it's been a pretty long day."

"Okay." He studies me for a long minute. "Good night."

I slowly ascend the stairs until I'm out of his sight, and then I race to my bedroom door. He didn't say anything about Journey and neither did I. The question is, will he tell Rachel?

# ▸ 25 ◂

Life always finds a way.

—MISS PETERS

Saturday is Victor's first weekend home since I've been part of the family, and Rachel has the whole day planned. First, pancakes for breakfast, then a drive through the old neighborhood and lunch at her favorite restaurant.

She invites Sydney to meet us for lunch, which turns out great because the conversation between Victor and Sydney is better than any crime-investigation class ever. Victor goes into great detail about all the amazing equipment he has in his lab at the FBI while Syd grumbles over Chief Culson's reluctance to bring that same technology to our city.

"It's the cost," Victor says. "Setting up a crime lab is expensive."

This supports what Journey said about Miss Peters's idea to share a lab with the school and the police department. But Sydney shakes her head.

"Cost isn't the whole story on him, I'm afraid," Sydney says. "Charles is your basic gumshoe. He's all about old-school detective work and truly believes a well-followed hunch is far more valuable than science." She uses air quotes around the word "science."

Wow. That's surprising. What police officer wouldn't want hard, cold science to support his cases? But I don't ask the question out loud.

"Chuck only says that because he got stuck here in a Podunk police unit." Victor sits back and sips his coffee. He waves his cup at Rachel for emphasis. "You remember, back in the day, he and I were going to go to the FBI together."

There's a clunk under the table.

"Ow." Victor casts a wary look at Rachel.

"Sorry," she mutters. But I know the exact meaning of her pinched expression and the quick side-eye motion she makes in my direction.

She doesn't want Victor talking about all this in front of me.

The adults veer off into talking about less exciting memories of the past. To make them more comfortable, I slip my headphones on and listen to some music until lunch is over.

More sightseeing follows lunch, this time a drive to the beach. On the way we pass the turnoff to the old cannery where Journey lives. Victor mentions the legends of the old place and gets another side-eye from Rachel. Poor guy. Everything he wants to talk about is on Rachel's off-limits list.

We end the day with dinner at home. Rachel's cooking another family favorite, enchiladas with green sauce, and I'm making a salad. She urges me to invite Spam and Lysa to join us, but I tell her they already have plans. I didn't actually check with them, though. It's not that I don't want to see my best friends, it's that I'm missing Journey. I want the freedom to think about him with no distractions.

I used to only think about Journey when I was at school. My weekends were pretty much Journey-free. But suddenly, having to go two whole days without seeing him is making me itchy. I don't know why, but while I'm slicing vegetables for the salad I'm remembering how he chews his fingernails. As I set the table, I'm picturing him slam-dunking his trash. Journey never just throws something away; it's always a slam dunk. I don't even want to get started thinking about his eyes, or how popular he is.

It's only Saturday. How will I survive Sunday?

▼ ▼ ▼

Sunday morning starts early with a whole new household sound track—the *thup, thup, whang* of a basketball warm-up in our driveway. But it's the smell of bacon that ultimately draws me downstairs. This also brings Victor in from his morning workout.

Maybe it's my imagination, but Rachel seems different since Victor's arrival. She's actually humming while she cooks, and I can't remember Rachel ever humming while doing anything. As I set the table, Victor keeps the conversation flowing with jokes and stories about their past. I bask in his uplifting energy. He's the breath of fresh air this family has needed.

When we're done eating, Rachel packs up for the office. She says she's hoping she won't have to work a double shift. I take over kitchen cleanup and Victor pitches in to help. Just as we finish, Spam shows up at the back door.

"I'm going on a delivery for my dad and I thought you'd like to ride with me," she says.

I shrug. I didn't have any other plans for today. "Okay."

Once we're in her car and she's backing out of the driveway, her plan unfolds a little further. "I've been thinking about your potential dads."

"And?" I approach this conversation with caution.

"I think we should check them out," she says.

"Check them out how?"

"Go by their houses. Snoop. Spy. Get a look at them."

"I see where this is going. You just want to *see* them, to see if you can match up some puzzle piece of their face with mine."

"No," she says. "Not exactly. I thought maybe we could crack their phone records, too."

I give her an exaggerated side-eye. "Let's do your dad's delivery first and then we'll see."

Spam's delivery happens to be to an office building in the older, historic part of town, which is always under construction these days. We've been silent for most of the drive but I know this doesn't mean she's given up on wanting to check out my P-dads. P for potential. I've decided that's what I'm going to call them in my head, although there's not much potential left now that Miss P is gone.

Spam and Lysa are my best friends but I'm not sure I want them involved with my P-dad investigation. Is that weird? It's like this is too personal or something. The only one I ever really trusted with all of this was Miss P. Hey, Miss P . . . for potential. Or not, as it happens to be now.

I picture her, circling the lab, hands raised over her head to draw our attention. "Remember this, people," she would say. "Life always finds a way."

One of the P-dads could be part of my life. I can't give up finding out for sure just because she's gone. She definitely wouldn't want that. But I have to set those questions aside. For now, my first priority is to figure out who killed her.

"Crap!" Spam slams her hand on the steering wheel.

"What?"

"The street's blocked. We can't get through."

I pull myself out of my daydreams and see what she's saying. There are cones and barricades keeping both people and traffic away from a large, crumbling old hotel on the corner and all the buildings on the street beyond it.

"Looks like they're tearing down the hotel."

"Well, goody for them," Spam says. "But I have to get to the other end of this block and this is the only access."

I stiffen as she noses her car all the way up to the barricade. "Spam, you can't—"

"Relax. I just want to see if there's someone around that I can ask."

"Hey! Back it up." A distorted male voice barks instructions through an amplified speaker. Suddenly, Chief Culson appears at the front of Spam's car, waving one arm and talking into a bullhorn.

Spam rolls down her window. "Hi. Excuse me," she says. "But we have office equipment to deliver to the green building down the block. How can we get there?"

Chief Culson walks up to the window. "Sorry. There's no access today. The mayor just finished a little ceremony and as soon as we get him out of here, we're under orders to clear the whole block so they can bring it down." He peers in the window and spots me. "Hey, Erin. I didn't know that was you."

"Hi, Chief." I give him a small wave.

"Is there any way?" Spam pleads. "Erin and I just need forty-five minutes to deliver this stuff and set it up. It's for my dad's store." She glances in the backseat. "Actually, I could probably even do it in twenty minutes."

The chief gnaws on the corner of his lip, contemplating her request. He checks his watch. "I can give you twenty minutes. But you have to park your car behind that Dumpster and walk it in. Can you do that?"

"Yes." Spam jumps at the offer. "Absolutely. We'll be in and out. You won't even know we were here."

Spam backs her car up and parks behind the Dumpster, where the chief directed her to park. Then she loads a stack of boxes containing computer components into my outstretched arms. "That's enough," I say, once the stack reaches my chin. "I have to be able to see."

"I'll guide you." Spam tucks a couple of boxes under her arm and slings her tool bag over her shoulder. Her idea of *guiding* is for me to listen to her tapping footsteps in front of me and try to follow them.

With my chin clamped down on the stack of boxes to keep them stable, my field of vision is limited. I can see up and slightly right or left. But that's it. The only way to see directly in front of me is to stop and turn sideways. Glancing to the side, I see the chief in front of the barricade, talking into a walkie-talkie.

"Thanks, Chief," Spam calls out.

He nods and points, instructing us to take a different—more secluded—route.

Spam happily follows his directions. "He's only letting us in because of you."

"That's not true," I say.

"It is," she insists. "His whole attitude changed when he saw you were in the car with me."

"Whatever." I'm not going to argue with her about it.

The route the chief pointed us to is a man-made walkway that skirts along the back of the hotel. It's essentially a tunnel constructed of plywood and scaffolding. One side is an open, steel grid and the other side is lined with solid sheets of protective plywood. The floor is made of wobbly strips of wood.

The tunnel is easily as long as a city block and we've barely traversed half of it when I hear a loud "all clear" shout in the distance.

Immediately, there's an ear-shredding buildup of vibrations and mechanical noise.

"What's going on up there?" I shout to Spam. "Is everything okay?"

It's so loud I no longer hear her heels tapping ahead of me. I strain to peer over and around the boxes. She's walking . . . and texting.

"Spam. Pay attention. What's going on up there?"

"What?" She continues staring at her phone.

I turn sideways and rest my armload of boxes against the steel railing to get a better view of what's happening ahead of us.

Just then, the protective wall about ten feet in front of Spam splinters without warning as the blade of a giant earthmover breaks through the barrier and grinds toward us.

"Spam!" I ditch the computer stuff and grab for her at the same moment she's grabbing for me.

We try to squeeze through the steel grid but the openings are too narrow.

We grab the grid and shake hard. It's too sturdy.

We have no choice but to turn and run.

It seems like we should be able to outrun an earthmover, but the freaking thing literally stays just a few feet behind us. As it chews through the tunnel we have to duck the chunks of wood and debris it flings at us. Even the wobbly floor rips apart under our feet.

The only way to continue moving forward is to pull each other along.

"Help! Stop!"

We scream, but no one's going to hear us. I can't even hear

us over the shrill whine of ripping wood and mechanical feeding.

I choke and cough on dust that collects in my throat.

I can't scream and I can barely run.

This is more surreal than any bad dream I've ever had. But Spam's nails biting into my skin and the absolute certainty that we're about to die keeps me fully aware that this is no dream.

The earthmover continues to advance, literally chasing us down the narrow chute by nipping away at the wood under our feet. Our only chance to escape is to outrun him and we still have half a block to go.

As my legs melt into rubber and my lungs refuse to gulp another speck of dust, Chief Culson suddenly appears on the path in front of us.

"Stop! STOP!" he shrieks into the bullhorn.

At first I think he's telling us to stop and I'm about to put my head down and butt him out of our way. But instead he barges between us and heads straight for the earthmover. In a frantic burst he maneuvers around the blade and bangs the bullhorn against the giant slice of metal as hard as he can. With each slam of metal against metal, the bullhorn erupts with a very loud, amplified metallic *whang*!

Seconds seem like hours, but within a few of them the earthmover sputters and the engine stops.

The driver of the earthmover stands up and looks over the top of the blade. "Holy— Chief! I thought you said it was all clear?"

Chief Culson points an angry finger at the driver. "You, shut up! Just shut up." Then he strides over to us. "Erin. Are you okay?"

"That was crazy messed up. But we're okay," Spam says even though she's gasping to catch her breath.

I give her a look. Seriously?

I'm bent over, hands on my thighs, begging for a breath that won't rip my lungs apart. And I'm not so sure. I'm not hurt. But I'm not okay, either. What the hell just happened? I shift my gaze between the earthmover driver and the chief, and then look over at Spam. I have *no clue* what any of them are thinking.

I also don't know how to explain what just happened or who's to blame, but I'm pretty sure someone just tried to kill me . . . again.

# 26

Being extremely thorough—especially if you think it will prove nothing—is the number-one rule to remember when processing a crime scene.

—VICTOR FLEMMING

While Spam and I pull ourselves together, the earthmover driver scrambles over the piles of debris and gathers up Spam's tool bag and all the scattered computer equipment. He apologizes profusely when he brings the stuff back to us.

He says he couldn't see us. We were in his blind spot. *Blah, blah, blah.*

My scrutiny is on the chief. The way he's standing off to the side, with his back turned to us, talking on the phone. He definitely looks upset. But there's a part of me that wonders, is he upset that he screwed up and almost got us killed, or is there something more?

The chief hangs up his phone and slips it into his pocket before he turns to face us. His shoulders sag as he shuffles over. "Erin. Samantha. I can't tell you how sorry I am. Thank God you're okay."

"We are. We're fine," Spam agrees. She looks over the boxes of computer gear, which also managed to survive. "Even the computers made it."

He looks to me for my reaction.

I nod. That's the best I can do. It may just be nerves but something about this feels hinky.

"I called Rachel," he continues. "She's on her way."

"What?! No. You can't do that." I grab Spam's arm. "We have to go."

The chief looks confused. "What about Rachel?"

"I'll take care of it," I snap.

Once we're in Spam's car, I get Rachel on the phone. It takes a lot of fast convincing for her to turn around and go back to work, but the last thing I need is for her to actually see what Spam and I went through and what could have happened. She's so overprotective and skittish about me that if she saw this mess I'd never be allowed out of the house again. Both of us will be a lot better off with her not knowing.

But as Spam pulls her car out from behind the Dumpster, I snap a photo of the precariously chewed-up tunnel and vicious-looking earthmover with my phone anyway. I want to show it to Journey and see what he thinks.

The ride home is pretty quiet. Both Spam and I are mired in our thoughts. She pulls into my driveway and we exchange a hug before I get out of the car.

"So all that back there was just some random, bizarre thing that happened, right?" she asks. I scan her face to discern if she wants truth or comfort. The folds on her forehead and slight frown to her mouth tell me she wants comfort.

"Oh yeah. Getting attacked by earthmoving equipment is about as random as you can get." I add a chuckle to make it convincing.

"Good." She exhales in relief. "That's what I thought, too. See you tomorrow."

"Yeah." I get out of the car and head into the house. Rachel said she won't be home until dinnertime, which means I still have a couple of hours to spend up in the attic. I can run the chroma test on the scrap of paper I found in Journey's van. It probably won't reveal any crucial information. But being thorough is the number-one rule of processing a crime scene—just ask Victor.

Even though I'm certain I'll be done and out of the attic long before Rachel gets home, I prep my room by shoving the binder under my door just in case. It's a habit. With my laptop under my arm and my bag slung over my shoulder, I sneak up to my attic. The room is untouched from the way we left it on Friday night, so the rug is still pulled back, revealing my chalk outline. I know Spam and Lysa think it's creepy, but Journey nailed it.

These details are what make my mother real.

I stare at the outline for a long minute before gently covering it with the rug.

I set my stuff on the old wooden desk and open the padlock on the cabinet. Whenever I'm up here, I bring out the box and keep it near me. I just like the way it feels, having it close by.

I squint and flatten the scrap of paper I pulled from the seat-belt clasp in Journey's van to see if I recognize the handwriting. But there's not enough handwriting to tell. All I know is I need pens with blue ink. I check the ones I brought from Miss Peters's desk in the biology lab. Three are black ink and the fourth one kind of looks like the special pen Chief Culson gave me.

I paw through my purse until my fingers wrap around the chief's special pen. Now I inspect it more closely. The outside is black with a brass band and a brass lever and clip. I pull off the cap and test it. It's a fountain pen and the ink is blue. There's a decorative CS crest stamped into the top of the clip.

I compare it with Miss P's pen. They are identical, except instead of being black, the outside of hers is a green marble color. Both of them have blue ink, though.

I decide to test them both.

The FBI has sophisticated machines that do all the work breaking down ink. But instructions for do-it-yourself versions are all over the Internet. I've done it several times in our lab at school, and even demonstrated it live once for a science fair project.

The scientific part is that ink—or lipstick, or any other product with color—isn't just one color; it's made up of different dyes and compounds all mixed together. Each pen company has their own unique recipe. Who knew, right? Blue ink might look the same on the page, but a chroma test breaks the ingredients down so that they show up as bands of different colors. These bands of color are so specific they're like a serial number or fingerprint of the exact brand of ink. The colors can be pretty wild, too, like violet and rust.

In about twenty minutes, I'll know if any of these pens match the note.

The supplies for a chromatography test can be found in almost anyone's home. The important items are pure acetone (basically nail polish remover) and a coffee filter cut into strips about the same length and width as the scrap of paper.

I work quickly to prepare the strips. I label the back of each one with the type of pen and place a dot of ink exactly one-half inch from the bottom edge. I prepare the fourth strip by lifting some ink off of the note with a drop of acetone on a Q-tip and then transferring it to the bottom edge of a fresh filter strip.

When all four strips are lined up in a row, the location of the ink on the bottom is identical. When the strips are ready,

I attach them to paper clips and thread them onto a chopstick, which will hold all four strips in a straight row. I lower the whole row of strips into a measuring cup containing a small amount of the acetone. The chopstick rests across the top of the cup, allowing the strips to hang side by side—without touching each other—while only the ends soak in the liquid.

I kick my feet up on the desk and set the timer on my phone for twenty minutes, an amount of time which I plan to spend doing some deep wondering about what Journey is doing right now.

Almost immediately my phone vibrates. I drop it into my lap like a hot rock.

Holy crap! It's a Snapchat friend request from B-Baller386.

My heart vaults straight out of my chest. It has to be Journey. Right?

I quickly accept.

A moment later, a stunning photo of the lighthouse at Cape Disappointment appears on my phone. The caption reads: YOU = THE OPPOSITE OF DISAPPOINTMENT.

I leap up and pogo dance around the attic, waving my arms like a crazy person before racing back to my phone to read his message again . . . and again.

But, sigh, Snapchat. It's already gone.

I want to send him a message back.

My hair's a mess. No makeup. I look around the attic. There must be something I can photograph to remind him of us. Ah. I snap a photo of the spot on the rug where we were sitting Friday night.

Then add a caption: WE NEED TO STICK TOGETHER.

I pause before hitting send and read it back. Stick together? What am I thinking? Could I be more boring? This is like saying you gave me a cookie, let me reply by giving you oatmeal.

I change my response to read: THANKS, YOU TOO. My finger hovers over send. There's nothing wrong with that. I'm saying thank you for the compliment and you aren't a disappointment, either. No, wait. That's not what I want to say. I change it again: YOU'RE WELCOME.

I read it back. You're welcome—over the photo of a dark spot of worn rug. Are you kidding me? Who am I, his grandma?

Agggh. I tap my head with frustrated fists, actually accidentally snapping a photo of the tips of my hair sticking up from my messy clip. Arrgh!

What's wrong with me? Why is this so hard?

The timer goes off, signaling that the test is complete. I lift the chopstick off the measuring cup, carefully slide the strips off, and lay them on a paper towel to dry. I make sure that the strips don't touch each other, but I don't take the time to inspect them. I'm still panicking over creating the perfect response to Journey.

I'm trying to think of something witty to say and a new photo to take when I remember how the last time we were together he was playing with the tips of my hair. That memory sends some dreamy goodness through me and gives me a strange confidence. Over the weirdly angled photo of my hair I type: "My hair misses you." Yep. I'm going with that. I'm just going to hit send and not look back.

But then I do look back. My hair misses you? Really? How many layers of lame is that? Thinking . . . thinking . . . thinking . . . I glance over at my ink tests and realize—holy crap—I've got a match.

I'm so shocked that I hit send and my weird photo and hair-missing-you caption is off to Journey. And, while I'm mildly freaked out about that, I'm kind of amazed that I have one pen—no wait—*two* pens in my possession that match the ink on that scrap of paper. A weird, creepy realization comes over me. I turn the strips over.

Chief Culson's two pens are the winners. They both match the ink on the note.

Miss P would be so proud. Pulling clues together is hard work. I try to think through what this means. It means Miss P could have written the note. But it also means Chief Culson could have written it, too. And, if I'm being completely honest, and thinking like Victor, there are a bunch of other people who could have written it. How many of these pens has the chief handed out? Who has he been giving them to? Is it possible one of them is a killer?

"Erin?"

*Holy crap.* Rachel. Outside my bedroom door.

And I'm in the attic.

# 27

Forensic psychologists are scary good profilers. They can tell if a person is lying by reading their body language like a newspaper.

—VICTOR FLEMMING

I cram my laptop into my bag and skim down the stairs. My feet barely touch the rungs. I step out of the closet as Rachel manages to force my bedroom door open a few inches.

"What's wrong with your door?" she asks, struggling.

"Hold on. There's a binder on the floor." I have to shut the door all the way before I can pull the binder out. Rachel opens the door, steps in, and looks around.

"You should be careful about leaving your binders on the floor like that," she says. "It could be dangerous."

"Good point." My heart's pounding and I suddenly don't know what to do with my hands. But on the outside I try to appear normal. "So, what's up?" I ask.

"Nothing," she says, her gaze flitting around the room. "I'm just letting you know I'm home early."

"Great," I say, trying to sound casual.

"Okay." She shrugs, looking around my room again.

"I'm going to take a shower." I twist the ends of my hair nervously.

"Okay." She grips the edge of the door and hesitates as if she has something else she wants to say.

I brace myself, lecture or an interrogation. It could be either, especially with all the craziness that's been going on.

"See you at dinner," she says finally.

"Yum." It's my stupidest response so far, but I can't think of anything else. I'm struggling to rein in my tension.

Once she leaves I collapse on the bed. Rachel almost caught me in the attic. That's huge. And it's certainly a much bigger deal than sending a lame message to Journey. I need to get a grip.

▾ ▾ ▾

After the longest weekend in history, Monday finally arrives. Thanks to Rachel's friendship with Detective Sydney, finding out what the fingerprints reveal about Journey's van won't be that hard. But first I have to get through the day. At least I'm here at school where I can see Journey.

English and algebra are boring as usual. I only survive because I've mastered the fine art of sleeping with my eyes open. At the nutrition break, I head for the café express line because I won't survive without a bagel. I pass Spam coming out of line as I'm going in. "I got the last sesame," she says, raising her hand for a high five. I mouth *brat* but slap her hand anyway. When I do, she palms a wad of folded paper from her hand into mine.

I settle for cinnamon raisin and grab an empty table so I can concentrate on what Spam slipped to me. The wad of paper turns out to be three pages. I unfold them and smooth them out on the table. The first page is a list summarizing the files she copied from the computer in Miss Peters's lab. I scan down the list of headings: homework (8 files), class research

(3 files), quizzes (2 files), labs (4 files), answers (8 files, Spam drew a happy face next to that entry). The last item is labeled PROJECT (2 files). Spam has drawn a star next to this folder and added a note to see page two.

I shift page one to the back of the stack and scan page two. The top reads, TEST RESULTS. It's a list. A sequence, actually. Numbers across the top of the page are labeled MARKERS. Below each marker are coded entries. Each entry contains a string of numbers. The numbers are all different, a jumble with no distinct pattern, a list that wouldn't mean anything to anybody . . . unless you know what DNA test results look like.

My nerve endings rev up and the *swish-thod, swish-thod* of my pulse is loud in my ears. I count the markers. Thirteen.

The exact number most commonly used to identify and compare human DNA.

I was right; Miss Peters had already run at least one DNA test using four samples. But will I be able to figure out whose DNA she tested?

The results page contains four entries labeled with letters: JM, EB, CC, ME. Initials, maybe? JM could be Journey Michaels, and EB could be me—Erin Blake. Miss Peters and I did play around with those sponge lollipop swab things that they use for getting DNA from your mouth, but I want to believe that if she had actually run my DNA, she would've told me.

There's a light tug on the back of my hair. I whirl around. Journey, along with a couple of his basketball bros, has strolled past and is heading toward the quad. He glances back with a quick, brilliant smile.

"Just saying hi to your hair," he says.

Agh. I laugh and shake my head, but turn back around quickly. My cheeks burn. I don't know what it's going to take, but I have to get smoother at this communicating with boys thing.

I get through the rest of the day by alternating between contemplating the mystery aspect of Miss Peters's test results and reveling in Journey saying hi to my hair. When the final bell rings, I head out toward the bus stop. A Snapchat comes through from Journey showing a photo of the empty passenger seat in his van. The caption says: *Got the van back. I'd give you a ride but I have a job interview.*

He's so cute.

I reply with a photo through the windshield of the bus that includes the back of the bus driver's bald head. I include the caption: *No sweat. Caught a ride with this guy.* The truth is that taking the bus downtown to Rachel's office is part of my plan.

Rachel's office has a separate entrance, but it's in the same building as the police station. As I'm walking in, I run into her coming out with her purse and keys in her hand. She's surprised to see me. "Hi, sweetie," she says. "What brings you here?"

I give her a pitiful look. "I didn't want to walk home, so I took the bus over. I figured I could hang out here and catch a ride home with you." I have to be careful not to oversell this or Rachel will get suspicious.

She looks a little pained, like this is somehow inconvenient, but she leads me back into her office anyway and stashes her purse and keys back in her desk drawer. "Were you going somewhere?" I ask.

"Not really," she says. Her voice sounds light, like it's no big deal. But there is a faint frown on her lips. "Not yet, anyway."

"Do you think Syd will let me use the new computer? I'd like to get a jump on my homework."

"We can ask her," Rachel says.

Syd's let me use it before, but it's not the computer I'm after, exactly. It's what's attached to it. A few months ago, the department purchased the new IAFIS system, which hooks into the national fingerprint database. I was so psyched, I begged Sydney to show me how it worked. Turns out it's exactly like making copies, which means it's unbelievably easy.

We walk from Rachel's side of the building through a door, down a hallway, and into the squad area, where Sydney and the other officers have desks. The copy room is at the far end, right around the corner from Chief Culson's office.

Sydney spots us as we come through the door. "Hey," she says, hurrying over and putting an arm around my shoulders. "I heard you had another close call yesterday. You okay?" She and Rachel exchange bug-eyed worry looks. Sydney's sudden attention causes everyone in the room to look at me, too. I keep my head down and answer her question with a nod and a shrug.

"Thankfully, she's fine, but we haven't replaced the scooter yet," Rachel says. "She took the bus over to catch a ride home with me, but I'm going to be tied up for an hour or so. Can she use the computer to get a jump on her homework?"

"Sure. If no one's using it." Sydney lowers her voice. "FYI, we're probably going to be releasing all the stuff from your room tomorrow morning anyway."

"Yay!" Rachel and I grin at each other.

"So that means she's clear?" Rachel asks. "That part is over?"

Sydney bobs her head. "Yeah. More or less. We didn't find anything, obviously. The timeline is a little faster than normal protocol, but the chief's insisting on it, so why not?" Sydney motions toward the back of the office. "Anyway, go ahead and hop on the computer, hon, you know the drill."

"Thanks, Sydney." I hurry off. But my brain is whirling.

Lately nothing is going where I think it's going to go. Both Miss P and the chief had pens that matched the note. Miss P ran a DNA test *before* she was killed. The chief screwed up and nearly accidentally got me killed and now he's insisting they give me back my stuff.

I can't wait to see if we got anything on the fingerprints.

The new computer, with the Integrated Automated Fingerprint Identification System (IAFIS) software installed, is located in the copy room, an all-purpose area where they keep the fax machine and the copy machine, office supplies, and now a computer that anyone can use. A desk is wedged in beside the copier.

On the desk next to the monitor is a latent print scanner. It looks and works exactly like an ordinary scanner, only it's connected to IAFIS, which is maintained by the FBI.

Someone's fingerprints will show up in IAFIS if they're in the system already. When Sydney did her test, she showed us how Rachel's prints came up because she works for the police department. Mine were in there, too, because of the investigation into my mother's murder. In both cases, the search brought up our names and photos from our drivers' licenses.

Since everyone in this building has access to this area, someone could pop in to make a copy or send a fax at any second, so I have to be on my toes. I waste no time scanning the two full hand prints from Journey's van into the system and set IAFIS to search for a match. I make sure that I stash the original fingerprint cards back in my bag. A slipup here might lead to some embarrassing questions.

Now I wait. A real IAFIS search takes about twenty minutes to an hour, not the bogus instant results you see on TV cop shows. I'd like to put my headphones on and zone out to some music, but I don't dare. I keep a file that looks like a book report up on the computer as a cover.

"How's it going?" Rachel appears behind me in the doorway and I jump about a mile. My knees shake when I realize Chief Culson is with her.

"Oh. You scared me."

"Sorry." Rachel hangs by the door but Chief Culson saunters all the way in. I freak as he goes straight to the scanner and straightens it on the desk. "Aha! I have you now."

Gripped with fear, I glance around. Is there a security camera in here or something? My insides quake, but I struggle to keep my outside looking calm. "M-m-me?" My voice is a ragged squeak.

The chief idly lifts the cover on the scanner, but finds it empty. "That depends, Erin," he says. "Have you done something I should know about?" I look up as he raises a pair of giant caterpillar eyebrows in my direction.

"Ah . . . just homework," I joke, gesturing at the computer screen and the two fake paragraphs of my book report.

"Well, that is a crime on a day like today. Shouldn't you be out having fun with your friends?" He tosses a laugh over his shoulder to Rachel.

I don't know how the two of them can avoid hearing my heart hammering from across the room, since the sound is deafening inside my head.

"Don't encourage her," Rachel says. "She works hard for her grades."

I flash her a grateful smile, since I'm still trying to get my breathing under control.

"I'm going to lock up my office," Rachel says. "Get your

stuff ready, Erin, we're going to leave a little early and give Charles a ride to pick up his car."

"I'm ready when you are," Chief Culson says. As Rachel leaves, I poke around on the keyboard, trying to form my face into a neutral mask even though I'm freaking out inside. I have to figure out how to cancel the IAFIS search before it's finished.

Chief Culson wanders around the copy room, lining up pins on the bulletin board and nudging stains in the carpet with his toe. Rachel returns. "Ready?"

"Um. Yeah. Almost," I say.

I'm so stressed I can hardly breathe. This is *so* not good.

I can't clear the IAFIS search from the screen without them seeing it. And I can't very well leave it running and walk out of here for someone else to find.

I'm so royally screwed.

# 28

A profiler studies a crime scene and makes educated guesses
about the personality and identity of the perpetrator.
This helps to narrow our search.

—VICTOR FLEMMING

My terrified brain is forced to multitask. One: Look normal. Two: Breathe in and out. Three: Pray for a cataclysmic distraction. A volcanic eruption would be nice . . . or maybe a homicidal maniac alert. At this point I'd be happy with a basic robbery in progress.

"Earth to Erin," Rachel says.

"Sorry." I wave over my shoulder, eyes glued to the monitor. "I messed up trying to send this file to myself. I just need a second." Or a miracle. Yeah. That's what I need, a freakin' miracle.

"I'm in no rush," Chief Culson says as he busies himself tidying things up around the copy machine.

His chatter reminds me that I know the number to his private line by heart. It's two numbers away from Rachel's. With my phone concealed against my middle, I key in his number and hit send. "Okay. I'll hurry," I promise.

A phone begins ringing in a nearby office. Someone hollers, "Hey, Chief . . . it's your private line."

"I better get that." Chief Culson moves off.

*One down . . . one to go.*

Rachel fluffs her hair and digs in her purse for her lipstick while I gather my books at the speed of Jell-O melting. Finally, she checks her watch and says, "I'm going to stop at the bathroom. Meet us up front."

"Okay," I say.

Just as Rachel leaves, the computer beeps, signaling the IAFIS search is complete. Thank God. I glance at the door before checking the results. IAFIS only matched one of the two prints, but it was the most important one. It was the full handprint I found on the back seat of the van. According to IAFIS, that print belongs to Police Chief Charles A. Culson.

Bah. I went through all of that to get the prints of the chief of police. The only thing that's a surprise about this is that he touched Journey's van without putting on gloves.

Maybe Victor's right. He *is* incompetent.

I forward the results to my e-mail for safekeeping, clear the cache on IAFIS, and power down. I grab my stuff and head out the door just as an exasperated Rachel is coming back for me.

I ride in Rachel's backseat and Chief Culson rides next to her. They make pleasant conversation between themselves while I stay quiet. Victor's car is in the driveway when we pull up, so Rachel doesn't even turn in; she just pulls over to let me out. She leans around her seat.

"I've got plans for dinner; do you think you and Victor can fend for yourselves?"

"Yeah, no problem." My mind is still kind of blown over the way the evidence seems to be tilting. I was hoping one of those prints would reveal something important. I wave good-bye to Rachel and the chief and amble away from the car without looking back. I climb the back stairs and bang the door into the wall as I enter the kitchen.

I start to smile because Victor's sitting at the kitchen table. But a second later, I see what's sitting on the kitchen table and it stops me cold.

The evidence box from up in my attic.

My bag thunks to the floor.

"Erin," he says, "we need to talk."

Giant Blue Angel jets filled with every lie I've ever told scream through my head at Mach speed. They fly loops and angles across the back of my brain. I force my mouth closed because I have nothing to say.

Victor pulls out a chair at the table. "Please. Have a seat."

Numb, I walk to the chair and flop down.

He doesn't look mad or crazy-psycho, which is how I imagine Rachel would look. Instead, there's softness around his eyes. He seems truly interested in what I have to say.

"I think you know what this is and I think you know where I found it."

I prop my elbows on the table and bury my face in my hands.

Victor sits back in his chair. "So, what would you like to tell me about it?"

I tilt my head back, pushing my chin out and getting just the right sweep of the hair veil over my eyes. "You haven't been around even once in my whole life and now you show up and start going through my stuff?" My voice cracks with emotion, which I hope he will believe is anger, not fear. My expression is scornful. "I can't believe you cut the padlock off."

Victor reaches into his pocket and pulls out my combination lock. He lays it on the table. "It was sitting out on the desk." He pokes a finger in his chest. "My old desk, in case you'd like to know."

I sink lower in my seat. I was so flustered when Rachel came home early yesterday that I forgot to lock everything back up.

"I know it seems like I'm spying on you, but honestly, I wasn't. I kept hearing noises in the attic late at night. I thought maybe there were rats up there or something. I went up there to help you and Rachel."

I hear what he's saying, but I'm too tired to process it. A huge blanket of brain fog settles around me. Nothing has been the same since I brought that box home. Maybe Lysa's right. Maybe it is my Pandora's box.

I can't think of anything to say, so I stare at my hands. Victor gets up and paces the room.

"Look," he says, "I get the violated privacy issue and all that. Maybe if I had found something else up there, I might have turned a blind eye to it. Or, if I thought it was serious enough, alerted Rachel." Victor plants his hands on the table and leans across until we're almost face-to-face. "But Erin, this is the evidence from your mother's murder."

"Yes." My eyes become watery.

"And there's other evidence up in that attic, too."

I nod.

"I am a forensic expert. You *want* to talk to me about this. In fact, there is no better person for you to talk to."

He's right, of course. This is my dream come true. He uses his foot to pull out the chair across from me and sits down, pressing his elbows into the table.

"I knew your mother."

I study his eyes. They're a rich blue with a slight shimmer of gold.

"She was a fixture around here. She and Rachel were inseparable. I called her my other little sister." He gets a faraway look. "She was quite the beauty, too."

His gaze settles back on me.

He doesn't say it, so I do. "I know, I don't look like her, but she was strong and independent and in that way I'm just like her."

His mouth twitches up at the corners. "I think you look quite a bit like her, actually. Even when she was nine or ten years old she was tall for her age, and she walked with this regal attitude. I used to call her the queen. You have her height and shape: slender like a dancer, and you move with that same regal attitude. I'll bet Rachel tells you that all the time."

I try to imagine what a regal attitude looks like. "Rachel never mentions her at all." I take a moment to wonder if what I'm about to do makes any sense or if I'm just too tired to try to stay ahead of things. "Okay. I'll tell you about the box, but you have to promise not to tell Rachel."

He shakes his head. "I can't make that promise. How did you get this, by the way? Through some access with Rachel's job?"

I slink my shoulders up around my neck. I know how bad it sounds and how much I have put Rachel at risk for my selfish needs. Victor softens at my reaction.

"Okay. I can't promise to keep this from Rachel, but I will help you present things to her in a way that won't send her too far over the edge."

I grip the edge of the table. I want to speak . . . tell him everything . . . spill my guts. But I can't seem to get the words swirling in my brain to come out of my mouth.

"Erin," he says. "Just say it. It's okay."

"Why? Because you say it is?" It's not what I expected to say, but it's what comes out. I sound like I'm blaming him.

"I know you don't know me very well, but you can trust me with your feelings . . . especially about this."

"You don't get it." My whole body begins to tremble.

"I don't have to get it. Just tell me what you're feeling."

"I'm not allowed to have feelings!" I bellow the words as loud as possible, and when the words are gone I just keep making the sound of rage until all the air in my lungs is expelled and my voice fades. When it's gone, my anger leaves with it. I flop back in my chair, spent.

There. That's the truth. I've admitted it and I dare him to deal with that.

Victor sits back in his chair, his voice neutral and his face a mask of calm. "Okay," he says. "We might be getting somewhere."

# 29

People lie to avoid getting caught. It's that simple.

—VICTOR FLEMMING

Victor and I are in a stare-down.

No one, not Rachel or any of my many therapists, has ever provoked me to this level of rage. All Victor did was talk about my mother like she was a real person and not a curse on my life.

He stands up, breaking our gaze.

Is he going to walk out and leave me hanging? If I screamed at Rachel like this, she would be fluttering all over. She would do anything to keep from having to let her real feelings out or having to deal with mine.

Victor doesn't leave, though. Instead, he takes off his jacket and walks to the nearby closet to hang it up. "Does my sister know this is how you feel?"

I shake my head. "I've tried to tell her but she always comes back with *How can you feel alone when I'm right here?* Or *I'm sorry I'm not enough for you.*" I wrap my arms around my middle. "Oh, and I'm supposed to not care who my father is, either. *He's just genetic material,* she says. Any questions about who killed my mother? Whoa. That topic is way off-limits."

Victor rolls up his sleeves and slides back into his chair. He rests his elbows on the table, rubbing his hands over his face.

"How about this?" he says. "I'll tell you a dark secret of mine—something that no one else knows."

Uhhh. I didn't see that coming. I peer at him through a safety curtain of hair. "That's kind of random."

"It's not random. It's an exchange. This way you'll have the same power over me that you're afraid I will have over you if you talk to me about this box and your stuff up in the attic. How's that sound?"

I shrug because I don't know how it sounds. I can't imagine what he could tell me that would give me any power over him.

"I think I'm about to get fired."

*"What?"*

He nods. "Yeah, no one knows that. But I'm pretty sure it's coming."

"Why?"

He pulls his phone off of his belt and checks it, then turns it upside down on the table. "I helped to put an innocent man in jail."

"On purpose?"

"Not on purpose. But in this case, intent isn't the issue."

"Why not?"

"Because the man was killed three days after he was incarcerated. It was a setup. Somebody tampered with my lab in order to make sure he went to jail, where they could get to him. I can't prove it, not yet, and since he's dead, I can't fix it, either."

"But if it wasn't your fault . . ."

"That's the whole point of what I do. It's all about what you can prove. And everything that happens in my lab is my responsibility."

I sit back. I don't know if Victor's overshare makes me trust him more. But I do feel for him. "So, what are you going to do?"

"I haven't decided yet." His phone vibrates and he ignores it.

"Is this why you came home?"

Victor shrugs. "I came because Rachel asked me to come. Something she's never done before. She's worried about you. But, now that I'm here, I can see that it's not a bad thing to know you have some family who's got your back."

He presses the fingers of both hands together as if trying to squeeze out the words. "I'll admit, I don't quite know how to address the way my sister handles your situation. I'm not a therapist . . . or a parent."

I gnaw on the corner of my lip.

"But I do believe that a lifetime spent blocking feelings can lead to sociopathic behavior." He stops and looks at me. His expression is not the normal angry adult look, but more like he thinks I'm an interesting puzzle. "You don't strike me as the serial-killer type."

I didn't expect that, so of course I laugh. "Whew. That's a relief."

"If what you need is the free space to talk about your mother, I'm here. I can be your uncle and your friend. I can also just sit and listen. Or, you can tell me to go to hell."

I raise my eyebrows.

"But if the unsavory things that have been going on lately have anything to do with what's in this box, well, then you really do need me." He smiles, and it's not a creepy I'm-trying-to-be-your-friend smile, but a real I'm-here-for-you smile.

"I'm thinking that first you'd like to know more about your mother, right?"

"Well, there's almost no way I could know less." The snort that follows is automatic. I can't help it. "Sometimes at night I play this game where I lie in bed and try to think of everything I can remember in my whole life. I work my way back year by year. I start by trying to remember all the things that happened when I was twelve . . . then nine . . . then six. I keep working back to the very earliest thing I can remember. Then I lie quietly, eyes closed, and I let my mind float, like a feather in a breeze, hoping to latch on to something. Maybe I'll remember how she smelled, or the tone of her voice. . . . I go back really far in the remembering game. I can remember a lot of things: a special dress, a favorite bunny toy. But she's like an itch I can't scratch—a memory of her is there, but I can never quite latch on to it."

Victor pinches his lips together. The skin at the corners of his eyes folds up. "That's sad, because she was such a beautiful person."

"When I saw the box, I had to take it. Just so I'd have something that was close to her." I lean forward. "Rachel never even showed me that all my mother's things were in the attic. I found them by accident."

"And you don't remember anything about the murder?"

I give him a grim smile. "Only the smell of blood."

He nods. "No one forgets that."

I pose my index fingers in the shape of an *X*. "And there's something about seeing the shadow of a cross on the floor, like when the sun shines through a French door at an angle."

"That's all?"

I nod.

I lay my hands flat on the table and press down. My knuckles are white as bleached bone. "So, yeah, you could say I have some questions."

Victor shifts positions in his chair. "Then let's start at the beginning."

"Well, I didn't just lose my mother, I lost the identity of my father, too."

"It was my understanding she was planning to raise you alone," Victor says.

"Maybe. But if she were here I could at least ask her questions. Think about it. I share DNA with a stranger. She might have loved him, or maybe he was just some random dude, but I came out of that and I have no idea who he is. Sometimes I walk down the street and just look at face after face after face and wonder, *Am I related to you . . . or you?*"

Victor smiles at the way I wave my hands around.

"I believe I have a right to know who my father is. I also think I have a right to know who killed my mother and why."

"I agree on both counts," he says.

"There's one more thing I want to know . . . well, it's more than a want, it's a need. I *need* to know my father isn't the one who killed her. That he wasn't the one who took away our dream of being a family."

Victor stays silent for a long minute. Then he ticks each item off on his fingers. "So, if I heard you correctly, you want to solve a murder, establish paternity, and rule out a suspect?"

I nod. "That pretty much covers it."

"That's what we call the DNA trifecta." He nods at my mother's box, still sitting in the middle of the table. "And, while it's all doable, it's going to take more juice than you've got up in your attic playroom."

"I know. That's why Miss Peters was helping me."

Victor sits forward. "The biology teacher who was murdered? She knew about all of this?"

"Yeah. Well, I'd say most adults in town know about me and what happened to my mom. But Miss P was the first to actually show me how I could get some answers on my own."

Concern forms in the creases of Victor's forehead. "That sounds highly inappropriate for a teacher. What did she show you . . . exactly?"

"She knew I was playing around with forensic stuff and she showed me—like you just said—how DNA could answer all of my questions. She helped me. Maybe you'll help me now."

Victor runs his thumb over a spot on his wrist, finally meeting my gaze with a look that's just as intense as mine. "I'll take a cursory look into the case. But first, I'm curious to know how you started 'playing around with forensic stuff.' "

"Your books kind of started it." I grin and he rolls his eyes in response.

"The attraction was always about finding the answers to my questions." I adjust my position in the chair by curling one leg up under me. "But first I had to get the techniques down. And that takes a lot of practice."

Victor rests his elbow on the table and props his head on his hand. "Some would say it requires more than practice, but go on."

"Well, a friend of mine at school was afraid her boyfriend was cheating on her, and I thought maybe we could use forensics to prove it. I started by looking at hair samples. Then taught myself to lift fingerprints and do chromatography tests on lipstick and stuff."

Victor looks surprised. "Wait a minute, you taught yourself to lift prints and do chromatography?"

"They teach it in high school now, so how hard can it really be?"

"I'll be sure to tell my boss that," he mutters. "Keep talking."

"We helped a lot of our friends at school with problems, which prompted Miss Peters to try to get a forensics class or club on campus."

"Wow, you've gone to a great deal of effort. Old Carl must be impressed with you," Victor says.

"Yeah. Not really. I mean, Principal Roberts gets it, to a point. He says science fair projects are okay, but forensic experiments are forbidden on campus."

"You're kidding, right?" Victor asks.

"I wish. Mr. Roberts claims my forensic experiments could have unpleasant consequences. So, if I get caught doing any investigations on campus, it's an automatic three-day suspension."

Victor rolls his eyes. "He's not wrong about the consequences, but if I told you some of the pranks we pulled when we were in school . . ." He gets up from the table. "Hey, I'm starving and I make some serious scrambled eggs *à la* Victor. What do you say?"

I nod an enthusiastic yes.

Victor heads for the refrigerator and starts unloading ingredients. "Your mother loved eating breakfast for dinner. In fact, last time I saw her we had eggs *à la* Victor." He gets a distant look on his face.

"When was that?" I ask.

"I think it was June 1998, something like that. You weren't born yet and I was home for my mother's funeral. How's that for the circle of life?" He musters a sad smile. "Not the happiest of moments. Your mom handled everything for Rachel, though. She was a rock."

I don't know what to say. I let the quiet in the room swallow us up. After a while it gets to be too much. "So you wouldn't have a problem with my investigations?" I ask.

Victor whirls to face me; he's got four eggs in one hand and a package of grated cheese in the other. He kicks the refrigerator door closed. "Oh, I didn't say that. I am impressed with how smart and resourceful you are, but unsupervised investigations aren't a good idea. And especially not with real evidence." He nods toward my mother's box.

"I wasn't trying to investigate her murder . . . not yet, anyway."

"What does *that* mean?" Victor turns his attention back to the stove. With a series of sizzles, I hear each egg hit the skillet. Next he opens the cheese and grabs a huge handful. I can't see where it goes but I assume he's dropping it on top of the eggs.

I clear my throat. "Not yet, because I'm thinking of making this my career."

Victor waves the spatula over his shoulder. "You should. But take classes or go to CSI camp or something. I don't like the idea of you doing these things unsupervised."

I watch in quiet amazement as he moves in front of the stove, rolling the skillet from side to side while vigorously pummeling the eggs with the spatula.

"But you still think it would be good for me, right? Critical thinking and all that." Rachel would never agree to CSI camp or anything having to do with forensics. She's afraid exposure to that stuff will "set me off." Whatever that means. But maybe if Victor thinks it would be good, he'll plead my case with her.

"Yes. Your inquisitive nature drives you to research and learn, and that's good. What you lack is the experience and maturity to understand that this kind of information is power, and there are people in power who won't think twice about using it the wrong way."

He scoops the eggs onto two plates and brings them to the table. "Like the person who keeps calling my phone. I don't want to talk to him. But as you can see, he's not giving up. He thinks he can badger me into picking up my phone, otherwise he'd stop trying."

Victor's words spark something. *People in power who won't think twice about using it the wrong way* is a tremendous thought. I scoop up a bite of egg and nibble it off the tines of my fork as the odd pieces of my evidence suddenly start to come together in my head.

"What's wrong?" Victor asks.

I'm distracted and thinking this through. But because I don't answer him, he picks up his plate and inspects the eggs, as if there's something wrong with them.

"I have a question," I finally say. "What did Sydney mean when she said the chief prefers 'old-school' police work?"

Victor takes a couple of bites of egg, scraping the extra-gooey cheese off his fork with his teeth. "I think what she means is that Charles isn't really up on the latest forensic science tech. She said 'old-school,' and by that I think she means 'old-fashioned.' "

"But could there be a reason why he would be against forensic science, like maybe a reason he would get super upset over having a lab here in Iron Rain?" I scoop up more egg onto my fork. These eggs look simple, but Victor's right, the taste is amazing.

He gives me a questioning look. "I can't figure out where you're going with this, so do me a favor and just tell me?"

I set my plate aside. "Okay. Total trust. I wasn't investigating my mother's murder, I was looking into who killed Miss P."

Victor's head snaps up.

"I felt responsible for what happened to her and, you know, for getting Journey involved, too."

"From what I understand, Journey got himself involved." Victor finishes his eggs and sets his plate aside. "He was there on his own accord. But when you say *investigate,* what do you mean exactly?"

"We've been gathering clues," I say. "Miss P was going to run DNA tests for me and Journey and we think this is why she was killed. Here's the thing—so far all of our evidence points to only one person."

Victor ferries our plates to the sink and returns to the table. "Who would that be?"

"Don't laugh or make me feel weird, but . . . I'm just going to say it. Chief Culson."

I spread my hands out on the table. It sounds even more ridiculous when I say it out loud.

"I have evidence that links Chief Culson and Miss P."

# 30

You won't go wrong if you always follow the evidence.

—VICTOR FLEMMING

For the first time Victor gives me a look of total disbelief. "Linking Chuck and your teacher doesn't mean anything. They're two adults. I'm sure they knew each other. They might even have been dating."

The thought of adorable Miss P dating droopy Chief Culson is not a pretty one. "What if I can prove he was at her house the night she was killed?"

Victor looks skeptical.

I pause to wipe off the table. "Alright, I know it sounds crazy, and I'll admit when I was gathering the clues they seemed more like accidents. But when you said that about a person in authority using their power the wrong way . . . it triggered something for me. Think about it. The chief is a person in a position of power."

Victor sneers. "I wouldn't exactly call Iron Rain a power center."

"But did you know that Miss P was working to create a forensic lab here, in Iron Rain?"

Victor frowns. "Actually, that wasn't mentioned in regard to her murder."

"Well, she was. She wanted the school and the police department to share it. I assumed the chief was psyched about it—I mean, who wouldn't be? But thinking back to what Sydney said, maybe he wasn't. And, he *is* a person in power."

Victor makes a calming gesture. "Don't get hung up on the power thing. What I said was just something you say. I don't see Chuck having any kind of motive—or the balls, for that matter—to murder anyone."

"But in your books you always say 'you've got to go . . .' "

" '. . . where the evidence takes you.' " Victor slaps his hands on the table. "Yeah. Yeah. Okay. Let's see what you've got."

I grab my mom's evidence box. "What should I do with this?"

Victor thinks for a moment. "Put it back in the attic . . . but just for now. Okay?"

"Okay." I dash up to my room and carefully return the file box to the attic. Now that Victor knows about it, I don't know how long I will get to keep it. I haven't told him about the matching shirt tie that Journey found in his van. I have a feeling that if he knew this was connected to my mother's murder, he'd start acting like Rachel. He'd take it all away and I wouldn't get to see any of it.

I return to the kitchen with my laptop and a smaller shoe box containing the evidence I've been collecting on Miss Peters's murder. Victor has cleared the table, and propped his huge brown leather briefcase on a chair beside him. The top of the briefcase gapes open and Victor is flipping through a notebook. I pause to reflect on just what a perfect moment this is. In all of his books, Victor stresses the importance of keeping detailed notes. And here he is . . . in my house . . . at my table . . . waiting to see mine.

I set the shoe box on the table and hand over my notebook. It's not leather-bound like his, but it's what's inside my cardboard cover that counts. "I kept a detailed journal on everything, just like you describe in your books."

He gives me an appreciative smile as he flips through the pages, stopping to jot something here and there in his own notebook. When he's done, he sets it aside. "Okay, hit me with it."

I open the box and begin to spread things out on the table. "Remember those fingerprint cards you spotted the other night? Well, one of those sets of prints belong to Chief Culson."

"How did you . . . ?" Victor frowns.

I bring up my e-mail from the IAFIS search and swivel the laptop so he can see it.

"I'll explain everything, but just listen first." I rummage in the box and find the Ziploc bag containing the scrap of paper. I slide it across the table to Victor.

"I found this lodged in Journey's seat belt. He says it's not his handwriting and an ink test shows it matches the chief's special pen."

Victor snorts. "Chuck and his special pens. What else?"

I pull out the pages Spam gave me and put them on the table. "Phone records. Miss Peters received a buttload of calls from the chief's private line in the days right before she was killed."

"Wait. How did you get private phone records?"

"Um. I don't want to reveal all my sources just yet. Just let me keep going."

Victor rolls his hand in the air for me to continue.

I'm down to the last two pieces of paper in the box. "Last but not least, DNA results from Miss Peters's lab computer." I push the DNA printout to the middle of the table and slide the page with the footprint I found in my room off to the side.

Victor nods at the footprint. "What's that?"

"It's a footprint, it connects, I just don't know exactly how." Actually, I know how. I'm pretty sure the person who left this footprint was looking for the tie that matched my mother's shirt. But since I don't want to tell Victor about the tie just yet, I can't really explain the shoe print either.

Victor frowns. "Where'd you find it?"

"In my bedroom."

Victor uses the smooth end of his pen to slide the footprint back into the middle of the table. "For now, it stays in. Everything stays in until we eliminate it."

I shrug okay and curl onto my chair. I watch him review one item after another on the table. His hand hovers over the group until he picks up the page Spam printed from Miss Peters's computer files. Donning a pair of reading glasses, he gives me a pointed look over the rims.

"What makes you think these are DNA results, and why do they implicate Chuck Culson?" he asks.

"Duh." I lean in and point out the obvious. "Subjects are down the left and markers across the top—thirteen of them. The exact number needed for comparison DNA."

Victor gives me a slight nod. "Impressive. But what about these letters: EB, JM, ME, and CC?"

He's testing me. "Initials. EB is probably me. And JM could be Journey Michaels. ME could be Miss Peters."

Victor peruses the page. "It fits."

"What do you mean?"

Victor lays the paper on the table between us and uses his pen to point to the markers at the beginning of each string. "Well, these early markers here indicate the sex. EB is female. JM is male. ME is female as well."

"What about CC?"

"Male." Victor gives me an appreciative nod.

I turn my palms up. "CC . . . Chief Culson. Works for me."

"Or it could just as easily be Charles Culson," Victor says with a slight grin. Then he adopts a serious look. "I don't know, though. DNA tests require special equipment and some expertise. I'd be surprised if your science teacher had the know-how to pull this off in the classroom."

"Yeah, except Miss Peters had a degree in chemical forensics and I'm pretty sure I found the actual samples in the lab freezer at school."

"You what?" Victor sits forward. "Where are those samples now?"

"In a safe place."

"How safe?" he asks.

"What's your position on peas?"

"I hate them. I'd rather die than eat peas."

I point to our refrigerator. "They're that safe."

"You're just an endless well of secrets, aren't you?" Victor sets the paper aside. "So, you have a theory that your teacher was conducting secret DNA experiments for someone—we don't know who yet—and that led to her being murdered, which you are starting to suspect somehow involves Chief Culson?"

I nod. "I have fingerprints, an ink sample, phone records, and maybe a DNA test. And, I'm sure you heard that he practically tried to kill me and Spam yesterday."

Victor looks skeptical.

I unlock my phone and swipe to bring up the photo of the earthmover and destroyed walkway.

"First, the chief *let* Spam and I in there and then, when we were in really far, he called out 'all clear' and this was the result." I hand him my phone. He pinches to enlarge the photo before handing it back.

"We barely made it out alive. It's a lot, isn't it?" In my head it feels like a lot, but I'm clearly not igniting any flames in Victor.

"To charge the chief of police with murder? No. Everything you have is circumstantial. It doesn't prove anything."

I think for a minute. "What about Miss P's forensic lab?"

Victor shrugs. "Schools and police departments sharing a lab is a new paradigm for smaller communities. Cities like San Mateo, California, are making a real go of it. I would think Chuck would welcome a deal like that. But then again, he is kind of an egotistical weasel."

"But isn't it weird that all my evidence points to him?"

"Weird, yes," Victor says. "But evidence of murder? Not by a long shot."

Victor picks up the Ziploc bag and closely examines the shred of notebook paper with the words "ur" and "DNA." "Erin, this scribbling looks more like it was written by a high school kid than the chief of police."

"I agree, but it matches his special pen. Miss P had one, too, so I guess it could be her writing. Either way, I think he's involved." I turn to the page in my notebook where I've taped the results of my ink chromatography test.

Victor takes the book and peruses the results. "Do you still have the pens?"

"Right here." I pick them up out of the shoe box.

He chuckles. "Oh, God. That's right. I was there when he gave you the black one. Ha! I'm a witness."

"I'll admit that when it came back that the fingerprints in the van were his, I was disappointed because I figured he just goofed up and touched Journey's van without gloves. But think about it, would he really do that?"

"To be honest, I don't know why he would touch Journey's van for any reason. His people are trained and tasked with lifting prints . . . not him." Victor inspects the cards and studies my laptop screen before giving me a very stern look. He taps the cards on the table. "You realize this is tampering with evidence, young lady."

I scoff. "If it wasn't for me, no one would even know there *was* evidence."

He shrugs. "And you ran these through IAFIS by yourself?"

"Well yeah, it's like using a copier."

Victor looks back through everything. "I'm not buying your theory, but I'll admit you have put in some first-class detective work."

Swoon. Victor always knows the right thing to say. "So what am I missing?"

"A motive." He sits back in his chair.

"Do we always need a motive?"

"If we want to indict the chief of police, we definitely need a motive." Victor stops and looks up as Rachel walks in the back door.

"What's all this?" she asks, a frown forming quickly around her mouth.

Victor helps me slide all the evidence together and clear the table. "Sit down, Rachel, and I'll explain," he says.

She looks suspicious as she walks over to the hall closet to hang up her coat and purse. "I don't like the looks of the two of you. You're up to something." But she comes back and takes a seat anyway.

I'm wiggling in my seat, straining. Champing at the bit. I can't wait to spill my guts. But Victor puts his hand on mine to slow me down.

"First," he asks, "how was your dinner?"

Rachel shrugs. "Fine. How was yours?"

"Incredible. We had eggs *à la* Victor," he says, oozing charm.

Rachel is not impressed.

"Can I get you some tea or coffee?" Victor offers.

Rachel narrows her eyes. "Stop trying to work me and just tell me what's going on."

"Well." He speaks with a very soothing tone. "It seems our Erin here has been doing a little detective work—"

Rachel explodes. She locks the look of fury onto me. "I knew that little trip to Journey's house wasn't about homework!"

"Calm down, Rachel," Victor says. "She's fine. There's no harm done. And, while I'm not sure I buy her theory, I think she's brought up some interesting points."

"Oh really," Rachel snaps. "About what?"

"Miss Peters's murder," I interject. I'm hoping Victor will continue to have my back.

Rachel turns her volcanic gaze on Victor now. "Are you out of your mind? Given what she's been through, Erin is the last person whose head you should be filling with your creepy forensic fantasies. I don't even let her watch those shows on TV because of how susceptible she is to this stuff."

I snort. What I've been through? I'm susceptible? The person she's describing is herself. I knew this wouldn't go over well with her, so I just slink a little farther down into my chair and keep quiet.

"There's no need to be cruel, Rachel," Victor says. "But now I'm going to ask you a question. Can you think of any reason why Chuck Culson might be threatened by a forensic lab in Iron Rain?"

Rachel's reaction is way off from what I had expected.

She laughs, but it's an angry, bitter laugh.

She's now angrier with Victor than she is with me. She leaps from her seat, shaking a finger in his face. "I see how it is. You saw us out at dinner together and cooked up this childish joke. You're a forty-five-year-old man, Victor. When does it stop? I asked you to come back here and help me keep her out of trouble . . . not ruin my life."

Victor and I exchange puzzled looks. It's a dumb move, I know. But I raise my hand and wait for Rachel to call on me. She glares in my direction.

"Um, Rachel. We haven't left the house all night."

Victor takes a different path. "You were out with Chuck?"

"Yes, I was out with Charles, and trust me. He's not the slightest bit threatened by you," Rachel shouts. "He's the chief of police, for God's sake. I know the FBI looks down on the lowly local police, but that's not how you were raised."

Victor stands up and shouts back. "This is not about how I was raised, it's about where Chuck Culson was the night Erin's teacher was killed. I doubt you can testify to that, now, can you?"

At first I think Rachel is going to slap him, but she just glares—first at him and then at me. She speaks, low and deliberate. "Not that I owe either of you an explanation, but I *can* testify to that, because he was with me." She points toward her bedroom. "Right in there. In fact, he's there with me whenever we can wedge in a few hours before he has to tiptoe out so he's not here when she wakes up or I have to come home and be a single parent." She spins angrily in my direction. "That *intruder* you saw on my patio the other night was Charles Culson! Happy now?"

"You're dating him?" This seems incomprehensible to Victor.

"Yes. I am. Don't even think about bringing up that silly old rivalry you two had. I don't give a damn about that. It's not like you were here for me when my best friend was slaughtered like an animal, her blood spilled out all over the floor, and I was too late. Too late to help her. Too late to change any of it. Too late to do anything but pick up the pieces and soldier on . . . which is what I did. Where were you then, huh?"

Victor and Rachel are going at each other and all I can think is how it never occurred to me that Rachel would want or need anyone else in her life but me. What's wrong with me? I'm terrible to her. I lie, and I refuse to call her Mom even though she's been here for me every second of every day. Why couldn't I see that she needed someone, too?

How stupid am I?

I clearly ruined her whole life. I bolt from the table and race up the stairs and into my room. It takes four binders to span the entire bottom of my bedroom door. I shove them in place one after the other, leaving no space between them. Then I head up to my attic and plug into some music.

# ▸ 31 ◂

In order to charge a suspect you must be able to establish
three things: means, motive, and opportunity.
Without all three your case will likely
never make it to court.
—VICTOR FLEMMING

I wake up in my attic about 3:00 a.m., shivering from the cold.

My emotions—like the battery in my phone—are completely drained. I slip down the ladder into my bedroom and listen for a second. The house is silent. I put my phone on the charger, slip off my jeans, and fall into bed. Then there's nothing until my alarm wakes me at seven.

After three snooze cycles, I'm dressed and downstairs. Both Rachel and Victor are gone. There's a folded piece of paper in front of my spot at the table. *ERIN* is scrawled on the outside in Rachel's handwriting. I open it.

> *I didn't mean any of that the way it sounded. You are the best thing that's ever happened to me.*
>
> ♥ *Rachel.*

Somewhere inside I *do* know.

I grab a couple of PowerBars from Rachel's stash and head out the door. I make it all the way to the bottom of the stairs before I remember. . . . Damn it.

No scooter.

Really? How effed up is this? I can completely forget that my scooter is a mess of tangled metal, but every time I close my eyes I still see Miss P the way she looked that night. There's no way I will make it to school on time.

I hit the driveway moving fast. Maybe I can launch myself into a wormhole, and then through some miracle of time and space, magically arrive on campus just before the tardy bell. As that absurd thought pops into my mind, a familiar van rumbles across the end of my driveway and stops.

Journey opens the passenger door and his brilliant, crooked smile beckons. My feet barely touch the ground as I rush to the van, toss my bag between the seats, and climb in. "You are my knight in rusty steel."

"Happy to oblige, m'lady," he says.

I settle in and fumble for my seat belt. Journey is so quiet that I'm hit with a sudden pang of concern. I look up and find him staring at me.

"What's wrong?" The air between us fills with dread.

"I was going to ask you the same thing," he replies.

"I'm fine. . . ."

His expression doesn't change. If anything, he looks even more serious.

He leans toward me, sliding his hand over the back of my seat and up into my hair. He buries his fingers in the strands. As he closes the space between us, a warm flush spreads over my body. His breath tickles my cheek. I try to focus on where I should put my hands.

I tilt my head forward, allowing strands of my hair to mingle with his. My eyes flutter closed as his lips crush against mine. I hold perfectly still, hoping time will do the same.

Finally, even though I'm not ready, he breaks the spell and pulls away.

We don't go far, staying face-to-face, a few inches apart, our breathing matched and ragged. His eyes are soft and full of questions. My lips tingle with the memory of his.

"You weren't online last night," he whispers. "And you didn't reply to any of my Snapchats. I was worried."

My phone? I pat my pockets. It's still on the charger. "Hold on. Don't move." I leap out of the van and race back into the house, up the stairs. I grab my phone off the charger, then I stop and check my reflection in the mirror. My face is splotchy and dotted with beads of sweat. But it doesn't matter, Journey Michaels just *kissed* that face.

I race back down the stairs and throw myself into the van.

Journey offers a hand to help me in. "So what happened?"

"Last night? Rachel and I kind of got into it, so I went to sleep early. That's all."

"About me?"

"No. This was some other weird family drama. Sorry you were worried."

He puts the van into gear and we rumble off toward school. "But everything's okay, right?" He glances sideways at me.

I nod, tipping my head slightly right and left. Should I tell him my suspicions about Chief Culson? Rachel says she was with him. And she has no reason to lie. Which probably means I'm wrong. But still . . . questions about the chief nag at me.

"What do you know about Chief Culson?" I ask.

"Only that he's a giant a-hole," Journey replies, his knuckles whitening on the steering wheel.

"Really?"

"He was involved in my father's case. He wasn't chief then, but my mother said he never cared about the evidence, only the results. Why, what are you thinking?"

"I don't want to say just yet. But I have a feeling about him."

Journey pulls into a space in the school parking lot and turns off the engine. Instead of getting out of the car, he turns toward me again, taking my hand in both of his and rubbing my fingers. For a brief moment I wonder if he's going to kiss me again. But instead he pulls back.

"I thought we were partners? A team?"

"We are." I squeeze his hand. "I just need to think things through a little more, then I'll tell you. I promise."

His quick nod says okay, but I can tell that it's not. He gets out on his side, then comes around and opens my door. He offers his hand to steady me as I step down.

Neither of us has much to say as we walk toward the school buildings, but he does drape his arm over my shoulders, which is a first.

Suddenly, my worldview has changed. I get to experience what it's like to be Journey. Everyone he passes offers a nod, or a high five. Small gifts of food are still involved. This time, instead of being invisible girl walking, I'm part of the show.

"Hey, Journey. Hi, Erin." The greeting is repeated at least ten times, from people I know but have never spoken to. I even score a snack pack of Mini Oreos. How cool is that?

The topper comes when a girl with a camera asks us to pose for a photo in front of the flagpole. "It's for the yearbook," she says.

Journey's all like, "Of course."

Meanwhile, I'm worried that we're barely ten feet from Principal Roberts's office window. His blinds are closed now, but I know what a dedicated spy he is. And, while I fully expect something to come along and ruin this amazing moment, I don't want it to be Rachel overreacting to a tip from Principal Roberts.

# 32

The leading cause of wrongful convictions in our country
is eyewitness IDs that are wrong.

—VICTOR FLEMMING

The memory of my morning classes is a vague fog compared with the memory of Journey's kiss and the worry on his face. On the other side of my brain is all the evidence stacking up against Chief Culson. There must be a way that these pieces fit together.

Tomorrow marks two weeks since the horror of Miss Peters's murder, and the weird suspicion about us being the ones who killed her has nearly died down. Spam and Lysa and Journey and I have fallen into a lunch routine, meeting up at the secluded table behind the building. And even though my best friends are really polite to Journey these days, I sense there's still a little bit of he and I on one side and them on the other.

Today, we sit at our usual table unwrapping our lunches. No one is really talking when, all of a sudden, there's a cell-phone sound. It's not a cute ringtone but a loud vibration. In unison, Journey and Lysa pull out their phones to check. I shrug. "Not me."

"Me, either," Journey says, stuffing his phone back in his pocket.

"Me, either," comments Lysa, returning her phone to her purse.

Spam's phone was already lying on the table facedown. She lifts it, looks, shrugs, and keeps eating.

The phone not only continues to buzz, but it also starts to ping. Journey, Lysa, and I look around, trying to figure out where it's coming from.

Spam stands up. She's wearing a pair of bright red Wellington rain boots that match her T-shirt. She props her foot up on the bench and digs deep into the boot.

"It's just my ankle phone," she says.

"Since when do you have an ankle phone?"

She pulls out a smaller phone with a slide-out keyboard, sits down, and starts reading the messages. "I set up a little gossip hotline," she says. I notice she's not making eye contact. "I wanted to keep it separate, so I sent it to a different phone."

"Gossip hotline?" I can't hide the surprise in my reaction.

She shrugs. "Well, we completely stopped getting Cheater Check requests after the thing with Miss P, and I had some time, so I figured I would start a little schoolwide *TMZ*."

"I love gossip," Lysa says, squirming in her seat. "What are they saying?"

Spam flips through a couple of screens with her thumb, tilting her head right and then left at each one. "Yep. Thought so," she says. Finally, she turns the phone around to show us. "It's all still about you two." The photo is a shot of Journey and me from this morning, in front of the flagpole, with our arms around each other.

Journey and I exchange a look. I turn a little pink, because my first actual boyfriend—I guess I can call him my boyfriend now—happens to be the boyfriend that every girl wants. Was it my imagination, or is there a bit of bitterness in Spam's voice?

Just this morning, Journey kissed me for the first time, and my best friends still don't know. On a normal day, we would have spent the entire lunch—and a full day's worth of text messaging—dissecting every detail of that one kiss. Obviously, we can't do that with him here. But even if he wasn't here, I'm not sure Spam would be on board with my new romance.

Spam shakes her head and gives me a little eye roll. There's no way she knows what I'm thinking, but her reaction makes me wonder if I'm putting out the wrong vibe.

"What's with the silly smirk?" she asks.

I shrug. What does she want me to say? My cheeks turn warm and my grin stretches from ear to ear.

Spam scowls. "You look like one of those creepy Disney princesses who's about to start singing to birds." Not only is Spam's tone mean, but she flutters her hands under her chin in an extra mocking gesture.

Ouch. I blink back the hurt. "Geez, Spam."

Lysa, who normally stays pretty neutral, jumps to her defense. "Maybe she's waiting for you to tell us what you found out about the fingerprint scans. I know I'm dying to know. Journey, aren't you dying to know? You did run them, right?"

I glance at Journey. There's an uncomfortable hesitation. He's torn. I know he wants to support me, but he also wants to know what's going on. "Erin says she'll tell us when she's ready."

"And there's the problem," Spam says. I don't have to wonder this time; there is a definite sting to her voice. "We're not a team if we have to wait until she's ready to tell us what she's found."

"Spam, I always tell you eventually."

"Right. Emphasis on *eventually,*" she says. "Meaning when you *eventually* need our help again."

"I promise I'll tell you everything as soon as I can, it's just that Victor and I . . ."

"See, this is how you are," Spam snaps. "First it was all Journey and I, Journey and I, and now it's all Victor and I, Victor and I." She gets up from the table and wags her finger between she and Lysa. "We are the ones who have been in on this with you from the beginning. When Journey and Victor bail on you, you'll come crawling back to us. Until then, peace out."

Spam turns and walks away. Lysa glances back at Spam and then at me. "I'll talk to her," she says as she gets up, and she leaves, too, slapping the table once in solidarity.

"Oh my god. Did you see that? I mean, did you hear her?" I turn my palms up.

Journey slides his arms around my waist and pulls me to him. "The question is, did *you* hear her? I trust you and I believe you, but you aren't telling us everything."

I give him a guilty look. "I think she's jealous of you."

"It's not that," he says. "I think she's worried about you. We all are. You want us to work with you to help you stay safe, but how can we if you won't tell us what you know?"

"Don't worry. I'll be fine. My uncle won't let anything happen to me."

The bell rings, signaling that lunch is over. Journey kisses the top of my head, balls up all of our trash from lunch, and makes a long lob into a trash can. "Two points," he says, flashing a brief smile. He gives me a quick hug and then heads off in one direction while I head off in another.

# 33

We have a joke in our business that forensic science is like climate change. There are those who believe it and then there are the people who think it's a load of crap.

—VICTOR FLEMMING

Spam has always had strong opinions, so storming off at lunch isn't exactly out of character for her. But the fact that she hasn't answered my last ten text messages is a bad sign.

Lysa hasn't answered, either.

My final class of the day is biology, which Spam and I share. She won't be able to ignore me straight to my face. I'll convince her to ditch class and go somewhere to talk everything out. I'll even tell her about my theory about Chief Culson. Bio's been a complete flush anyway. In two weeks, we've gone through four substitutes and eight movies. Yesterday the sub told us to work in small groups, which meant everybody just talked for the whole period. I'm sure today will be the same. Wash. Rinse. Repeat.

But when I peek in the door to the classroom, I'm not prepared for what I see.

Victor is standing at the whiteboard, writing his name.

I step back and flatten my back against the wall. I'm trying to catch my breath when Spam sails past me into the room.

"Whoa." She steps back into the hall to face me. "What's he doing here?"

"I have no clue." My face flames. It's one thing to have a cool uncle who works at the FBI. It's another to have someone who lives in your house teaching your class.

Since ditching is out of the question, I grab Spam's arm and pull her in the door. Using her as a shield, I press her into the seat in front of me. Then I take out a large folder, prop it open on my desk, and prepare to hide for the entire class.

The bell rings, but barely half the class is even in the room. The rest of them straggle in slowly, talking and laughing and pushing one another. They slam their books on their desks and mill around the room. There's an unwritten law that says students aren't allowed to show respect to a substitute teacher. I keep my head down behind the folder.

I'd rather no one knows that Victor and I are related.

For the next forty-seven minutes, the class pays no attention to Victor. I sneak a peek over the top of my folder at his face and I see terror.

Victor might be an awesome forensic scientist, but he pretty much bombs as a high school teacher. There's a knack to being just cool enough to make thirty high school students sit and pay attention, and he doesn't have it.

He tries to appeal to their sense of reason. "Just because you don't want to learn doesn't mean the person next to you isn't interested," he attempts.

Yeah, except they *know* the person next to them isn't interested.

He tries negotiating. "You give me what I want, which is for you to sit down and be quiet, and I won't summon Principal Roberts."

They don't care. Bring him.

He tries threats. "Okay, that's it. I'm taking names." The entire class, except me, does exactly what they want for the whole period. And I'm guessing Victor—like most substitute teachers who venture into the high school system—won't be back tomorrow.

In the wrong circumstances, one hour can feel like a week. Today's biology class has dragged on forever. When the bell finally rings, Spam bolts out of her seat and heads for the door. I don't even try to catch up with her.

Instead, I catch a ride home with Journey. I want to talk to him about the blowup with Spam, but there's no time. He's frantic over not being able to find his cell phone.

"I'm 100 percent certain that I put it in my locker after lunch," he says. "And it's not there."

"Maybe it slipped between some books or something."

"Impossible. I completely emptied my locker," he says.

"We can go back. I'll help you look for it," I say.

"I can't," he says. "I have to start my new job in twenty minutes."

"Aggh. Sorry. Do you want to take my phone?" I say as he pulls into my driveway.

"No. But that's sweet of you." He gives me a quick hug. "I'll figure something out."

We say good-bye and I slip out of the van. I'm not surprised to see that Victor's not home. I wouldn't show my face around here tonight, either. It's at least two hours before Rachel will be home, which gives me some time to go back through my evidence on Chief Culson and see if I missed anything.

I charge up the back stairs and bang open the door with my hip. Rachel is sitting at the kitchen table, which scares the hell out of me.

"I didn't know you were home," I say, once I've recovered from the shock. Rachel parks her car inside the garage, so there's no way I would know. "Are you sick?" To tell the truth, she doesn't look good.

Rachel gives me a warm smile, but that doesn't hide the bags under her eyes. She obviously didn't get much sleep last night. She pulls out the chair next to her and moves a carton of orange juice in front of it. "I'm fine, Erin. Come. Sit down and let's talk."

"Is everything okay?"

"Everything's fine. But I think it's time for us to be 100 percent honest with each other."

Uh-oh . . . the honesty speech. As I move toward the chair, I run through all the lies I've told recently, in order to get my stories straight in my head. Just in case. Maybe Principal Roberts saw Journey and me together and reported it to her. Now I'm going to have to listen to what happens when I break her trust. I cringe inside, while at the same time keeping my expression neutral. "Rachel—I . . ."

"No. Let me go first," she says. "I'm sorry about yesterday. What I said had everything to do with my frustration with my brother and nothing to do with you."

"It's no big deal." I shrug.

"No, it is a big deal," Rachel insists. "You know how I'm always telling you that it's important for us to be honest with each other because we're all we have?"

I keep my gaze down because here it comes. The Journey lecture.

"Well." Her voice trembles. "I'm the one who broke that trust, Erin. Not you."

What? Her eyes are watery and her mouth quivers. I start to protest and she holds up a hand.

"Let me finish before you say anything, okay?"

I nod.

"Charles Culson and I have been friends a very long time. He was one of Victor's best friends in high school." She pauses and blows her nose into a Kleenex. "I don't want to go into details about those days, it was a very long time ago." She flashes me a smile. "I felt very grown-up, though, dating my big brother's friend. But then when a problem developed between Charles and me, Victor took my side." She smiles and looks down, picking at her nails. "It's what a good brother is supposed to do."

I wanted Rachel to open up. But this much all at once is making me squirm. Is this Rachel's version of Victor's "I'll tell you my secrets and you tell me yours"? I shudder just thinking about it.

Rachel looks toward the ceiling, summoning the courage to continue. "But a few years later, when your mother was murdered and my own brother didn't even come home for her funeral, Charles was there for me every moment of every day."

I suck in a sharp gasp of air. In the entire time Rachel and I have been together, I've never heard her say the m-word in front of me. Not once.

It's a showstopper.

Rachel studies my face. "I'm sorry," she says. "I shouldn't have been so blunt."

"It's okay." I take her hand to support her, but my voice is shaky.

"It's not okay." She switches it around so that she's holding my hand. "All those years, when I was taking you from one therapist to another, well, I was seeing one, too. In fact, I'm still seeing one."

Wow. Apparently, everyone in this house is keeping secrets.

"You're not the only one with survivor's guilt." She examines her nails again. "Your mother was my very best friend. She was like a sister. She's gone, and I got to live her life. I got to raise you."

I, of course, knew this. But this is the first time Rachel's admitted it. I prop my elbow on the table and rest my chin on my hand, anything to control the tremors taking over my body.

"I was so lucky to have you, Erin. You are—and have always been—the sun and the moon and the stars in my life. You were such a gift, and I felt compelled to do it right. No mistakes. I wanted to make up for everything you lost. I wanted your life to be perfect. That's why I'm so protective . . . and it's why I can't talk about her." She lowers her head. "I feel guilty for every breath I get to have that she didn't."

I squeeze her hand. "Rachel . . . I . . ."

Her expression is intense. "There's more. When Charles . . . um, you know, Chief Culson and I started dating again a year ago, I hid it from you. I'm the one who broke our trust, Erin. Not you."

Trust is a very strange word.

Every day I do things I can't tell Rachel about, and she does things that she can't tell me about. I think I'm protecting her and she thinks she's protecting me. For a brief moment, I consider confessing everything, including the box and the DNA/dad investigation that led me to find Miss P's body. Getting it all out in the open would be transformative for me. I even think for a wild moment that Rachel will understand and want to help. But then I see the pain and longing in her face to rewrite history, and I decide not to go there.

I don't know why she thinks I wouldn't want her to date. If anything, it's the exact opposite. I used to wish she would date just so she wouldn't be so focused on me all the time. It's not a good thing to be someone's sun, moon, and stars. Rachel needs to spread that intensity around a little.

I slowly become aware that while I've been processing stuff in my head, she's been waiting for me to say something back.

"Don't worry about me. I'm good," I say. "And I really think it's great that you have someone—" I catch myself, almost saying "someone, too." But she doesn't seem to notice.

Her face brightens like the sun breaking through a thick bank of clouds. "You mean it? You won't mind if I start dating someone . . . well, not someone." She actually giggles. "Charles. You won't mind if I start openly dating him?"

I don't know what to think. I want to make Rachel happy but I still have a lot of unanswered questions about him. I choose my words carefully. "If he makes you happy, I'm happy."

She giggles again and I'm struck by how I've never seen this side of Rachel before, which means she must really like him.

"I knew I could count on you, Erin. You are an amazing gem. My life wouldn't be the same without you." She looks at me for a minute, considering. "Now I need your help on an important decision." She jumps up from the table and rushes off to her room. "Don't go away. I'll be right back."

She returns with an elegant black dress on a hanger and two pairs of shoes: one a pair of simple black pumps, and the other a pair of very high, strappy copper sandals with stiletto heels. She stands before me, eyes glistening. "We're going to the opera in Portland tonight. Which shoes should I wear with this dress?"

Wow, high heels *and* the opera. This is so unlike Rachel I hardly know what to say. I'm drawn to the copper sandals because they're sparkly. "I've never seen those before."

"They're Sydney's. Aren't they great? She let me borrow them. With the right jewelry, what do you think?"

I shake my head. "Go with the black. They'll look classy and they'll be more comfortable—look at the heel on those copper ones. Your feet will kill."

Rachel sighs. "You're right. I was willing to suffer for one night, but . . ." She opens the hall closet door and hangs the sandals on one of the hooks. "I'm going to take a bath and get ready. Charles is coming straight from the gym. He'll shower and change here because we have a long drive." She forms a sour face. "I'm hoping we can get out of here before my brother gets home. Will you be okay for dinner? There are leftovers in the fridge."

"Don't worry about me; I have homework to do. I'll just take leftovers up to my room." I pick up my bag and head for the stairs. Rachel stops and comes back.

"Oh, um. Can you do me a favor?"

"Sure, what?"

"Can you work on your homework down here until after we leave? I want Charles to see that you really are okay having him around."

I sigh. "Sure."

# ▸ 34 ◂

The smallest lie will taint the truth.

—VICTOR FLEMMING

I'm sitting at the kitchen table, working my way through an e-mail from Lysa.

Manifesto would be a better word for it.

She says I need to patch things up with Spam. That I must call—not text—her. She's included a list of talking points, all the things she thinks I need to say. She's even outlined how I should say these things and what tone I should use.

Wow. She must think I'm a complete idiot.

I know how to patch things up with Spam. I just need her to understand that the evidence was really confusing and I wasn't ready to talk about it at lunch. I can't just blatantly accuse the chief of police of murder. If it turned out he didn't do it, my credibility, and our evidence, would be shot . . . and if he did, well, he could probably silence all of us and make it look like an accident.

Victor strolls in the back door.

I hate to say it, but he has that beat-down dog look. His collar is open and his shirt is rumpled. He's carrying his briefcase and a large brown shopping bag.

I take pity on him. "Subbing for a high school class is like getting tossed into a pit of snakes."

"That was one tough room." He dumps his stuff on the floor behind his chair and kicks it into the corner. I note how this is more like my behavior than Rachel's. Victor rummages in the refrigerator and comes up with a soda.

"Trust me," he says, joining me at the table. "If you took every piece of evidence that went down in flames after I swore to it in front of a jury . . . and then added every shred of data that I was convinced would reveal some important secret, but didn't . . . if you rolled all of those disasters together, the resulting humiliation wouldn't come close to what it felt like to stand in front of that classroom today." He leans back, tipping the chair on two legs.

"I wanted to help you out, but . . ."

He stretches his arms up over his head. "It wasn't your job, it was mine, and I royally sucked." He tips his head toward Rachel's room. "Is she over her snit yet?"

I shrug. "More or less."

"Can you believe she's dating Chuck Culson? I mean, c'mon. Rachel still looks great . . . and he's . . ."

Victor presses his fingers to his face and pulls the skin down to resemble a melted mask. He stops when he hears Rachel coming. She steps into the kitchen and nearly takes my breath away. She has makeup on and her hair flows around her shoulders. She looks gorgeous. She's even wearing perfume. She frowns at Victor.

"I need you to be nice tonight, and if you can't, you need to leave. It's that simple."

Victor throws his hands in the air. "I'll be nice. You didn't even have to ask."

Just then the front doorbell rings. All three of us stiffen.

Rachel hurries to answer it. Victor and I listen as she invites Chief Culson inside. Victor grimaces when he hears them kiss. I have to fight back a giggle. As they enter the kitchen, Victor pops out of his chair and offers his hand.

"Hey, Chuck. Good to see you again so soon."

The chief is holding a garment bag in one hand and a pair of wing tips in the other. He shrugs helplessly, unable to return Victor's handshake. He's dressed casually in sweats.

"Oh yeah, hey, no handshake, no sweat," Victor says, withdrawing his hand. "But then, you look like you just came from the gym, so maybe there *is* sweat." Rachel and the chief just stand there as Victor cracks himself up.

He looks at me. "Get it—no sweat . . . sweat?"

I don't want to take obvious sides here, but I can't just let Victor hang. I offer up my palm. "Got it. High-five."

The chief mumbles something lame to me about homework. I smile and agree. Then he asks for a glass of water so I get up and get him one. With that, Rachel leads him off to her room. She pauses at the door. "He's going to take a quick shower and then we'll be out of your hair for the night."

"Roger that," I say, and return to my homework.

▾ ▾ ▾

When Rachel and the chief return to the kitchen about thirty minutes later, they shine. And not just because of their dressy clothes. They seem really happy, especially Rachel.

Victor stands, sliding his hands into his pockets. "You look beautiful, sis."

"She does, doesn't she?" the chief says as he crosses the kitchen and sets his water glass on the counter next to the sink. "Don't wait up for us. We'll be late."

As they leave through the back door, I'm watching Victor.

He stays quiet and tilts his head, listening for their car to leave. As soon as they're gone, he leaps up and claps his hands together. "Okay, let's get to work."

I let the surprise register on my face.

He stops. "Wait. What am I thinking? First, where do you stand with your homework?"

"Done."

"Good. When I planned this I thought we'd have to work up in your attic, but since they're gone, we can work down here."

I blink a few times. "Work?"

"Yeah. What are you waiting for? Grab that evidence box and let's get busy."

"Which one?" I ask.

"The bio teacher."

My heart pounds as I race up the stairs toward my attic. It sounds like it's going to be an interesting night. By the time I return with the shoe box containing all of the evidence I've gathered about Miss Peters's murder, Victor has cleared the table. He rummages in his briefcase and pulls out a handful of buccal swabs. "Know what these are?" he asks.

"Elephant Q-tips," I say, adding a sassy grin so he'll know I'm kidding.

He holds a giant lollipop-sized Q-tip up next to his ear and makes a funny creaking noise.

"Buccal swabs. All the forensic TV shows use them for getting DNA samples from inside someone's mouth. Miss P even had some," I say.

"Correct," Victor cheers. "So, do you have any idea what I have in mind, Erin?"

"Something to do with DNA would be my guess."

"That's my star pupil." He snaps his fingers at me. "Where's your notebook with the DNA results from Miss Peters's computer?"

His urgency prods me into action. I grab my notebook and flip to the correct page before handing it over to him.

Victor points. "We'll need pizza, extra cheese and any toppings you like. You call it in and I'll pay for it. Then I'll give you the full rundown of our agenda for the evening."

He had me at "star pupil" but pizza's not a bad bribe, either.

I use speed dial to order a large ham and pineapple with extra cheese. When I'm done, I curl my leg under me on the chair and sit back to watch.

Victor paces the room, rubbing his palms together. "For starters," he says. "Fancy pens aside, I don't buy your theory of Chuck Culson as a murder suspect. Because if I did, I wouldn't have let my sister leave with him." He squints. "Where were they going again?"

"Portand. To the opera."

He tosses his head, expressing a clear lack of excitement. "Okay. You have no motive *and* Chuck has a pretty solid alibi for that night from Rachel, someone we believe is ironclad credible. . . . Wouldn't you agree?"

I nod. If Rachel says she was with Chief Culson when Miss Peters was killed, I wouldn't dream of questioning her.

"But last night Rachel admitted she has been concealing this relationship. You knew nothing about the two of them, correct?"

"Zip," I confirm. "That night she went to bed early, saying she thought she was coming down with the flu. I felt bad that the police had to call her to come to the station. But when she got there, she didn't seem sick at all."

"Aha. You see? Alibis are hard enough to prove, but combine them with a lie and you have a problem with motivation.

Why was the person lying to begin with, and why should we believe them now? Even the tiniest lie will eventually taint the truth."

He's not talking about me, but I feel the weight of his words. Hopefully, he won't pick up the guilt rays I'm radiating. "So, what are you saying?"

"I'm saying that part of your theory is flawed. But the other part is genius—dabbling with DNA testing probably did get your teacher killed," he says. "So tonight we're going to try to re-create her DNA test and see what it tells us."

"Wow." I'm about to fall over in a dead faint . . . or float to the ceiling and bob there out of extreme bliss. Watching Victor actually do a DNA test = mind-blowing.

There's even an extra side of surreal because I know most of the steps he'll be taking before he takes them. I just can't believe he's doing it with me.

"I'm just going to throw this together quickly, so if you have any questions or want me to explain anything don't be afraid to ask." Victor moves around the kitchen gathering supplies: a pitcher, measuring cups, spoons. He dumps them at one end of the table.

My guilt is starting to weigh me down. Victor's treating me like an equal, but I'm still holding back information. I decide I'll tell him about the strip of fabric and the link between the murders *after* we finish running the DNA.

I don't want anything to detract from this moment. I slide my chair closer to Victor. "I want to write down each step." I open my notebook. "What will re-creating her test tell us?"

He drags a shopping bag over next to his chair and starts unloading things onto the table. "The first thing we try to do in a murder investigation is come up with a profile of the victim's behavior and activities that occurred in the days or hours right before she was killed. You had the right instincts about the DNA samples in the refrigerator. If we can duplicate that and match even one or two of the profiles from her test, it will tell us something about what she was thinking and the evidence you've been gathering."

"So, we're going to the lab at school?"

"Nope. We're going to do it right here," Victor says, wiggling his eyebrows.

"But I thought you said it required special equipment and a bunch of stuff to pull off an accurate DNA test."

Victor raises his hand. "Yeah, for the don't-try-this-at-home crowd. But I am a trained professional. I've pulled off many a field DNA test in a hotel room and even once in the trunk of a Lincoln. It's tricky, but possible."

"So where do we start?"

He grabs a buccal swab in each hand. "I have one for you . . . and one for your boyfriend." He pins me in a serious gaze. "I'm assuming Rachel's edict fell on deaf ears and he's still your boyfriend. Can you lure him over?"

My cheeks flame. I think he just officially became my boyfriend today. "You're a bad influence. But actually Journey started a new job today so he probably can't come."

Just then the front doorbell rings.

Victor and I exchange surprised looks for a second.

"Right, pizza!" Victor hurries to the door and I follow. I wasn't expecting that because our normal pizza guy always comes to the back door. Victor swings the door open and Journey is standing there, holding a stay-warm pizza-delivery box.

"Somebody order pizza?" He flashes me a crooked grin.

I'm stunned. "You didn't tell me," I say.

"It was supposed to be a surprise," Journey says. "I know Papa John's is your favorite."

Victor rubs his hands together. "Erin, look who's here." He ushers Journey inside. "We were just talking about you. Come in. Come in."

Journey looks adorable in his uniform, a white coat with a bright green armband bearing the logo for our neighborhood Papa John's Pizza. He unsheathes two boxes from the wrapper. Victor rummages in his pockets for money.

"Will twenty-five bucks cover it?" Victor asks, shoving bills into Journey's hand.

"Oh yeah. Let me get you some change," Journey says.

"No. Keep it." Victor insists.

"Why didn't you tell me you were delivering pizza to my house?" I ask.

"I lost my phone, remember?" Journey says.

"Oh, right." I inspect the boxes in Victor's hand. "Um, I only ordered one pizza. Ham and pineapple."

"For real?" Journey makes a face. "Who eats pineapple on pizza? The second one is mine—which I didn't charge you for. It's time for my dinner break and I thought maybe we could eat together." He smiles at me. "But if I shouldn't be here, no worries. I can always eat in the van."

"Your timing is perfect." I take the pizzas from Victor and lead the way into the kitchen. "Victor just asked me to get you over here anyway."

Victor and Journey follow me in and take seats around the table.

While I get out plates, napkins, and drinks, Victor gives Journey a thumbnail of what we're getting ready to do. I notice that he chooses to leave out the part about Chief Culson.

Victor unwraps a buccal swab and holds it by the outside paper. He offers it to Journey. "I know this requires some trust, but would you mind giving me a DNA sample? I promise I'll only use it to compare with the results Erin found on your teacher's computer. Nothing else."

Journey shrugs and takes the swab. He scrubs it around the inside of his mouth. Victor hands one to me and I do the same. When we're done, we pass the swabs back to Victor and he pops each of them into a test tube with a stopper at the end and marks each one with our initials.

As exciting as it is to actually see how this stuff works, there's also a sinking sadness that always creeps in. "What about Miss Peters? We can't get a sample from her."

Victor slides the test tubes around on the table. "True. But I met with her sister today and asked her for a sample. It's called familial DNA. So, while it won't be an exact match, we will be able to confirm if one of the original samples was hers."

"Are you working on her murder case?" Journey asks, scooping up a slice of pepperoni and sausage pizza.

"You could say I'm consulting. Unofficially," Victor says.

He lifts the lids on both pizza boxes and takes a long look. "Sorry, Erin." He chooses a slice from Journey's meat-laden pizza and ferries it to his plate. "There is one more thing. . . ." Victor pulls a plain folder out of his briefcase, lays it on the table, and flips through, avoiding smudging pizza grease on any of the papers. He finds a photo and spins it out of the folder and onto the table in front of Journey. "What can you tell me about this?"

Journey folds his slice of pizza taco-style. The photo is a close-up of the side view of the sole of a well-worn Michael Jordan mid-top basketball shoe. "That's a photo of my right basketball shoe," he says, reaching for a napkin.

"How can you be sure?" Victor prods.

"Well . . ." Journey uses his little finger to indicate an area near the toe of the shoe. "See that spot where it's more dirty and worn than the rest of the sole? It's kind of an OCD thing, but when I line up a shot I scrape my right foot on the court three times. My shoes always wear out there first."

I lean over Victor's shoulder. "They gave you the evidence from Miss Peters's murder?" I'm practically drooling.

"Easy there, Sherlock." Victor gives me a pointed look over his shoulder. "I asked for copies of *some* of the photos." He slides another photo out for Journey's view. This one is a close-up of the bottom of the right shoe. There's a two-inch-long smooth spot right at the spot Journey identified.

Victor slides the photos back into his file. "Okay. That's consistent with the report."

"There's a report? What's it say?" Journey gives me a wary glance. I know he's worried, but Lysa told us his shoes came up clean.

"It says . . ." Victor paws through the pages for the report. Once he finds it, he gives Journey a straight, hard look. "And, for the record, this came from my department at the FBI. It says that the shoe prints found in the blood in the victim's house *are* consistent with this exact style and size of shoe."

A knot of worry develops in my stomach and I push my pizza aside. My gaze stays on Journey's face. He blinks a few times, swallows hard, and licks his lips. "Why would the FBI do a report on *my* shoes?"

"Because Sydney probably sent your shoes to the FBI so they would analyze them as part of the evidence, right?" I look to Victor for confirmation.

"She's right. The FBI is available to local PDs, who don't

have crime labs, to process and analyze evidence. So anyway, about *your* shoes . . ." Victor continues. "It was determined that the prints did not come from this exact shoe."

I breathe out a sigh of relief. Journey's shoulders relax as well.

"Good news, of course. But how do they know for sure that it wasn't Journey's shoe?" I ask.

"Because the shoe that left the prints had a faint kidney-shaped smear on the outside of the right shoe, but it was lower, more toward the heel. The smooth spot on Journey's shoe is at the top, near his big toe." Victor points out the areas as he talks about them. "Also, just so you know, your shoe was tested for blood residue and it came up negative."

"So, if you knew it wasn't a match, why did you ask Journey to identify his shoes?"

"I was spot-checking to see if the evidence was what they said it was."

Journey and I share measured smiles across the table. It sounds like this issue with his shoes is settled.

# 35

Intentionally withholding or destroying evidence in a legal proceeding can result in dire consequences.

—VICTOR FLEMMING

After we finish eating, Victor cleans up the kitchen while I walk Journey out to his van to say good-bye.

"Your uncle's cool," Journey says, leaning back against his van. He rests his arms on my shoulders and pulls me to him. I lay my head against his chest. I listen to the faint thrum of his heartbeat and wish I could sync mine with his. Mine is racing. I've never been close to another person this way, except maybe Rachel.

"Yeah, he is." I drift into Journey's circle of warmth, loving how his fingers twist the very tips of my hair.

"Maybe he'll solve this thing and we can stop worrying about psycho killers."

"Mmm. That would be nice," I whisper.

Journey moves me away from his body so he can look at my face. "Have you told him about the—you know—connection?"

"Not yet." I step back. "But I think I should. What do you think?"

Journey pulls me back against his chest. "I think we're safer if you don't tell."

"Why?" I pop my head back again, studying his face.

"Because that connection between the two murders is the one thing no one else knows. Even the killer doesn't know we know it," Journey says. "And, since we're not sure who we can trust, I think we should keep it that way."

"Except we know we can trust Victor."

"Probably. Yeah." Journey rakes a hand through his hair, sweeping it off his forehead. "But can we trust who Victor would tell?"

I haven't discussed my suspicions about Chief Culson with Journey, but I see what he's saying. If I give the tie to Victor, he'll tell Rachel and she'll tell the chief. Even though Victor thinks he's safe, I'm still not so sure.

"That makes sense." I de-stress by forcing the air out of my lungs and then taking in a long deep breath. Thoughts of possible motives for murder used to be a silent dark knot that lived quietly inside me. It was not something I ever talked about openly. I don't have to hide any of this from Journey, which is a relief. But our lives would be better if we didn't have to worry about it at all.

Journey pulls me to his chest again and rests his cheek on top of my head. "I have to get back to work." He whispers this into my hair. In one swift move he pecks me on the cheek and climbs into the van. "I'll call you later."

The van finally rattles to a start on the third try and he backs down the driveway toward the street.

"How?" I wrap my sweatshirt a little tighter around me, my voice buried by the rumble of the van. "You lost your phone." I watch him back into the street and pull away.

Returning to the kitchen, I find Victor in full-fledged field

DNA test mode. The table is littered with all kinds of stuff and he's slumped in his chair, going through my notebook. I take a seat.

Victor sets the notebook aside. "So we know your bio teacher collected samples from you and from Journey. And, I can maybe buy that she would put herself in the mix, too. Can you see her doing that?"

"Definitely. Miss Peters used to say we are our own best test subjects."

Victor gnaws on a hangnail. "So, if she had a degree in forensic chemistry, she probably knew what her own DNA string looked like."

"We all knew what it looked like," I say with a laugh. "She had it blown up, framed, and hung on the wall."

"She included her own DNA in order to validate the test. That's logical," he says.

"She was a stickler for things like that. I can hear her voice in my head. 'Always include a control sample.' "

"She's her own control sample. I'll buy that." Victor stabs the notebook with his pen. "I don't expect to match the last sample because we don't have enough information. But let's say CC indicates it was Chuck. Why would she include him?"

"Because . . . she wanted to impress him, show him she could do it."

Victor points at me. "You really are my star pupil." He thinks for a minute. "It's too bad we can't get a sample of Chuck's DNA, because then we could settle your theory once and for all."

Victor stops and gives me a wide-eyed look.

Which is funny, because I'm giving him the very same look.

Two great minds . . .

Both of our heads swivel to the counter next to the sink and land on one plain, gleaming, half-full glass of water.

We leap up and make it to the sink in a matter of steps. Neither of us touches the glass, but we both know it contains the chief's DNA.

"Looks like we'll get to test your theory after all." Victor returns to the table and slides my notebook over to me. "Clean page, write this down: today's date . . . gel test. Samples one through four. We'll label them the same as Peters's. That glass on the counter will be CC."

Victor shoves all the crap to one side of the table and grabs an unread newspaper from our recycling stack. He unfolds it, covering half of the table. "My lab table has a stainless steel top, easy to clean and sanitize," he explains, "but out in the field we use newspapers. Here's a lesson for you: An unread newspaper is sterile. Want to know why?" He doesn't wait for my answer but keeps talking. "Because printing presses get up to about one hundred and thirty degrees. That's enough to kill most bacteria."

"Wow, that's *news* to me." I giggle.

Victor groans.

I peer into his open briefcase. "You carry around the stuff to run DNA in your briefcase?"

"I do for certain things, like the agarose gel and buccal swabs. But the rest of this stuff I picked up at the superstore on the way home. They sell everything there."

"So, it's just normal stuff?"

"Pretty much." Victor reaches into the bag and pulls out a brick-sized chunk of green foam, which he sets in the middle of the table. "Like floral foam, for example."

"You're going to use that?"

"It makes a perfect test tube rack."

I peer over the edge of his shopping bag. "You found test tubes at the superstore?"

He smiles. "The buccal swabs come with their own tubes."

"Oh. Good to know."

He ticks a list off on his fingers. "But I will also need rubbing alcohol, tape, a sharp craft knife, some aluminum foil, and, oh yeah, baking soda and a pitcher."

While I gather the requested items from various places in the kitchen, Victor twists open an unused swab kit. He then retrieves the glass we saw Chief Culson drink from. He hoists it to me and we nod to each other—a silent confirmation that we agree this was the chief's glass.

Victor vigorously runs the swab along the rim of the glass, first along the inside and then the outside. When he's finished, he drops the swab into the test tube. He lines up each of the samples by sticking them into the block of floral foam.

"Okay, these samples are in the same order of Miss Peters's test."

I give him a raised-eyebrow look. "There has to be more to it than that."

"There is. I'm just going to power through. Stop me if you have questions, or you can just sit back and watch."

I prop one leg up on the chair to rest my notebook against. "Best show in town."

He shakes some baking soda into the pitcher and then sloshes in some distilled water from a bottle in his shopping bag.

"How much did you put in? That didn't look very precise," I say.

"It doesn't have to be. I'm just making an alkaline buffering solution." He rummages to the bottom of his shopping bag and retrieves a small testing kit for home aquariums. He scoops a bit of the buffering solution into the kit, adds a few drops of something red, and shakes it. Then he holds it up to the light and analyzes the results. "Close enough," he mutters. He puts the lid on the pitcher and hands it to me. "Stick this in the fridge and put the alcohol in the freezer."

Victor upends his shopping bag over the table, dumping out the rest of his purchases. It's a bizarre assortment. A small plastic container about the size of half of a sandwich, and a smaller plastic soap dish, with a flimsy, hinged lid. Two small spools of electrical wire: one red, one black. Two packages of alligator clips, some wire strippers, six 9-volt batteries, and a bottle of meat tenderizer.

"Guess what this is?"

"Junk on sale that you couldn't resist?"

Victor chuckles. "I like the sense of humor. It's cute. This, my star pupil, is our electrophoresis chamber. Or it will be once we build it. Now pay attention. You don't want to miss anything."

# 36

Fifty percent of human DNA is identical to the DNA of a banana.

—VICTOR FLEMMING

Victor's right. I don't want to miss any of this.

"I don't know how much you know about running gel," he says. "So I'll just skim the basics."

"Pretend I don't know anything. Tell me everything." I scoot my chair in close.

"The test is called electrophoresis. It's a process that uses electrical current to move particles through a fluid or, in our case, a gel."

Victor snaps the lid off of the plastic soap dish then uses the knife to carve away each end, creating a U-shaped shell. He holds it up and rotates it. "This is the gel casting tray. The gel goes in here." He picks up a slightly larger plastic container. "This is the buffering chamber." He demonstrates how the smaller tray fits inside the larger one. "That alkaline solution I put in the fridge goes in here."

I make a quick sketch of these items in my notebook and label them.

Victor rips into the packages of wire, cuts off an eight-inch piece of red and one of black, and then proceeds to strip off the coating at each end and attach the shiny copper tips to the alligator clips.

"It's starting to look electrical." I remember the new equipment in Miss P's lab. There was a clear acrylic tray that had similar red and black wires attached to it.

Victor sets the wires aside and creates two strips of aluminum foil, which he folds over each end of the buffering chamber. "The aluminum foil makes the contact point on the buffering chamber," he says.

He clips a black wire over the foil at one end of the chamber and the red wire over the foil at the other end. "Black is negative and red is positive." He sets the contraption in the middle of the table. "That is pretty much all there is to an electrophoresis chamber."

I turn it over and inspect it from all angles. It looks exactly like a plastic soap dish inside of a sandwich keeper, wrapped in aluminum foil and wired up. But even though it's primitive, it closely resembles the one I saw shoved aside in Miss Peters's lab. "Why does it need a current?" I ask.

"The current mobilizes the individual DNA strands, moving them through the gel. The smaller the strand the farther it will travel."

"But you don't plug it in, right?" I ask.

"Nope. Six nine-volt batteries will run this baby in about forty-five minutes." Victor unwraps the economy pack of 9-volt batteries and builds a little battery pyramid—three batteries on the bottom (tops up) and two batteries on top (tops down) all plugged in to one another. This arrangement leaves one terminal open on each end. "In the field test you can't always rely on having available power," he explains. "So, you need an alternative."

I sketch his battery arrangement in my notebook. "I didn't know you could plug one battery into another."

"It's called connecting them in series." Victor touches the alligator clips. "I won't do it now, but all I have to do is clip the red side to the positive terminal on your stack of batteries and the black side to the negative terminal and voilà, electrical current."

I check the time on my phone. It's still early; Rachel and the chief are probably just arriving at the opera. We have plenty of time.

"Now we make the agarose gel." Victor is standing near the microwave and mimes a slight mad-scientist expression as he tears open a small envelope of powder he retrieved from his briefcase. He taps the contents into a glass measuring cup that already contained distilled water. He stirs the two ingredients together for a minute then holds up the cup for my inspection.

"It's cloudy," I say, wrinkling my nose.

He pops the measuring cup into the microwave and heats it for a few seconds.

"We actually have to melt it to be sure all the particles are removed," Victor says.

While the cup containing the gel is heating, I notice Victor applying tape to the open ends of the soap dish. "Wait. You just cut that off. Was that a mistake?"

"Hey. You're paying atttention," Victor says. "I like that." He holds the plastic tray up, gesturing to how it is formed. "Remember, I said this is the gel casting tray. When we run the test the ends need to be open so the current can pass through the gel. But we need to tape the end until the gel forms into a solid."

The microwave dings and he removes the measuring cup and pours the melted mixture into the tray. "This'll take thirty minutes to set up," he says. "Now we prep the samples."

While Victor messes around with the buccal swabs and test tubes, I page back in my notebook, reviewing the notes I've made. "I had no idea there were so many steps."

"Fortunately, I don't have to run DNA every day. But in my lab I have a lot of high-tech stuff that streamlines this process," he says.

I watch as he uses a drinking straw to pipe the buffering solution into the first two tubes. Then he hands me the straw and I add it to the last two tubes. "So what do you do every day?" I ask.

Victor shrugs. "Solve mysteries any way I can . . . and go to meetings." He rolls his eyes. "You have no idea how many meetings. By the way, here's one for you: Did you know human DNA is 50 percent identical to the DNA of a banana?"

"Is that why bananas are so a-peeling?"

Victor groans and chuckles. "Enough with the puns. That one stunk up the room."

I laugh along with him, all the while contemplating how this kind of casual, silly, hanging-out fun is what normal families do. But it's not something that comes naturally to Rachel and me. She's loving and concerned and protective, but there's always a barrier. We just never seem to get real with each other. Clearly, Victor's just being Victor and I'm just being Erin and we're just here hanging out together, running DNA and making up bad puns. But this feels completely real.

He puts a few drops of dishwashing detergent into one of the test tubes and then plunges the swab up and down, scraping and scrubbing it along the sides of the test tube.

"You're getting kind of aggressive there."

"This isn't a gentle process. In the lab I'd put it in a blender," he says.

After he's soaped, scraped, and ravaged all four swabs, he sprinkles a few grains of meat tenderizer into each tube. I pick up the bottle so I can add it to my notes. I can't resist giving him a strange look. "Meat tenderizer?"

Victor grins. "What is meat?"

I shrug. "Food?"

"It's protein. In order to run it, we need to free the strands of DNA from the protein. Meat tenderizer destroys protein." Victor makes an explosive gesture with his hands. "Boom. The DNA is left behind."

"Wow. You should have been rapping on this stuff in biology today. People might have paid attention."

"I have analyzed my performance in the classroom at least a hundred times. If I were to do it again I would approach the whole thing differently." He puts out a hand. "Alcohol, please."

I retrieve the alcohol from the freezer and set it on the table.

"You're going to do this part," he says. "Use the straw and float a small amount of alcohol on top of each of these tubes. By floating, I mean very slowly drizzle the alcohol down the side, so that it doesn't sink, but floats on top of the buffer."

I push the bottle of alcohol back to him. "You better do it. I might screw it up."

"You got this. Just go slow," he insists.

I wonder where his confidence in me is coming from. Nonetheless, I take a deep breath and add the alcohol to the first tube. It's nerve-wracking, but I do it. By the last tube, I'm handling it like a total pro.

Victor's final purchase from the superstore is a package of long, thin wooden skewers. He uses the skewers to show me how the DNA floats up in the tube right to the point where the buffering solution and the alcohol meet. With a skewer, he pulls up a small ball of milky white goo that almost looks like snot.

"And there you go," he says. "You just successfully extracted DNA."

Blink. Blink. I'm amazed, yes. And a little grossed out, too. Because the essence of life looks like it came out of someone's nose.

# 37

Fingerprints and eyewitness testimony will connect a suspect to a crime scene, but if you want to really make it stick, find their DNA.

—VICTOR FLEMMING

The gel is set. The DNA extracted. The chamber's wired up, loaded, and ready to go. I should be on-the-edge-of-my-seat excited about this—and I am. But I'm also obsessing about Journey. It's weird not to be able to text him or send him a Snapchat and get an answer back.

This isn't normal. I'm extracting DNA and still can't stop thinking about *him*.

"You seem quiet," Victor says. "Are you okay with all of this?"

"Yes. All of this is amazing. I was just thinking about Journey, that's all."

"He seems like a pretty nice guy." Victor rummages in his briefcase, retrieving his notebook. "What is it that you like about him?"

My face turns pink. I didn't expect that question. This boyfriend stuff is still pretty new to me. "Um, I guess I like that he's not afraid of me."

Victor does a slight tick with his head. "Why would anyone be afraid of you?"

"You know, afraid of who I am . . . my history. Everything I've been through. People ask about you, about your family. But when you tell them what I tell them, they get weird. That didn't happen with him." I think for a minute. "It also didn't happen with you."

"I'm glad," he says, giving me a heartfelt look. "Because you are a delightful and brilliant young lady. My only regret is that I took so long to meet you." He rubs his hands together, viewing the setup on the table. "Okay. We're all set. You ready?"

"No. I'm not ready at all," I joke.

"Let 'er rip." He motions for me to hook the alligator clips to the batteries. Within seconds, bubbles form in the buffering solution. "See those bubbles?" Victor asks. "That tells us it's working."

Now we wait.

Victor brews a pot of coffee and I make my favorite dessert, a vanilla ice cream and orange juice float. Then Victor busies himself by organizing the contents of his briefcase. He sets out a bag of disposable rubber gloves and a fingerprint kit. I place my crime-scene kit on the table next to his. I, too, have gloves, a fingerprint brush, lifting tape, and cards. I click the switch and shine my ultraviolet penlight at him.

"Where'd you get all of that stuff?" he asks.

"The Internet . . . or just around the house."

Victor holds a small spray bottle between his thumb and index finger. "Bet you don't have any of this." He spins it so I can read the label.

"Luminol!" I've wanted to play with this stuff forever.

"I'll show you how it works." He grabs a clean wooden skewer and pokes his finger, drawing a small spot of blood.

I cringe. "Dude, no."

He scans the kitchen for something to wipe it on. Finally,

he kneels down next to a strip of tile by the door and squeezes his finger. A couple fat drops of blood roll out and splatter on the floor. "I'll clean this up with water and show you what happens."

He scrubs the spot with a wet paper towel. "It looks clean, right?" But then he spritzes luminol onto a swab and runs it over the area. The tip of the white cotton turns bright blue. "Bam! Blood evidence."

I jump out of my chair and do a little flailing-arms dance. "I'm not going to lie, that was impressive."

"It's very sensitive, too," Victor explains, tucking the luminol back into his briefcase.

"You have to promise me that you'll do that again for Spam and Lysa and Journey. Pleeeease?"

Victor chuckles. "No problem."

While he finishes organizing his stuff, I run upstairs and get my laptop, checking again for Journey, but he's still not online.

At the thirty-minute mark, Victor points out some early bands forming in the gel. They look like ragged slashes of dark color across the clear gel.

Wow. It's really working.

"When this is done, I'll stain it with a blue solution and the bands will show up even better." He keeps an eye on the process while skimming through my notebook. He zeros in on my notes about the footprint in my bedroom. "I'm impressed that you took the initiative to go to a shoe store to find the style and size of shoe that matched the print you found in your room. That's some excellent detective work."

"It didn't lead to anything, though."

"That doesn't mean it won't at some point. You have to follow up on everything, and you did."

"What do you do when you can't figure out how something fits in?"

Victor shrugs. "Some things never drop into place, so at the end of the day you have to accept that they don't count. That they were scene, not crime. You just hope that you get enough clues that do count."

It's been about forty-five minutes since we started running the gel. Victor turns to the page with Miss Peters's DNA results in my notebook and arranges it next to the chamber. Then, it's as if he sees something he hadn't seen before. He places his hands on either side of the chamber and notebook and leans in, studying them both.

I sit up. "What is it?"

Victor's reaction is small, but I pick up the signs anyway. He rolls his lips together and tightens his jaw. His coffee refill is forgotten. He stares at the process for a long time. After a while he lifts the notebook and studies it by itself.

I stare at the chamber from across the table, but of course it just looks like a big blob to me. I stay quiet for as long as I can. Finally, I'm about to burst. "Did we get a match?"

Victor is distracted. He disconnects the chamber from the batteries and slides the gel out onto a plate. He takes it to the sink and runs water over it.

"The swabs from you and Journey match," he says. "So you were right about them. And it looks like we were right about Miss Peters, too."

"What about Chief Culson?"

Victor brings the plate back to the table and retrieves a small, dark blue bottle from his briefcase. He squirts a few drops of that over the wet gel. "No match to Chuck."

There's something edgy in Victor's manner. "You're not lying to me, are you?"

He gives me a straight-on look but doesn't deny anything.

I'm not sure he's lying, but I'm 100 percent positive he's not telling me the whole truth.

Victor pulls a small ultraviolet flashlight from his briefcase and shines it over the gel. Then he stuffs everything back into his briefcase and carries it to the closet. He grabs his jacket. "I'm going out for about an hour."

I reach for my jacket, too. "I'll go with you."

"You should stay here."

"Why?" My voice is high-pitched and worried.

Victor gives my shoulder a gentle squeeze. "Erin. Trust me. Everything's fine. I just want to run over to the station to check on a couple of things."

"But . . . what about our tests and everything?"

Victor takes the entire floral foam holder with the samples and sticks it into the freezer. "Just leave everything on the table; it'll be fine."

"This stuff can't be here when Rachel gets home. She'll flip."

"Don't worry." Victor pauses at the back door. "I'll be back before Rachel gets home. They're going to be late, remember?"

I'm boiling with emotion, but keep my face blank. "I'll stay in the car."

"I promise, one hour," he says. My lips tighten, proof that I don't believe him, so he repeats it. "One hour."

And then he's gone.

This sucks.

I've done my homework.

Eaten dinner and dessert.

Run DNA.

Now what?

I call Spam, but her phone goes straight to voice mail. This doesn't surprise me. When she plays her online games at night, she turns off her phone. Lysa's parents have huge issues with her cell phone. She's not allowed to bring it to the table during meals, and no calls after eight o'clock on school nights. I can only reach her through e-mail.

I check my laptop again. Still no Journey online. Lysa's not on, either.

I glance at the clock, hoping Victor will be back soon . . . only to realize he's barely been gone fifteen minutes.

I don't want to think he blew me off. We were getting along so well. Then, out of nowhere, he got that distant look in his eye. I know it very well. It's the same expression I get from most of the adults who have known me since I was little. It says, *I know something terrible happened to you but I'm afraid I won't know what to say if we accidentally start talking about it . . . so I'm never going to ever look you straight in the eye again. Instead, we'll just pretend everything is normal.*

From the very first moment I met Victor, he never gave me that look . . . until tonight. Now I'm pacing the kitchen exactly like him.

He says it helps him think. I think it's making me paranoid.

I have to do something to stay sane for the next forty-three minutes and twelve seconds. I sit down with my shoe box full of evidence and take everything out, one piece at a time.

First, the shoe print from my bedroom. I never focused on it before, but it *is* the right shoe. And even though the heel of the print isn't as clear as the toe, it does kind of look like there's a smooth spot on the lower right-hand side, near the heel.

There's definitely not a smooth spot up by the toe. So for sure this print didn't come from Journey's shoe. Realization mingles with fear because there's a good chance this print was left by the killer! That psycho was bold enough to come into my room late at night. Who would do that? Who *could* do that?

The chief is dating Rachel, which means he knows the inside of our house. He might even have a key. In fact, Rachel admitted that he was here that very night.

The tie that brought Journey and me together links the murders of Miss P and my mother. Only the killer or someone with access to my mother's evidence box would know that. Chief Culson had access to my mother's evidence box.

The fingerprints in Journey's van matched Chief Culson and the ink on the scrap of paper matched his special pen. Even the phone calls Miss Peters received in her final days were mostly from his private line.

Only the DNA didn't match. Or at least that's what Victor wanted me to believe.

Damn! Where is Journey? I check e-mail again. Are they making him work a double shift on his first day?

My frantic mind-hopping takes me from worrying about Journey to remembering that Chief Culson's gym clothes are here. I peek into Rachel's room; the gym bag is on the chair. I bring his shoes out to the kitchen. I'm both surprised and not surprised to see they're also the Michael Jordan brand. What is it with these guys and Michael Jordan shoes?

I'm also not surprised to see they're a size eleven. These guys are all about the same height, so I guess that makes sense. The soles are pretty worn on both shoes so it's hard to tell what a print would look like.

I need to do a test.

I set the shoes on the table while I whip up a batch of fake blood. Miss Peters used fake blood for a class one time on latent evidence. I mix about half a cup of light Karo syrup with a few drops of red food coloring. Yummy.

Where should I do the test? Stamping fake blood on paper won't look the same as a hard surface like a floor. But it has to be a place where Rachel won't kill me if the food coloring stains a little. My choices are the garage or the back patio.

Grabbing the kitchen flashlight, I leave the shoes on the table but bring the fake blood and a couple of Popsicle sticks. As I head down the stairs, my movement activates the motion detector on our outdoor lights. They blink on, startling me and bathing the driveway in twin pools of light.

I freeze. What if the killer's watching me?

No, wait. He's off with Rachel.

Ugh! That makes me feel worse.

Scurrying to the side door of the garage, I swing it open. The creak is a mocking whine and the musty smell engulfs my head like a helmet.

I nervously bounce the flashlight beam around the garage. Everything looks normal. Rachel's Honda Accord is parked in her spot. With my finger I dab a little fake blood on the floor, but the cement is too slick to get a good impression.

The patio it is.

At the farthest edge of the patio, behind the table and umbrella, I take a leaf from the yard, dip it in the blood, and stamp it on the cement.

It leaves a perfect outline of the leaf and all its veins.

I can test Chief Culson's shoe here and, according to Victor, as long as I don't clean the shoe with oxygen bleach I won't even destroy any real blood evidence.

Just as I'm about to stand up, headlights from a car lurch into the driveway. It's moving fast and the brakes make a squealing stop.

I'm relieved because for a second I think it's Victor. Then I recognize the hulking shape of Journey's van. Even better. He can help me do the shoe print. The driver jumps out, leaving the engine running and the headlights on. But it's not Journey. I stare, confused.

Principal Roberts?

Truth be told, I'm relieved to see any adult at this point. And at least he's one I know I can trust. I'm about to throw myself at him when he staggers to the front of the van. His movements are jerky and frantic. He dabs at a dark stain on his forehead. There's a stream of something dark seeping from the side of his lip, too. He presses a bright green rag to it.

Is that blood?

Wow. Now I notice that his hair is disheveled and the shoulder of his sleeve is torn. He scrubs at a spot on his hand with the bright green rag, which I slowly realize isn't a rag at all, but the green delivery-person armband Journey was wearing.

Something's not right.

I duck back down behind the table. That fear I earlier wrote off as crazy paranoia is back like a runaway freight train with no brakes. Victor should be home any minute and I'm not coming out until he gets here.

Just when I think it can't get worse, I notice how the headlights cutting through the decorative rail around our back stairs cast a long, skinny, shadowy cross that points directly to my hiding place.

For my entire life, this image has been the one thing capable of sending me into a full-scale panic attack. But I've worked on it with my therapist. *It's just a shadow, nothing more. Just a shadow.* I repeat the mantra over and over in my head and try to loosen my chest so I can breathe.

Once Principal Roberts finishes cleaning his hand, he tosses the armband into a bush. Taking out his phone, he punches in a number, then waits, agitated, pacing back and forth in front of the van.

"Pick up the phone, Erin," he says out loud, frustrated.

There's a vibration in my pocket, I slip my phone out just enough to view the screen. It's Journey. First, there's an excited flutter. Then I remember—Journey lost his phone. I study Principal Roberts, pacing angrily, phone in his hand, and my stomach sours.

# 38

Footprints and tire tracks can be left on—and also found and lifted from—nearly any surface.

—VICTOR FLEMMING

I'm home alone.

An angry and aggressive Principal Roberts is storming around in my driveway. He looks like he's been in a fight. He has Journey's van *and* cell phone.

I can't find Journey. Rachel's unreachable. Victor is MIA.

I crouch lower behind the table.

Suddenly, Principal Roberts whirls and strides straight toward me. I cower, squeeze my eyes closed, and hope for the best.

The clatter of metal scraping against concrete is deafening.

I peek. He's grabbed a chair from the other side of the table and turned it around to face the back of the house. He sits down with an agitated thump. His rapid foot tapping on the cement mirrors my terrified heartbeat.

Seriously, what the hell?

I quietly turn my phone off. He's sitting close enough to me to hear it if it vibrates, and he might try calling again.

Through the gauzy glass tabletop I watch him inspect his hands. He finds more wounds oozing blood. He pulls a folded square of notebook paper from his pocket and uses it to dab at his wounds. After a few minutes and some frustrated grumbling, he pulls a plastic glove from his pocket and slips it onto his right hand. Then he lurches off the chair and heads for our back stairs, mounting them two at a time. At the top, he wrenches open the door without knocking. "Erin? Rachel?" he calls into the house.

When he doesn't get an answer, he just barges in. Through the window I see him climbing the stairs. I'm shocked. Why is he going up to my room like that?

After a couple of moments, he comes down the stairs. When he exits he's calm, almost happy. He's carrying Chief Culson's shoes. Something flutters from his pocket as he passes in front of me. He's whistling as he climbs into Journey's van, revs the engine a few times, and backs out of the driveway before pulling away.

Once he's gone, I race toward the house, stopping only to pick up the green armband and the paper he dropped. I get inside but my hands are trembling so violently I can hardly secure the lock.

It's nine-twenty. Victor should have been back fifteen minutes ago. At this point I figure I'm entitled to call him, and besides, I have new information.

That man was not the Principal Roberts I know. And why does he have Journey's van and his cell phone? Why would he steal Chief Culson's shoes? Why did he look so beat-up? I turn my phone back on and call Victor. I immediately hear a cell phone ringing nearby.

I open the hall closet. Victor's briefcase is sitting on the floor, the top gaping open. His phone is inside ringing and lighting up. Great. I take it out. He's had seven calls, only one of them mine. I drop the phone back into his case.

Next to Victor's briefcase is a gym bag and, just visible

inside, another pair of white basketball shoes that look to be about the right size.

I grab the shoes and turn them over.

Horizontal rays that cut through a circular tread. These are Victor's shoes and they're also Michael Jordan AJ1s.

Looking at the sole of the right shoe, there's a smooth, kidney-shaped spot near the outer edge, toward the heel. It looks like gum or something sticky got on the sole. The sticky part is nearly worn off now, but the outline of where it was is clearly visible. There's also a faint rust-colored residue along one edge of the shoe.

Shaky, I drop into my seat at the table. I'm instantly stung by a terrible realization. Oh my god. It was Victor! He did it! He killed Miss P. That's why he acted so weird and took off suddenly, because I was going to know.

But wait . . . I wasn't going to know. I don't know how to read DNA stuff. And, Victor wasn't even in Iron Rain until after—

These aren't Victor's shoes.

They belong to Principal Roberts. I remember now, he *loaned* them to Victor.

I lay the shoes and the things Principal Roberts dropped in the driveway out in front of me.

My face is feverish, but my bones have turned to ice. The fear that has been a constant companion my whole life fades. In its place molten anger rises.

Journey's green armband, stretched out and soaked with blood, speaks volumes. I know it's a long shot, but I'm hoping all of this blood belongs to Principal Roberts.

The square of notebook paper twists my insides, too. It's damp, tattered, and spotted with blood. But I instinctively know what it is even before I open it.

It's a handwritten note from Miss P.

*Carl–*

*Just an update. Charles and I have spent a lot of time this week prepping a presentation re: the shared forensic lab concept. Melding our budgets to a common goal is definitely a viable option.*

*I've run some preliminary tests to show the ease and contribution to the community using Erin Blake and Journey Michaels—as you know, their families would greatly benefit from having access to this technology.*

*I even lifted yo from a coffee cup you left in my office—just to see if I could. And it wo ty cool, huh?*

*Laura*

I'm not surprised to see a strip torn out of the middle.

I dig around in my evidence box to find the Ziploc bag containing the scrap of paper I found lodged in Journey's seat belt. It's an exact match, which completes the words: "I even lifted your DNA from a coffee cup you left in my office—just to see if I could. And it worked. Pretty cool, huh?"

Coffee cup.

CC.

Miss P's fatal move must have been testing Principal Roberts's DNA just to prove that she could.

There's only one thing left.

With cold precision I retrieve the bottle of luminol and a swab from Victor's briefcase. I repeat the test that he just demonstrated for me by rubbing the swab on one of the rust-colored spots on Principal Roberts's shoe, then squirting a few drops of luminol onto the tip of the swab.

The swab turns bright blue.

This evidence throws me back to two years old. Vulnerable and alone. I shrink in on myself. What if he comes back? What will I do?

The betrayal is overwhelming, followed by extreme sadness. Somehow I have to grasp that a man I have known and trusted my entire life is responsible for ruining it.

Not once . . . but twice.

I don't know why, but I do now know, without any doubt, that Principal Roberts not only killed Miss Peters and tried to kill me—he also is the one who killed my mother and left my two-year-old self locked up alone with her body.

Why? Why would he do this to me?

I can't reach Victor, but I'm certain Principal Roberts has Journey, no idea why, and I need to get to him before . . . well, I'm not going to think about that. I just need to get to him.

I don't know what happened to Mr. Roberts. But he's reasonable and I'm persuasive. I'm sure I can talk this through with him.

I race up to my room and change clothes: dark jeans, dark turtleneck, tennies, heavy jacket, and knit cap. Ready for anything. Before I leave, I pause in front of my laptop. I quickly send an e-mail to Lysa that just says, *"Something's going down. Call me if you can."* I race downstairs and stuff the shoes, the armband, the note, and the luminol into my bag. I pick up the extra set of keys to Rachel's car, lock up the house, and hurry into the garage.

Information is power, and I'm armed with a buttload of it.

It's nine-thirty and the streets of Iron Rain are quiet as a tomb. The only places still open are clubs and bars. I drive past a few, looking for Victor's bright red rental car. Then I remember he said he was going to check on something at the police station.

I make a U-turn in the middle of the street.

At the station, I park in front and hurry inside. I recognize the sergeant at the desk, but don't remember his name.

He gives me a smile. "What can I do for you, little lady?" I shoot him a smile, too. It's forced, but I don't think he can tell. Then he blinks and gets that look. "Oh. Hey. You're Rachel's daughter, aren't you?" he says.

And there it is, the "I-remember-what-happened-to-you look-away" look.

I sigh. He can't help it.

I offer my hand. "Yes. Hi. I'm Erin."

"Mike," he says, giving my hand a shake.

"Thanks, Mike. Listen, I'm in kind of a hurry. Is my uncle Victor here?"

"The FBI guy?"

"Yeah. He said he was coming over to check on something." I shift from one foot to the other, trying not to panic over how much time this is wasting.

Mike shakes his head. "I haven't seen him, but I just came on half an hour ago."

"Could he be using the computer in a back room or something?"

"I doubt it. It's pretty quiet here tonight, but I'll check." He picks up the phone and dials an extension, says a few words, then looks at me and shakes his head no.

"Okay. Thanks." I whirl and race down the hallway to the door.

Mike calls after me, "Hey. Are you okay?"

"Fine," I say, twisting my hand over my head in an effort at a crazy backward wave. There's no time to explain. I shoot out through the door, allowing it to bang behind me.

I'm really not fine, though. Not fine at all.

The only place I can think to go is to Spam's house. Was it just this afternoon that she said those words to me? *When Journey and Victor bail on you, you'll come crawling back to us.*

With a sigh, I start the car. She won't refuse to help me. Not straight to my face.

▾ ▾ ▾

I race up Spam's stairs to her back door and tap lightly. Mr. Ramos peeks out from behind the curtain. When he sees that it's me, he opens the door. He's in the kitchen in his bathrobe eating ice cream.

"Hi, Mr. Ramos, sorry to come by so late."

"No problem, Erin. She's in the computer room. Pow-pow, pow-pow." He pretends like he's firing a gun with his finger. "She drives me crazy with those games."

"Thanks." I enter Spam's computer room, which looks a lot like command central in the Batcave. Her desk is a wide semicircle with a spot carved in the middle for her to snug up in her desk chair. She has an array of three flat-screen monitors on the desk, two keyboards, and a laptop. And they're all running views of some colorful, altered universe.

"Die!" Spam mutters as her fingers tap her keyboard.

"Spam?"

"Ahh-hahahaha," she crows softly. "Got you. And you."

"Spam?"

She ignores me.

I cross the darkened room and place my hand on her shoulder. She explodes out of the chair and rips off the headphones.

"Erin. You scared the crap out of me."

I press my hands against my chest because I swear it's the only thing keeping my heart inside. "Sorry." I gulp air, trying to catch my breath. "I called your name, but . . ."

She tosses her headphones on the desk. "What's up? You look freaked."

I lean against her chair because my knees are shaking so hard I can hardly stand. "I need your help."

"Okay," she says, patting the chair. "Sit down. We'll talk."

"No time. We have to go."

She stands up. "Where are we going?"

I flail my arms. "I'm not sure. I just know we have to go."

She grabs my hand, pulling me toward a chair. "Explain. Start from the beginning."

I pull her up. "I'll tell you in the car."

She stumbles out the door behind me. The house is dark as we slip through the kitchen. We pause at the back door while she pulls on her red Wellington boots, tucking in the bottom of her red flannel pajama pants with the giant moose heads. She also puts on a heavy coat. Her hand hovers over a garish, hot pink Hello Kitty knitted cap with earflaps and pom-pom kitty ears. I shake my head and she leaves it behind.

I twitch, watching her dig through her purse for her wallet, which she drops into the pocket of her jacket. Then, she drops one cell phone into her pocket and the other one into her boot.

"Let's go."

Once we're in the car, I squeal away from the curb and let the words tumble out. "Principal Roberts killed Miss Peters. I don't know why, but I have proof."

"That's crazy." She frowns. "So, we're going to the police?"

"First, we have to rescue Journey. Then we can bring in the police." I turn the car toward the school.

"What do you mean, rescue Journey?" Spam asks.

"We have to get him away from Principal Roberts before he kills him."

"Wait, what?" Spam's voice quivers. "How are we going to do that?"

"How do you think? I'll distract him and you help Journey escape."

"Wait. Whoa, whoa. I'm a better distracter," she says. "You said you had proof. Why can't we just go to the police?"

"You don't get it. There isn't time to explain this whole mess to someone else. Plus, we don't have a motive. Without that they'll never believe us."

"But how do you know—" she asks.

"Principal Roberts came to my house. He was all bloody, like he'd been in a fight. He's driving Journey's van and using Journey's cell phone. Does that not tell you Journey's in danger?" I swerve around a corner, deciding at the last minute it's the way to go. Then I realize I'm driving in circles. "Do me a favor, look up Roberts's home address on your phone."

Spam glances at my speedometer. "Dude, you're doing sixty in a residential zone. Slow down."

"Address. Now." I stop at a light and look up just as a tow truck zooms through the intersection, towing Victor's rental car.

"Wait, never mind. There goes Victor's car."

"What are you doing?"

I hang a hard left and run the light. "Following it."

# 39

Sometimes evidence comes in the form of strange suspect behavior. It's important to follow your instincts.

—VICTOR FLEMMING

"Why are we following a tow truck?" Spam asks.

"To see where they're taking Victor's car and ask them where Victor is."

"But Journey's van just went the other way," Spam says.

My mouth drops open. "Seriously?"

She points.

I pull an immediate U-turn in the middle of the street and shoot back in the direction we came from.

"You should call Rachel," Spam suggests, gripping the car door.

"Can't. She's at the opera in Portland and her phone is turned off."

"What about Chief Culson? You could ask to talk to him."

"He's with Rachel at the opera."

Spam laughs. "You're kidding, right?"

I take a dip a little too fast and the car bounds up in the air. "Do I look like I'm kidding?"

"No." Spam cinches her seat belt a little tighter.

I'm just about to catch the van when it speeds through a

light on a late yellow. I know if I go through, too, he'll see me. I stop and slam my hand on the dash. But after a couple of seconds, there are no other cars, so I gun it and go straight through on the red.

Out of the corner of my eye, I see Spam give me a look of respect. "High-five." She offers up her palm. "We're Thelma and Louise now."

I follow my gut and muscle Rachel's car through a couple of sharp turns, hoping I'm taking a shortcut. "I never saw that movie."

Spam reaches over and swipes a chunk of hair off my face in a comforting gesture. "I'm actually really glad to know that," she says softly.

I skid into a last-minute turn down an alley, scattering gravel. It's reckless, but my hunch pays off. I'm just in time to catch a glimpse of the van shooting past the alley and turning off the main street onto the deserted road that leads to Journey's house.

"He's going to the cannery. This isn't good."

Spam whistles. "Can we call the police now? That place is creepy . . . not to mention haunted."

I shake my head. "Not yet." If we set one foot in the police station, the first thing they'll do is set Spam and I aside while they get into a whole debate over what action they should take. Right now, Journey's life depends on me being bold and taking chances. I kill my headlights and decide to hang out in the alley until we figure out our next move.

Spam's phone *be-boops*, shattering the silence. We both scream. Spam drops it between the seat and the console.

"Answer it." The tension is about to explode the car.

"I'm trying," she shrieks, contorting in her seat. First her hand and then her arm disappear into the narrow space. The phone continues *be-boop*ing.

Spam manages to retrieve it with two fingers. "It's Lysa," she says. "She's FaceTiming." Spam pushes the button, revealing Lysa's face on the screen.

Without even a hello, Lysa launches into a stern diatribe. "It's after eight, so I'm doing this from my iPad. You know if I get caught I'll lose my phone *and* my car for a month, so shut up and listen."

Spam starts to speak, "I know—"

"I got an urgent e-mail from Erin. I know you're upset with her—"

"Hey—" Spam tries to interject a second time.

"Shut up and let me finish, this is important," scolds Lysa. "I called her but she didn't pick up. Go to her house right now and make sure she's okay."

I pull my phone from my pocket. The ringer was turned off.

"But—" Spam says.

"No buts," Lysa orders. "Just do it. That's the deal with friends. We'll patch this up later. And send me an e-mail once you know she's okay, I'll check back with my iPad." With that, Lysa signs off and the screen goes blank.

"Lysa!" Both Spam and I scream her name at the same time. But we're too late. She's already gone. Spam tries to call back. No answer.

Spam half smiles. "You've got to give her credit, she tried."

I chuckle. "Yep. She did."

"What are you thinking?" she asks.

"That I'm glad you're here," I say.

"Of course you are, you idiot." Spam gives me a light smack. "That's the deal with friends. But I'm talking about this. Did

Principal Roberts fry some circuits or what? What's going on here?"

"I know it's hard to believe, but I think he did some bad things and now he's looking for a scapegoat. He tried to pin this on Journey once at Miss P's house and it didn't work. I think he's in there right now figuring out how to make it look like Journey is responsible for her murder."

I slip the car into gear but leave the headlights off and turn onto the road. Within a few minutes, the creepy abandoned building looms ahead in the dark.

"Do you have a plan?" Spam asks. "Because we're going to need one."

"We'll leave the car out here on the road so we can get away fast. We'll find a break in the fence. Sneak in and see what's up. Maybe take a photo or two, then sneak out and call the cops."

"Works for me." She shudders and uses her phone to shoot a random photo of the dark, hulking cannery, barely outlined in moonlight.

I crawl down the pitch-dark road at a superslow speed, looking for a good place to park the car. Just as I pull over, my phone vibrates. I take it out of my pocket and stare at the name.

Spam looks at the screen. "It's Journey. Answer it."

"It's not Journey." I click the button but I don't know what to say.

"Erin? This is Mr. Roberts." The calm has returned to his voice. I flick the button to put it on speaker so Spam can hear. She and I share an ominous look. I put my finger to my lips.

"What's up, Mr. Roberts?" I purposely try to sound light and bright.

"I know you followed us, dear."

"What are you talking about?" Playing dumb wasn't my plan but it's all I've got.

"Cut the crap. I left the gate open. Bring the car and join us at the cannery loading dock. You have five minutes before I start piling up the bodies."

Bodies, plural? Now I know he has Victor, too.

"See you in three." I flip my phone into Spam's lap and mash the accelerator.

Rachel's car skids sideways as we rocket through the gate and thunder over the wooden boards. I glance at Spam. Her extreme-roller-coaster-fear face is in place. Her left hand is braced against the roof of the car and her right has a death grip on the door handle. The bad news is I'm pretty sure we're not getting off this ride anytime soon.

"Hang on," I say.

She flashes devil's horns with both hands, shouting, "Go big or go home." Then she grabs the door handle and braces against the roof again. God, I love her, because I know she's just as terrified as I am but she'd rather spit than admit it.

I slow down as we round the corner of the building. At first I don't see anything.

"Over there." Spam points to the farthest cannery building, next to the water. I can just barely make out the shape of a dark figure standing near the gaping maw of the decrepit old building.

I roll slowly up to the building. When I'm no more than ten feet away, Principal Roberts steps into the beam of our headlights.

He's holding a gun.

Journey's van is parked just inside the loading-bay door.

"Turn off the engine. Leave the lights on and the keys in the ignition," he orders.

# ▸ 40 ◂

When processing a crime scene you'll pick up a lot of things. The trick is determining what is crime . . . and what is scene.

—VICTOR FLEMMING

Spam and I get out of the car. I step quickly toward the front, hoping to get a look inside the van. The back doors are closed and I don't see anyone, inside or out.

"Erin and Samantha. The two of you showing up together makes my job much easier." He points the gun at us. "Keep your hands where I can see them and hand over those cell phones."

I pull my phone out of my pocket and hold it up high. Spam scampers over to my side, clutching my jacket with one hand and holding her cell phone up high with the other. One glance at her screen tells me two things: One, she's calling Lysa on FaceTime, but she's reversed the camera so that it's pointing at Mr. Roberts and his gun. And two: She set the speaker to mute.

I need to stall for time and hope Lysa picks up.

"Where are they, Carl?" I stick out my hip and give him a hard glare. This is not a brave-girl act. I've imagined this moment my whole life. He can't hurt me any more than he already has.

"Oh, listen to the bravado on you," he says. "If you'd rather call me Carl than Principal Roberts . . . or Dad . . . then be my guest."

"What?" My voice cracks. So I was wrong. He found the one word that could destroy me. I glance at Spam.

Her face crumbles. "Mr. Roberts is your dad?"

I see a glimpse of Lysa's face on the screen just before Spam kills the connection. At least now she knows something's wrong.

"I don't believe you. There's no way. I have red hair. . . ." It's a struggle, but I manage to keep my voice steady.

"Your hair is the spitting image of my Aunt Grace's." Mr. Roberts keeps the gun on us as he moves in and takes our phones. He tucks mine in one pocket and Spam's in the other. "Step over here and I'll reunite you with your friends."

Spam and I cling to each other and take small steps closer to the back of the van. Principal Roberts swings open the back doors, revealing Victor and Journey slumped inside. Both of their eyes are closed.

I let out a yelp and start toward them.

"Not so fast," Principal Roberts says, raising the gun. "Come and sit on this bumper where I can take care of you properly."

I sidestep toward the van. Spam clutches my arm so hard she's squeezing the life out of it, and yet she stubbornly refuses to lift her feet. I'm dragging her along just to keep moving. I shift my gaze between Victor and Principal Roberts. Then I steal a glance at Journey and my heart drops. A trickle of blood outlines the side of his face.

"Are they dead?" Spam worries. "Are they? You've got to tell me."

Almost everything I care about is right here—almost.

Except for Rachel and Lysa.

We have to make it out of this. If for no other reason than for Rachel. She can't go through something like this again.

Spam and I help each other hop up onto the bumper of the van. I glance over my shoulder at Victor. His eyes flutter open and link to mine. He pinches his lips together, a silent signal for me to stay quiet.

Principal Roberts picks up a pair of industrial-strength plastic zip ties, already looped together like handcuffs. "Let's see those hands, little lady."

I stick my hands out in front of me. A sob catches in my throat. How can he do this using the pet name he always had for me?

"Behind," he orders.

I put my hands behind me and he tightens the loops around my wrists. Next he moves behind Spam. "Reach back and stick your hands through here," he orders.

She complies, but clenches her fists and extends her middle finger on both hands. He yanks on the ends, tightening the loops around her wrists.

"Not so tight, a-hole," she says.

"Oh, Samantha, really? Your mouth is atrocious," he says.

"And your mouth looks like a cat's butt," she retorts.

"You're disgusting," Mr. Roberts says.

"Bite me," Spam replies.

I'm happy to hear the famous Spam spitfire attitude. We're going to need it, plus every bit of guts and bravado I can muster to get out of this alive. I notice how he keeps the gun trained on me nearly the whole time and I decide that's something I can work with.

"So, what's the deal, Mr. Roberts? You say you're my dad but now you want to kill me. That's not very fatherly."

"Don't go there, Erin," Victor says from inside the van. "And whatever you do, don't make any deals with him. You can't trust him."

I'm relieved to hear Victor speak. He sounds okay. But his hands are bound behind his back and his feet are lashed together, too.

"Aww, Vic," Principal Roberts says. "You always thought you were better than me. It must've hurt when she chose me over you."

"Let the kids go, Carl," Victor says. "If this is about Sarah, we can keep it between you and me."

Sarah? What are they saying?

Principal Roberts shoves his gun right into our faces. "Erin. Samantha. Now scoot back into the van and stick your feet out so I can bind them, too."

"How do you think this is going to end, Carl?" Victor asks. "Someone is going to figure this out."

Out of the corner of my eye I can tell he's working to get out of the bindings.

"That's where you're wrong," Principal Roberts says. Using one hand and his teeth, he loops two more cable ties together. His other hand keeps the gun on me. "I've thought this through." He sweeps the gun briefly toward Journey. "I'm going to pin everything on that poor, crazy young man over there. His father's a murderer, too."

"Shut up," I blurt out. "I don't want to hear any more of your lies."

"They won't be lies when I'm done," Principal Roberts says. "Murder-suicide events happen every day."

I hate him with every pore in my body. I couldn't disguise it if I had to.

"They'll find your bodies here on his property. You'll be tied up and he won't. There'll be a note," he says. "What else do they need?"

"Some evidence, maybe, or a motive?" I add a sneer to my voice.

"Yeah. Not so much," Mr. Roberts says. "Especially not with Victor gone, too. The Iron Rain PD tries, but as you know, they don't have a crime lab. Most of their evidence just sits in a box for years. It really hurt to have to get rid of Laura Peters, but unfortunately she left me no choice. She ruined everything with that DNA test of hers."

My head is spinning and this is coming at me faster than I can process it. The only thing I know to do is to stall for time. "You should have been more careful with your trophies," I say.

He casually steps back, a cool customer. "I don't know what you're talking about." But his voice thins.

"Really?" I taunt. "You don't remember dropping a blue-and-white strip of fabric?"

"Oh, so you found that, did you?" he asks.

"We did. And we know where it came from, too."

"Well, that is impressive," he says. "But it won't matter. Once you're gone, there won't be anyone to follow up on those details."

That's when it sinks in. He really is planning to kill us.

It couldn't end any other way, but hearing those words from a man holding a gun in your face is life altering. I won't get to apologize to Rachel for all the lying and I won't get to tell her what a great mom she is.

I won't get to see how things work out between Journey and me.

Hopefully, there are enough clues in the trunk of Rachel's

car that Sydney or someone will be able to figure out who the killer is, though.

I'm determined to keep Mr. Roberts talking to delay the inevitable for as long as possible and hope Lysa comes through.

"I don't get it, Mr. Roberts. I've wanted a dad my whole life. If you were really him, why didn't you tell me or buy me a birthday present or something? Do you even know when my birthday is?"

"April sixth." He props a ridiculous smile onto his lips. "I know everything there is to know about you. I even know that—still to this day—you sleep with a stuffed bunny that I gave you when you were just a tot."

I suck in a ragged breath and try to look casual, but this guy is way too good. The ragged one-eyed bunny is the sole remaining relic from my childhood, but I had no idea where it came from. All Rachel ever said was that it was my favorite.

"Gross, Mr. Roberts. Creeping on people while they're sleeping is some depraved crap," Spam says.

"Spam, stay out of it," Victor warns.

"Yes, Samantha. Stay out of it," Principal Roberts says.

"You're not smart enough to pull this off, Carl," Victor says. "Thanks to Erin, your DNA is stored in a place where it will be found. I saw it. And by the way, I can confirm the fragile X gene. You wound up with your Uncle George's shaky hands after all."

I glance at Victor and wonder if he's just making all this up. The fragile X stuff is news to me, but it's having an impact. Mr. Roberts's hand was a little shaky before, but now he places his other hand over the top of the gun to steady it.

"You and your *investigations*. You were always such a little pain," Principal Roberts sneers right in my face. "Where'd you find it, in Laura's lab?"

"That's right," I brag. "I found it and only I know where it's hidden."

He slips the zip-tie loops over my feet and up to my ankles, savagely wrenching the ends tighter. Pain shoots up my legs, but I refuse to give him the satisfaction of even the slightest wince.

"I'm curious. You want us dead. But what do you get out of that?"

"It's good news, bad news," he says. "The good news is I retain my freedom. Once Vic showed up and started sniffing around, I knew I had to take action to insure nothing could come back on me. I might have to leave town and maybe even the country. But freedom . . . you really can't put a price on that. So yeah, that's the good news."

He assembles another zip-tie loop set. "The bad news, of course, is I'm losing an esteemed friend from my high school days and a daughter. It doesn't matter that no one knew about you. I knew. You held a special place in my heart, and it pains me to have to let you go." He cradles the gun against his chest in mourning. "And all because of a stupid, surprise DNA test. I made it fourteen years without anyone looking at me for anything, then all of a sudden my DNA could wind up in a database. I need you to tell me where it is."

"The FBI has it," I say.

"If that were true, we wouldn't be here right now. So, tell me and things will go easier on you."

"Pound sand. I'm not telling you anything."

"Go ahead and tell him, Erin," Victor says. "It'll be better if you do."

Furious, I give Victor a laser glare.

He's so confident that I slow down for a second and try to think like him. I get the vibe that he wants me to tell Principal

Roberts that the samples are in our freezer at home because that's where he put the ones we ran today. Is he forgetting that Miss Peters's samples are in there, too? Of course, Mr. Roberts probably won't go browsing into a bag of peas once he finds the first set.

Principal Roberts waves the gun in front of Spam's face. Her eyes are the size of golf balls and they move and follow the gun, but she sticks her tongue out at him anyway.

"What's it going to be, Erin? Hard, painful bullets, where I kill everyone else and make you watch? Or a nice, soothing, eternal, happy nap?"

"Fine!" I play the part, looking torn and broken. "In the freezer at my house."

"That wasn't so hard, was it? Is your spare key still under the mailbox?"

I nod. Creepy. I guess that explains how he got into my room.

He stares at Spam's feet and shakes his head. "Look at you with your ridiculous costumes. Why can't you wear normal shoes like everyone else?" Using one hand, he jerks off her boots, first one and then the other, and tosses them randomly into the back of the van.

Mr. Roberts bends to slide the loops over Spam's ankles, and as he does, a large crucifix necklace slips out of the front of his shirt. The way it dangles there, free around his neck, catches the light from the headlights on Rachel's car and casts a small shadow of a cross on my leg.

A sudden memory explodes in my brain, loud and painful.

I turtle my shoulders protectively around my head. If my hands were free I would bury my ears in them. I would do almost anything to block this pain. It's sharp and intense, like being shot in the skull.

There's a woman's voice . . . a voice I've never heard before but suddenly remember. It's a voice that's clear and bright and strong.

*She's not your daughter.*

I look around the van. Where's it coming from? I stare at the cross on my leg.

"I remember now. . . ." My voice is barely a whisper.

"What?" Mr. Roberts turns his head sharply toward me.

"Oh my god. It's her. My mother." It feels strange to finally say it and mean it. I stare at the shadow swaying on my leg. "I remember now. . . . She yelled at you."

"No. No." Principal Roberts fumbles, trying to lash Spam's feet together.

"She did. She said: 'She's not your daughter.'"

"No!" he roars.

"*Yes* . . . and then you hurt her."

He grabs me roughly by the arms, picks me up, and tosses me farther into the van. I land just beyond Victor's shoulder, near Journey. Spam scoots next to me, trying to stay out of his grasp.

"Shut up. Just shut up," he yells. "She only said that because he was filling her head with lies. You have been my daughter every day for the last sixteen years."

For some reason I know it in my bones; I feel it in my cells. There's no way this crazy psycho's blood pounds in my veins. He's not my father. I'm 100 percent sure of that.

"Liar!" I scream.

"Just shut up," he says, his voice cracking.

From my angle in the back of the van, I watch him duct-tape a three-inch flexible hose to the exhaust pipe and secure it to the bumper with heavy strips of tape. He then works the flex hose up through a piece of dry, rotted wood flooring.

He brings the hose up to about the middle of the van wall. Then he tapes it in place.

When he's finished, he slams the rear doors, locking us inside. A few seconds later, he opens the driver's door, reaches in, and attempts to start the engine.

The van sputters and dies on the first two tries and I'm hopeful. If ever there was a perfect time for Journey's van not to start, this is it.

But no such luck. Third try, the engine cranks over.

Mr. Roberts pounds on the side of the van. "Okay, chums. I'll be back in a bit to set the murder-suicide stage. Don't worry, I won't wake you."

And then he's gone.

Carbon monoxide pours down on us from the hose and begins to build up inside. The smell is strong, like sticking your head under a bus . . . only maybe worse.

# - 41 -

Keep this in mind, nearly everywhere you go, you're surrounded by a cloud of bacteria that is as unique as a fingerprint.

—VICTOR FLEMMING

Victor rocks from side to side, twisting around and worm-crawling to the back of the van.

"Somebody check on Journey," he says. "I need him working with me."

I try to roll to Journey's side, but it's awkward and I end up stuck, face down, because it kills my shoulder to roll over on it.

"I'm awake, I've just been laying back," Journey says. "Let's do this."

I'm flooded with relief. I roll onto my hip and struggle into a semiseated position. "Thank God," I whisper.

"Journey, back here. We need to bust out these windows to let in fresh air," Victor says. Journey squeezes between me and Spam to get to the back. I go first, rolling to the left. Then Spam goes right. Journey grunts as he makes a powerful crawl and manages to squeeze between us. I gasp for air. With all four of us trying to move in different directions, it's quickly getting tight and sweaty, and the exhaust fumes are getting thicker by the minute.

Victor surges up on his knees and starts to ram the back window. It's too high for his shoulder, so he's forced to slam it with his forehead. It sounds a lot like trying to break glass with raw chicken.

Journey has made it to the back, so now instead of one thump against the window I hear two: *thump, thump.*

"Erin, get to the front," Victor gasps. "You and Spam . . . away from the fumes. Find a way to turn off the key."

"Okay." My voice sounds thin and papery. If I stretch my head and neck forward and then bring my knees up toward my chest, I'm able to move across the rough wooden floor. Splinters gouge my skin straight through my clothes.

Spam stops. "Wait," she says. "Over here. I found the boot phone."

A crazy laugh escapes my ravaged throat. I turn to roll toward her instead of heading to the front of the van. "Coming," I say.

"Forget the phone," Victor orders. "Get to the engine."

"You don't know Spam." I don't know if they even hear me because I can hardly hear myself over the loud thuds of them banging their heads against the window. There's a high-pitched ringing in my ears and my mother's voice, which sounds like summer rain on a tin roof. *"Don't touch her. She's not your daughter."*

I don't know how, but I manage to scoot up to Spam's back. She presses her boot into my hands. "It's in there, I just can't get it out."

I get it. It's hard to think with all these fumes. I try to tip the boot upside down and it tipples over. I giggle a little bit. It doesn't tipple. It topples over. It must have been enough though, because far away, I hear Spam's voice.

"Got it."

Even farther away, I hear the rhythmic drumming of Victor and Journey still bashing their heads against the window. The sound is dull and wet, and the air inside the van grows hotter and thicker, so I know they haven't succeeded.

"Erin, damn it. Get to the front." Victor coughs.

I realize I've been holding my breath for a long time. I take in a huge gasp and it's like sucking a load of hot sand into my lungs. I cough. I'm so tired.

"I will . . . in a minute. I just need to close my eyes for a sec."

"No!" Victor shouts. "Do not close your eyes! Get to the front. Kick your feet. Crawl. If you don't find a way to shut off that engine, we will die in here."

Too late. My eyes are welded shut. But Victor's voice drives me to push on. I kick and struggle. I imagine that I'm one of those fish that live in the mud. I don't exactly have feet and I don't exactly have flippers.

I'm a mudfish.

I keep scooting, inch by inch, through a thick haze until I bump my head on the gearshift. The stupid, ridiculous gearshift in Journey's stupid, ridiculous van. I'm going to die here and I never learned how to drive a stupid ridiculous stick shift without stalling the stupid—

Ha! All of a sudden I go from stupid to brilliant, because even though I can't open my eyes or climb over the seat or figure out how to turn off the key with my teeth, I know how to kill the engine . . . if only I can stay awake long enough.

I press my side against the gearshift and use it as a brace to raise myself up into a sitting position. Once I'm sitting up, I lean back into it. My arms ache and my hands are so numb they feel like they aren't there anymore. I'm sweating and exhausted, but I struggle to lift my left side high enough to wedge the gearshift knob into my armpit. My plan is to twist and throw my body forward until I pull the van into one of the gears, but instead I begin to cough and gasp for fresh air.

I can't breathe and I can't stop coughing. My body convulses and lurches forward. My ribs are being crushed from the inside.

And yet somewhere, way in the distance, the van shudders and I hear the crunch of breaking glass. A draft of cool air skims over my skin. I breathe in a deep lungful. I'm too tired to cough anymore.

But my world is all mixed up, because now there's music playing and people dancing. Suddenly Officer Baldwin is here and he's carrying me. Rachel and the chief are here, too. Rachel is clinging to Lysa's hand, and Lysa's parents are pounding the chief on the back. But I don't know how they got here, because I have Rachel's car. And I can't possibly be seeing any of this, because my eyes are welded shut.

And I'm very, very tired.

▾ ▾ ▾

I wake up with my throat on fire, like I've gargled sriracha with a side of jalapeño juice. My head throbs and my lungs sound like a weak accordion.

I made it out of the van, though, because white light's seeping through my closed eyelids. I open them carefully. Holy crap, I'm in the hospital. I try to sit up but my muscles scream, *Don't even think about it.*

Just then Victor strides into the room.

"Ah, there you are, sunshine. Feeling better?" Except for the large bandage across his forehead, he looks a whole lot better than I feel.

He strokes the hair out of my eyes. "You okay?"

"Ow. I guess." I press my hands to my head.

"Keep resting. I'll be back to debrief you in a little bit."

I come straight up off the pillow, pain and all.

"No. Do it now. I want to know everything. How'd we get out of the van?" I gasp, considering what might have happened. "Is everybody . . . ?"

He comes back and pulls a chair up to my bedside. "We all made it out just fine."

"How?"

"We were quite the formidable team. You and Spam somehow alerted your third musketeer, Lysa, that you were in trouble. She and her parents called the police. The problem was no one knew where to look, so first they searched the high school."

"That makes sense."

"Spam—quite the clever one, that girl—managed to broadcast our exact location, and a bunch of kids showed up looking for a rave."

I chuckle. "Yeah, that's Spam. If you want the cavalry, you don't cry 'help,' you yell 'party.'"

"You probably recall that Journey and I were trying to break out the back windows of the van with our heads? We finally doubled down on one window." Victor rubs the bandage on his forehead. "That brought in a little fresh air."

"Oh my god."

"But *you* made the most amazing contribution by killing the engine before we were asphyxiated."

"I don't even remember."

"In a magnificent show of stamina, you hooked the gearshift under your arm and forced it into fourth gear. The engine died, and not a moment too soon. There was only two hundred and thirteen cubic feet of space in that van, and most of it was filled with carbon monoxide. We were close to a lethal dose."

"Yay for never learning to drive a stick," I say. "What happened to Mr. Roberts?"

"He was quite the clever one as well. Apparently, his night of terror began when he instigated a hit-and-run on Journey's mother's car."

"Oh no! Is she okay?"

"She's fine. But while everything was going down at the cannery, she was at the emergency room being checked out."

"Wow."

"Carl then intercepted Journey on his way back to the pizza place. The last thing Journey remembers was pulling into the parking lot."

"But why Journey?"

"With me in town following the case, Carl got nervous. He planned to stage Journey's suicide and leave behind a written confession to killing the bio teacher. I stepped into it when I showed up at Carl's house. That's how I became collateral damage."

"How did he think he was going to get away with all of it?"

"His plan was solid. He had a small boat stashed at the cannery dock. Once he got us set up, he used that to slip back into town. He even stopped by the bar he and I went to the other night, in order to establish an alibi. He left the bar and went to our house, used the key to get in and take the DNA samples from the freezer. He planned to come back to the cannery to make it look like Journey murdered all of us and then killed himself, but I think when he saw all the kids and the commotion, he just took off. Chuck's team picked him up at the Portland airport about an hour ago."

"How'd they know he was at the airport?"

"Your buddy Spam gave us that tip, too. We tracked your cell phones. He still had them on him."

I raise the back of my bed and pull the covers up. "So when you took off last night, did you know Mr. Roberts was the killer?"

"No." Victor stretches his neck, rolling his head right and left. "It was quite a puzzle. I should have seen it earlier, but when I compared our test results with the ones your teacher did, the fragile X jumped out immediately."

"You knew he had it?" I ask.

"I knew fragile X ran in Carl's family. He was always afraid he had the gene but refused to get tested. But even then, I didn't think he killed anybody. I still don't understand what CC had to do with him."

"It stands for 'coffee cup.' Miss P lifted Mr. Roberts's DNA from a coffee cup."

"You might have advanced yourself beyond star pupil. How did you figure that out?"

"Remember the scrap of the note that matched the chief's pen? Mr. Roberts dropped the rest of that note in our driveway. The note was from Miss P and she told him what she had done. Then I found his basketball shoes . . . the ones he loaned to you, in our closet. They not only matched the print in my bedroom, but they also matched the print you described in the blood. I tested them. They made the luminol turn blue. They're in the trunk of Rachel's car, if you need them."

He gives me an admiring look. "Amazing."

"How's Rachel, is she okay?"

Victor smiles. "She's been at your side all night. I just sent her home to shower and eat. She's fine, though not very happy with me. She blames me for getting you in the middle of all this."

"Pfft," I snort. "If Rachel had her way . . ."

Victor dismisses my comment. "Give her a break; she doesn't have the same stomach for this that we do."

"I guess that's true," I say.

"Plus, she now has to live through the story of your mother's murder all over again."

I flop back against my pillow. I hadn't thought about that. Finding my mother's killer will make us all notorious again. There's a lot I haven't had a chance to think through yet.

"And by the way." Victor's look becomes stern. "Journey fessed up about the tie in the van and how it linked the bio teacher to your mother's murder. You held back evidence from me."

Oops. "Sorry, I just thought—"

"I don't care what you thought, that's not how we do things," he says. "It doesn't matter if we're a family or a forensic team. We never hold back evidence. Is that clear?"

I cringe. "Yes, sir. Sorry. It won't happen again."

Victor pats my hand. "Anything else?"

"Yes. Why did all of my evidence point to Chief Culson?"

"Trust me, I wanted to clear that up, too. Because of his . . ." Victor struggles for the right word. ". . . affection for Rachel, Chuck personally followed up on every piece of evidence. He did actually go to Journey's house and inspect the spot where the van rammed the wall. He went to the tow yard and physically inspected the van, too. He was doing this for Rachel, and he was doing it for you, too. This is probably how his fingerprints wound up inside the van, but here's the lesson about evidence. At any crime scene, you will find a lot of it. It's our job to figure out . . ."

I finish the statement ". . . what's crime and what's scene." Victor includes that line in every one of his books.

"Keep it up and you'll become my star *apprentice*," he says with a proud smile.

It's tricky to pull off in a hospital bed, but I manage a little celebratory flailing-arms dance. It's not every day I get a compliment like this.

"One last question." I stall. "About Principal Roberts . . . he isn't really . . . ?"

"Your father?" Victor shakes his head. "No. I know it was creepy and it led him to commit very bad deeds. But I think he really wanted it to be true. He wanted to hold an important place in your life, and that says a great deal about what an amazing young woman you are."

Victor's right. It is confusing and creepy. Mr. Roberts had a place in my life. He was my constant. "How did he get my nail file?"

"We think he must've grabbed it out of your locker."

"Oh right. The infamous locker checks," I say.

"We have him on security video going into Journey's locker and stealing his phone."

"What a creep. Why would he do all of that to me?" I sit up.

Victor gives my wrist a squeeze and buries my hand between both of his. "Your mother was special, Erin. A lot of men were in love with her. But obsession is a strange beast. I honestly believe Carl became obsessed with the notion that you and your mother were his family. Sarah didn't share that notion and her rejection pushed him over the edge."

I have to look away or I'm going to completely fall apart.

"I know these are just words, but you can't blame yourself. None of us knew. Not even Rachel. She's blaming herself, too."

I pull my hands from the sheet and force them to rest quietly on top. "What about Spam and Journey?"

"They were both released a couple of hours ago."

I flop back against the pillow and snuggle into the warmth of the bed. "Does this mean you're leaving soon?"

"That depends." Victor scoots his chair a little closer to the bed. "I've done a little thinking about that, and I have an offer for you to consider." A grin spreads across his face. He looks a little shy, almost embarrassed. "First of all, I quit my job. I'm leaving the bureau and moving back to Iron Rain."

"What about . . . ?"

"Getting axed?"

I nod.

"This could be viewed as sort of a preemptive move against that action, but that's not why I'm doing it. I owe it all to you, Erin. You changed me."

"Me?"

"You're an amazing survivor. Even more than that, you thrive. But I think the clincher, for me, is how you clung to your mother's evidence in that box, up in that attic, with the conviction that someday you would solve her murder."

I look up at him through damp eyelashes and a tangled veil of copper hair. "And we did. We solved it."

"Yes, we did." He smiles. "Which is why I think maybe we should tackle the other mystery in your life."

Excitement thrums through me. "What other mystery?"

"Well, I don't know if it's possible, but if it is, I thought we should try to identify your father."

I can't take all this good news at once. The stress of the last twenty-four hours finally dissolves my defensive crust and a few fat tears slide down my cheeks.

Victor takes my hand. "Hey, this is what you want, isn't it?"

"Are you kidding? It's everything I've ever wanted."

"Hmm. I don't think that's exactly true." Victor adopts a teasing tone.

"Don't say that. It's totally true. You can ask anybody. Spam. Journey. Lysa."

"Actually, I think there's one more thing on Erin's Wish List."

I dab my eyes with the edge of my sheet. "Well, what then?"

"I think you've wanted a forensic class. And guess what, you're getting that, too."

I let out a shriek that's so loud a nurse pops her head in the door. Victor nods to assure her that we're okay.

"It's true. The district was having trouble finding a replacement for your biology teacher and now they have to replace the principal, too. I'll still have to get my teaching credential and figure out how to engage a group of zombie teenagers. But yeah, we're going to change it up. Biology 101 will become Forensics. That's the bad news; you get the class but me as your teacher. And, we're working out a deal with Iron Rain PD to kick in some budget dollars to trick out the lab. They get a part-time criminalist, the school gets a teacher and a new lab. It's win-win."

Holy crap. "I'm also getting an uncle."

"And I'm getting a family. I just hope you'll be my goodwill ambassador to let all those kids know I'm cool so they won't humiliate me again."

"Well yes, of course. I'll have your back; you can count on that. But, think about this . . . our school can now officially be called C.S. High—get it?"

Victor chuckles. "Funny."

This is so huge I start planning out loud. "We should change our mascot from an acorn to a giant fingerprint. We can have crime-scene tournaments . . . and . . ."

"Whoa, slow down. It's just one class. One step at a time." He pulls a buccal swab from his pocket. "If you're up for it, I thought I'd start with an official DNA sample. One I can send back to my buddies at my former lab for them to process and run through the DNA database. Are you ready?"

"I'm so ready," I gasp.

Victor opens the swab and hands it to me. I scrub it on the inside of my cheek.

"Do the inside of your lip, too." I scrub it around a little more and hand it back to him. He drops it into the tube and then into the box. He takes out a pen and writes my name on the side. Then he slides the box into a FedEx envelope. A nurse sticks her head in the room. He signals for her to wait a minute. "Okay, she's going to check your oxygen level. If it's okay, they'll release you. I'll be waiting right outside."

As he slips out of the room, I jump out of bed and rummage around for my clothes. They're beyond filthy, but I slip into them anyway. I could dance all the way home. . . . I wouldn't even need a car.

I can't sit still.

I open the door, intending to shower Victor with a huge hug to show my appreciation. However, instead of waiting right outside the door, he's standing at the nurse's station, a few feet away. His back is to me, but I watch in amazement as he breaks open another buccal swab and begins to scrub the inside of his own mouth. When he's finished, he slides the swab into the tube, scrawls his name on the side, and drops it into the same FedEx envelope with my sample.

As he seals the envelope, I close the door quietly and press my back against the wall. Little sparks of happiness turn everything bright. What just happened?

Is it possible that Victor's . . . no. Wait. Could he be? He must think there's a chance. There's no other reason for him to put his DNA swab into an envelope with mine. Right?

The door opens and Journey peeks his head in.

"Erin?"

Wrapped in his fist are the strings of a huge bouquet of balloons. It's a challenge, but he manages to wrangle himself and all the balloons the rest of the way into the room. "Are you in here?"

I hold my fingers in my ears, waiting for a balloon or two to pop. Once he's inside, I tap him on the shoulder. He whirls around and we hug, mashing the balloon strings between our bodies. Journey holds up the ribbons from the ends of the balloons, revealing a card tied there.

I touch the card. "What's this?"

"Open it," he says with a smile.

I slide out a white card embossed with our school logo and the word "PROM."

"Will you?" Journey asks. He pauses to wet his lips nervously. "Go with me?"

# 42

"Erin! I need you down here, now." Rachel's voice is shrill and anxious. For the first time in a long time, I'm not frozen in fear that she's stumbled over one of my deep, dark secrets or caught me in a giant new lie.

Rachel knows it all now. She knows how much I needed to talk about my mother and what happened to her. She knows about the attic, the box, my investigations. She even knows about Cheater Checks, though we have agreed to table those until I'm out of high school.

Victor brokered this landmark, two-sided confession, which he called our Family Fess-up Fest. Rachel had to come clean, too. And not just about her relationship with the chief. She had to fess up about my mother and her feelings of survivor guilt. Needless to say, the last couple of weeks have changed all of us.

With Victor around, Rachel is more relaxed, and the three of us function like a true family. I'm learning to open up and tell her the truth, and she's learning not to hold back.

"Erin!" she screams from downstairs. "Journey's here."

Oh yeah, Journey is no longer banished from my life, either, which is another good thing.

Now, if I could just twist myself into slightly more of a pretzel shape, I would be able to reach the zipper on this dress. Rachel and Lysa shopped for it together and were extremely proud of the fact that it goes perfectly with the strappy silver shoes Lysa made me buy at Shoe Haven.

Rachel has delivered a Cinderella's-godmother level of fussing and attention to getting me ready for my first prom. She did my hair up with tiny wisps trailing down. No hiding behind the veil of death tonight. Lysa found a delicate pearl headband, which is the perfect touch, and it matches the heart-shaped locket that Rachel gave me about an hour ago.

"Your mother was the prom queen, but she gave this to me to commemorate our first prom. Inside is a photo of the two of us when we were exactly your age," she said. "I've been saving it for the right moment."

Now, I squint at the dime-sized image and I recognize the familiar slope of her nose and the slightly almond-shaped eyes. "Hey, Mom," I whisper, touching the photo.

Everything has worked out just the way Rachel always said it would.

A kiss . . . a boyfriend . . . the prom. Not to mention a killer caught and a forensics class. There's even the possibility of a father. *My* father. In the end, there are only two things missing from this new perfect world: my mom and Miss Peters.

I can't deny the huge hole they left behind in my life. Losing them not only impacts who I am, but who I will be someday. My only hope is that I'm able to live up to the dreams they had for me. The same person took each of them from me at different times and for different reasons. But at least we caught him.

And he's *not* my father.

"Errrriiiinnnn!" Rachel shrieks from below.

"Okay!" *Okay.* I slip the locket over my head and stand, taking a few tentative steps toward the door. Trying not to wobble in these heels is a challenge. I shuffle onto the landing and peer down at the crowd gathered around the base of our stairs. Flashes explode from cameras and cell phones.

"Whoa. Who let the paparazzi in?" I shield my eyes with one hand and grasp the banister with the other as I try to make a graceful entrance, or at least avoid a face-plant.

Lysa and her date wait by the door. She blows a kiss. She looks amazing in a long, silk coral sheath and four-inch heels.

How does she walk in those things?

Spam rushes toward me, holding up the wide, full skirt of her simple, long white dress. I try to ignore the untied, tongue-out combat boots she's wearing below, because her dress is so completely normal. Maybe even a little dull, especially by Spam standards.

"Your dress is gorgeous," I say. "A statement of simplicity."

"Oh, wait." She feels around the fitted bodice waist, touching and pinching. "One sec." Spam pushes something on the waistband of her dress and the skirt lights up like a giant movie screen filled with bold, undulating color. Colorful, round shapes pulse and swirl and rotate to the right, only to be replaced with other colorful round swirls. "Get it?" she asks.

It takes me a minute to recognize the swirls are planets. Mars, Venus, Earth. Spam's dress is an animated display of our solar system.

She holds her arms out and twirls. "Booyah!"

I give her a hug. "You *are* the center of the universe."

Rachel rushes over with her camera. Spam and I put our heads together and offer up cheesy smiles.

Rachel responds with a quick volley of flashes.

Chief Culson steps in and takes the camera, motioning for Rachel and Lysa to get into the shot. "I want one with all the beautiful girls," he says. Then he pauses. "Erin, you are every bit as stunning as your mother."

While Spam and Lysa and I squeeze together, Rachel slides up behind us and drapes her arms around all of us, giving us a tight squeeze. "Both of your mothers would be so proud."

The chief fires off some shots.

"Where's Journey?" Rachel calls. "We need pictures of him, too."

I glance into the kitchen. Journey and Victor are standing together. Journey hands Victor a small, brown paper bag. Victor reaches inside and pulls out an old toothbrush. He holds it up and inspects it closely. He lets the toothbrush fall back into the bag and stuffs the whole thing into a FedEx envelope.

Then they spot me standing in the doorway. Journey smiles and moves toward me. But my gaze is beyond him, on Victor. He doesn't know that I saw him put his own DNA in the envelope along with mine. Our smiles meet and his grows, like a wedge of sunlight breaking through a cloud of despair. I swear I see liquid welling up in his eyes. "You are so beautiful," he whispers.

While they are clearly happy tears, I'm not sure if Victor—like me—is remembering the past . . . or imagining the future. Because I know I can't wait. It's going to be amazing.

Turn the page for a sneak peek at
the next Erin Blake novel

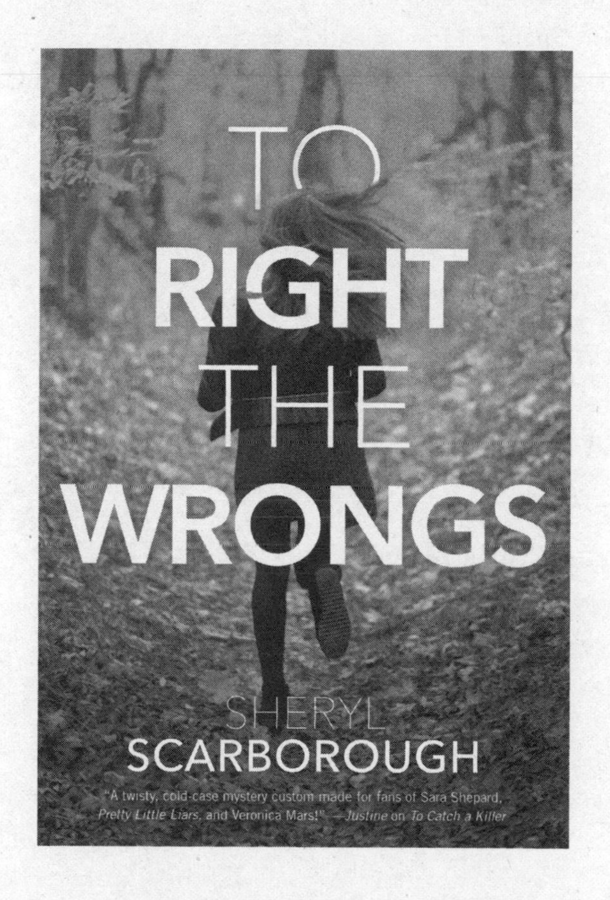


Available February 2018

# 1

Normal is an illusion. What is normal for
the spider is chaos for the fly.
—MORTICIA ADDAMS

Care to guess where you wind up after you and your friends help police catch a killer? It isn't Disneyland.

To my great relief, it isn't the *Today* show, either. They called to extend an invitation, but my guardian, protector, and de facto mom Rachel was solidly against it. She didn't want to have to relive the worst day of her life on TV any more than I did. Thankfully, our fame was distilled down to two and a half minutes on the local news, and a front-page article in the paper.

The important thing is we caught the man who killed my mother and my biology teacher. I stood up to him after a lifetime of looking over my shoulder and being afraid. And, I *remembered* something, too. A small sliver from that horrible night fourteen years ago.

Now, supposedly, I can go on with my life and just be normal.

How exactly does that happen?

Do I flip a switch, turn a dial?

Today begins the *normal* last three weeks of my sophomore year of high school. I'm pacing between my bedroom and the tree-shaded balcony that overlooks the street, watching for Journey's battle-scarred van to rumble into view.

The warm, lazy air makes me glad we're finally in summer countdown. Soon, I'll be able to spend my mornings lounging in bed with the French doors wide open and a stack of books I've been dying to read.

I check my phone again.

He's not that late. Maybe only a minute or two. I'm just anxious.

A few weeks ago, I thought I knew everything there was to know about him and he didn't even know I existed. Now, I'm officially his girlfriend. He said it right out loud in the TV interview. After those words came out of his mouth I couldn't answer any more questions. But it was worth it.

I'm wearing a new green tank top, which brings out the color of my eyes, and a pair of white shorts. The outfit may not look like that much of an effort, but before I started hanging out with Journey my morning routine was to pick the least rumpled navy blue T-shirt out of the laundry hamper—my T-shirts were all navy blue because that paired best with jeans, and navy blue and denim blend really well into the background.

It wasn't that I didn't have a sense of style before Journey. It's that my *normal* back then meant not standing out. When a tragic event steals your childhood, and puts your name in the headlines for weeks and months, you become *that girl* forever. Now I'm hoping that I can quietly morph into just a girl.

The worn-out shocks on Journey's van squeal as he pulls into the driveway. His brakes harmonize in protest.

I grab my purse and backpack. The small, round wooden heels of my sandals tap out my excited departure on the stairs. I blast through the kitchen, past Uncle Victor, who is camped out at the table with a cup of coffee and some paperwork.

"Bye. See you later." I barrel toward the back door.

I glance back in time to see him grin and hoist his cup.

The van has added a new, asthmatic wheeze to its soundtrack and the passenger door complains loudly as Journey opens it for me from inside. His hand remains there to help pull me up into the belly of this ancient beast. I slide into the seat and lean across the wide-open space. He meets me halfway and plants a quick peck on my lips.

Humph.

Our last actual date was prom, two weeks ago. Since then we have been pushed together and separated. We have been interviewed, interrogated, analyzed, and seen by specialists in PTSD. We've also been fussed over by family and friends and hounded by reporters. All of this activity has meant virtually no PDA. So now that we're finally allowed to go back to school and we're alone, I was hoping for a little more than just a peck.

"Sorry," he says.

"For the kiss?"

"What? No. Because we're late." The transmission crunches into reverse and he pilots the van out of the driveway.

I should just be happy that he's giving me a ride to school. I'm not exactly on his way. It takes him at least an extra twenty minutes to pick me up. Rachel has offered to buy me another mode of transportation to replace my scooter that got munched, and I'll take her up on that eventually . . . but for now I'm enjoying riding to school with the guy who has reclaimed his status as hottest senior on campus.

We ride quietly for a few minutes, each in the silence of our own thoughts, because that's just how we are with each other. We don't have to fill every moment with chatter.

"Three weeks and I'm free." Journey does a quick fist pump.

"How's it feel?"

"It'd feel better if I knew for sure I got into OSU."

"Don't worry. You'll get in." I don't know why I'm saying that. His grades are good, but his application was late.

As he pulls into the parking lot my gaze drifts to the spot where Principal Roberts used to stand and survey everyone's arrival.

It's weird. Same spot, new principal.

This one's tall, probably over six feet, with a back as straight as an ironing board and feet planted in a wide stance. The way her arms are crossed over her chest is more defiant than defensive. Her dark hair is wrenched back so straight that it looks painted on, the tight twist at the nape of her neck an afterthought. A dark band of sharply designed wraparound sunglasses cover her eyes. Her regal, "what's that smell" expression is the same look she gave the TV reporter when she was asked if she was proud to have a group of student crime fighters in her midst.

Miss Blankenship, our new principal, made her feelings very clear. She is impressed by high test scores. That's it.

"Can you snag a ride home with Spam or Lysa today?" Journey asks. "I have to leave early to drop my suit off at the cleaners for graduation."

"Yeah. No problem."

Am I imagining it or are her eyes following us as we drive by? I must be imagining it, since I can't actually see her eyes through her sunglasses. Anyway, I get it. Journey's van is a huge eyesore that groans and squeals. I guess anyone seeing it for the first time would be inclined to stare. I rub the well-worn door panel lovingly. We almost died in this wreck.

"Don't forget, you promised to teach me how to drive a stick this summer," I say.

Journey pulls into a parking space, pops his seatbelt, and wraps a long arm around my neck. He strokes my jaw with his thumb and gives me a sultry look through thick eyelashes. "Which stick are we talking about?"

I playfully bat his hand away.

But he leans in for the longer kiss that I was waiting for. At the first sign that he's pulling back, I gently grab his lip with my teeth to draw out the kiss. Then he does it back to me and we both try to keep from giggling. The warning bell rings as we're finishing up. We pull apart breathlessly and I catch something moving out of the corner of my eye. Holy cra— The new principal is standing right in front of the van, staring at us through the window.

I jump away from Journey as if we were doing something wrong. "What the heck?"

Journey bounds out of his door with the enthusiasm of a golden retriever. Hand out, smile on. I proceed more cautiously.

"Hi. Journey Michaels." His charm goes into overdrive. "You're the new principal, aren't you?"

She glares at him, arms crossed over her chest. "Where's your parking pass?"

"Oh." Journey digs out his wallet and pulls the parking pass from inside. He holds it up to show her. "The little thing that attached to the mirror broke off. Should I just put it on the dashboard?"

"You should go to the office and get a new one. Bring it out here and hang it on the mirror. Then hurry to class. If you're late it's on you."

Seriously? Her lips move but nothing else. I expect her voice to sound flat and metallic.

Her gaze swivels to me with such intensity that for a second

I worry that maybe I said that out loud. But I'm pretty sure I didn't.

Journey barely seems to notice her odd mannerisms. He sways slightly. "I'm on it," he promises her. "Don't worry. But I'm a senior. We're basically done with classes, so it's not that big of a deal."

She makes a pinched face. "You won't walk if you have any demerits on the books. If I were you I'd hurry."

I'm standing here witnessing crazy train in action when she again shifts her reptilian gaze in my direction. "Why are you still standing here?"

I open my mouth to explain or introduce myself and decide silence is the better option. I hurry off in the opposite direction from Journey. We glance at each other once and share a small wave.

And I thought our last principal was a psycho.

Actually, our last principal *was* a psycho.

But since there aren't any other unsolved murders lurking in Iron Rain's past, we're probably not in any real danger.

I hurry into the building where my first class is and a group of freshmen girls flock around me like birds on a scrap of bread.

"Erin. Erin. Look what we got. We ordered them from the website where you got yours. They just came yesterday." They're all talking at once and twirling multifilament fingerprint brushes like the one I use. The newspaper article mentioned the contents of my supply kit and where I got everything. Which is so funny because after Lysa and Spam and I admitted our forensic activities, our parents extracted promises from each of us that we won't be doing any more favors for our friends at school. Cheater Checks is DOA.

"That's cool," I say. "What are you going to do with them?"

"Lift fingerprints. What else," the blonde says. "Look. We

already did some." She holds up a white card that's covered with smeary, black smudges. "What do you think? Do those look like a match?"

I blink and back away. "Okay, so first you need to work on your technique. A lot. Those aren't fingerprints. They're black blobs."

She whips the card out of my hand. "Whatever, it was my first try."

She moves off with her friends in tow and I head for my locker. Strolling along the rows, I see splashes of black and neon colors all over the place. Geez, what's going on here? Then I come upon a couple of guys blowing neon green fingerprint powder against the metal door. Some of it sticks, but most of it is going to waste on the floor.

They laugh hysterically.

I pause and consider telling them they're doing it wrong, but when the second warning bell rings I shake it off and head to class. As I pass them I hear one whisper to the other.

"Hey, that's *her,*" he says.

Ugh. No matter what, I'm always going to be *her.*

I shudder and hurry to class.

Normal. What does that even mean?

# ABOUT THE AUTHOR

SHERYL SCARBOROUGH is an award-winning writer for children's television. She holds an MFA in writing for children and young adults from Vermont College of Fine Arts, lives in Washington State, and has always had an obsession with forensics. When she was twelve, her home was the target of a Peeping Tom. Sheryl diligently photographed his footprints and collected the candy wrappers he left behind. Unfortunately, he was never caught. But the desire to use evidence to solve a great mystery was sparked inside Scarborough all the same. *To Catch a Killer* is her debut.